The Moonless Night

BENJAMIN ANDRUS

The Moonless Night

Part one of the Veldorian Saga

Edited by: Michelle Tilmon and Joel Andrus

This is a work of fiction. Names, characters, places and incidents either are products of the author's imagination or are used fictitiously. Any resemblance to actual events or locales or persons, living or dead, is entirely coincidental.

Author photograph by Joel Andrus

ISBN-10: 0615-74230-0
ISBN-13: 978-0-61574230-4

Second Edition

12 11 10 9 8 7 6 5 4 3

For Ashley

BENJAMIN J. ANDRUS

ACKNOWLEDGEMENTS

I started writing this book on a snowy night just after the first of the year. At that point I had an idea in my head how I wanted things to go and how I would get people there. What I did not know, was what the whole story line was going to be. I just watched as the characters acted out. It wasn't until a few months later that I was given the whole story. Thanks to my wonderful muse I knew what was going to happen and I even have the plot for the next two books mapped out.

Let me tell you now it is all rot saying that writing a book is easy and anyone can do it. This has been a very exciting but difficult task to undertake. If it were not for some very important people, or person, in my life I would never have made it this far.

First I would like to thank my family. They are so supportive in everything I do, and they always help me out when I need it. Second I want to thank Ashley. I also want to thank everyone who has helped me on this project. My writers club, thanks guys! Mike for showing me how this all works. Professor Ramey for teaching me to love writing again. Amber for being willing to edit this manuscript on your free time, thanks so much. Matt for the countless times you came over and we just sat in the basement writing, or at least you were writing and I was playing online games feeling bad I wans't writing. That forced me to try to keep up, thanks. Michelles help with all the correction's of my uses' of apostrophe's proved to be invaluable, we both know I needed it. Marissa, and everyone else who helped me find all the little demons hiding in the details of such a long work, thank you. And last, but certainly not least, Azfar, it was your class that started this whole journey.

Anyone I didn't mention, or forgot to mention, but told you in person that I would mention you in the acknowledgements page, this one is for you. Thank you.

I am adding this to the end of the previous acknowledgments because it is just not worth it to redo the whole thing. I would like to thank both my brothers and my family that helped me to create this new and revised second edition. I know this is my first book and it turned out well, but with that being said I rushed through the final details and some things came up that were found wanting. Its ok I fixed them so enjoy this new edition!!

THE MOONLESS NIGHT

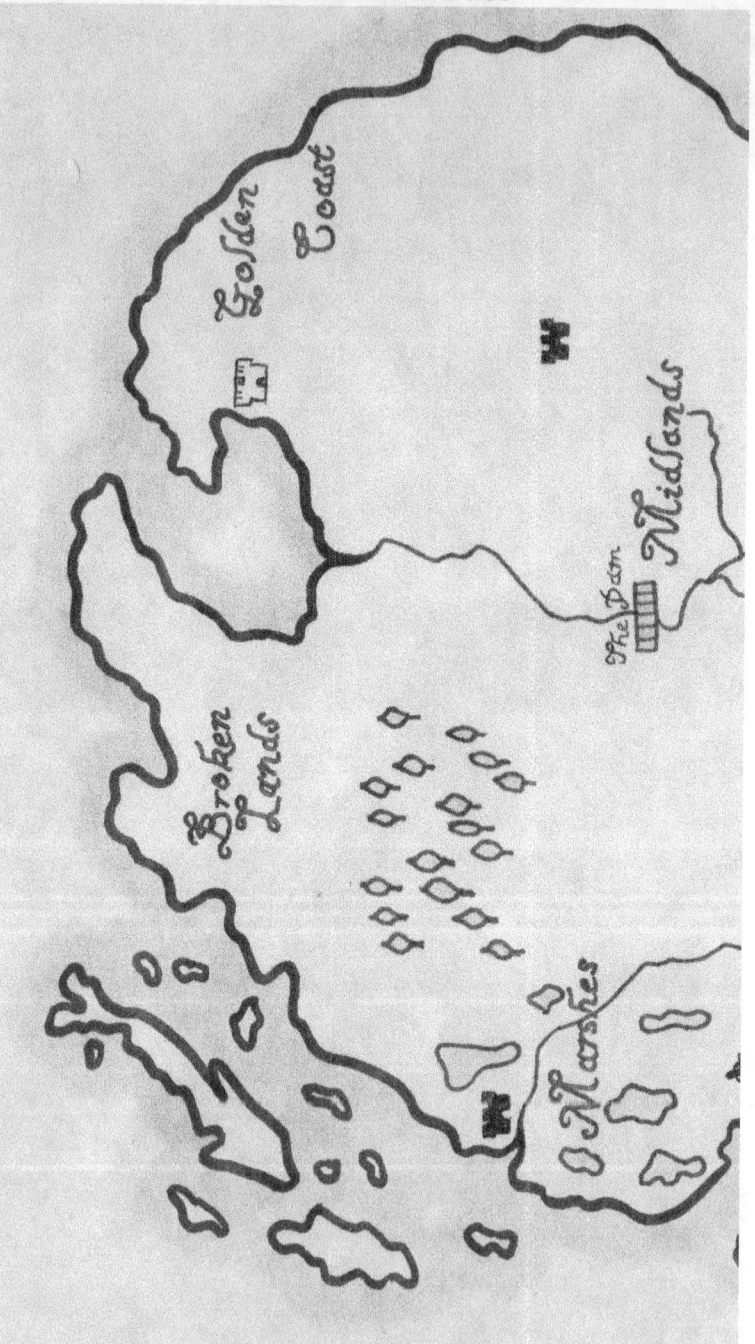

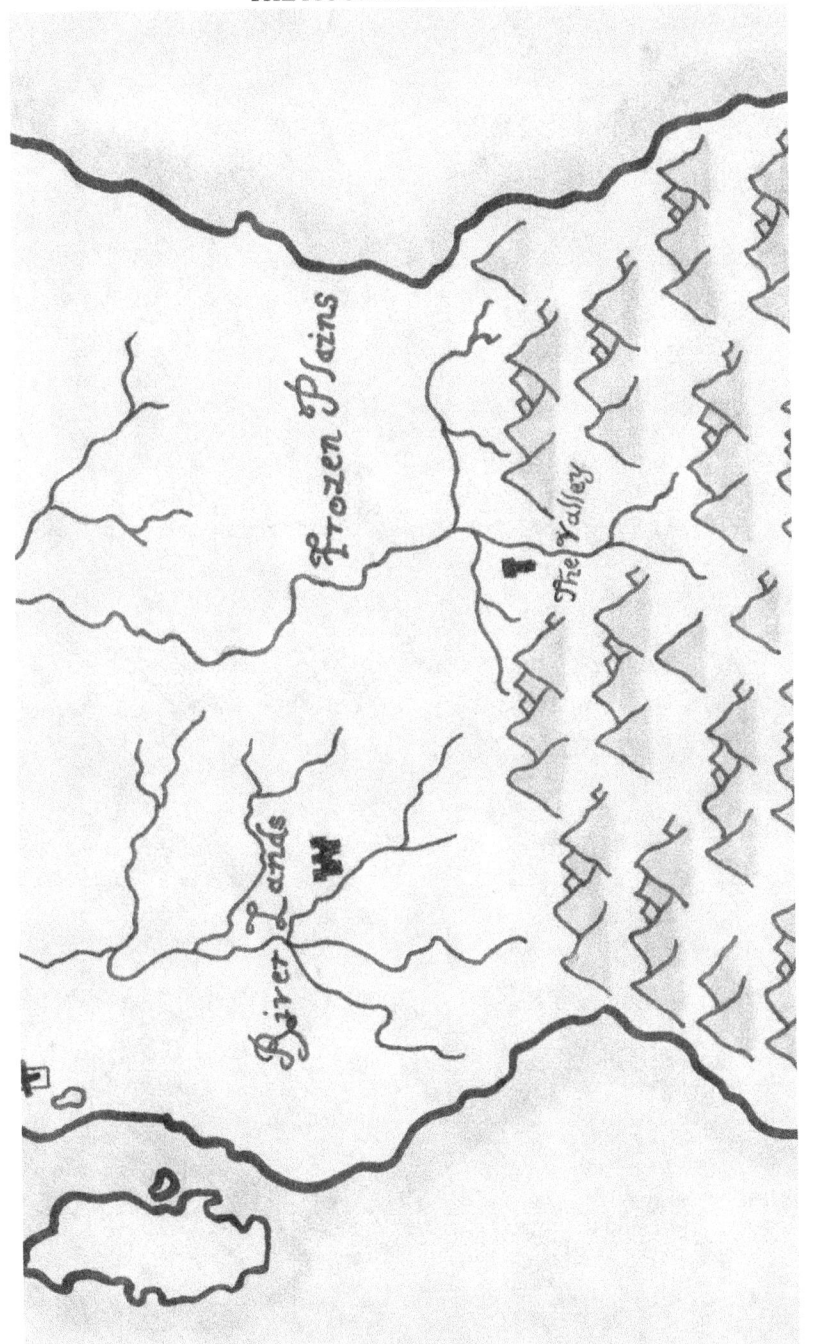

BENJAMIN J. ANDRUS

Prologue

The faint glow of the full moon cast a pale shine on the wood around him, and shadows danced wildly among the foreign trees. The sun had set a few hours ago, and night was steadily advancing on the frozen woods of the southern mountains. Waking amidst the howling and whistling of a frigid breeze, Renyard Storm was greeted by the crushing darkness of the alpine forest.

As he blinked away the fog that was trying to envelope his mind he focused on the moon, shining translucently through the thin, quickly moving layer of clouds. His head ached. Reaching up with a tentative hand he felt the side of his face, warm, wet; he knew he had to find help. He struggled against the unseen force holding him down and looked around frantically for his horse—his only friend out here—

his lifeline, and only means of survival. Panic crept in at the corner of his consciousness entreating him to give in to the growing night, and succumb to the darkness that was steadily enveloping him. *No, I must warn the others. They are depending on me,* he thought as he kept trying to stand. "I will not die until my oath is fulfilled," he yelled into the night. "This will not take me, I am descended from the bloodline of old Veldoria." He felt his face again, still warm, still wet. He knew enough from his experience as a warrior that his wound was fatal, but he refused to give in to the inevitable demands of death itself.

Picking himself up with a near fatal amount of strength, he found his footing and leaned heavily on a nearby tree. His eyes were wide with fear and frenzy, and a light layer of snow covered the landscape; he could see the dark red stain he had left on the ground. Gripping the hilt of his sword he struggled from tree to tree, lacking the power to hold himself upright on his own. "Lysee! Where is my horse?" Panic made a second attack, nearly defeating his dwindling resolve. With one last, crawling leap he fell heavily against a trunk of a smaller tree, and found the reigns of his horse tied carefully to it. "Gods and heaven smile on me this night." Pulling his boot-knife slowly from its concealed resting place he cut the leather straps and crawled onto the back of his faithful companion. "Take us home, Lysee. May your namesake, the goddess of the moon, keep us safe this night; that we may deliver our message to the others." The horse spurred into action by his touch, reared and sped forward, following her own path, winding between the closely knit trees in the direction of her stables; now that her rider had returned it was long past time she was safe and warm inside the castle walls. He clung to her mane with all but the last of his waning life. He knew if he could just get back to the city, cross the bridge into the castle, and shout to the others who waited for him there then he would have fulfilled his oath, completed his mission and saved countless lives. They needed to know—something had emerged from under the mountains.

He could feel the dark hand of death slowly wrap its icy fingers around his heart, but still he clung; no manner of tribulation would prevent him from delivering his message. He would laugh in the face of death itself—if it had a face—before he would give up his mission and fail his oath. The wind began to scream, like the voices of the dead around him. His legs went numb. "Just a little further, Lysee; we are almost home." The horse spurred forward, galloping wildly, from fear or urgency he could not tell. Cresting a hill, he could see the dim walls of the city Riverspring lit sparsely by torch light, and looming below him in the river valley. He fought against death's second advance with all that he could muster; his heart pounding maniacally in his chest, aching to be free from the burden the wounds had cost him. Trying to reach for his head again, he found his arm would not respond to the command; his fingers gripped the shredded reigns with the cold grasp of frostbite. He knew it would not take long for him to succumb to the unconsciousness of the endless slumber. If only he could reach the castle gates and tell the first person he saw what had happened out there today, he could then give in to the ever-growing call of the grave. After a few more yards, he could start to hear the conversation of the night guard and could almost feel the fire's heat on his face. "Not long now." Lysee did not slow her pace as she entered the bridge and nearly trampled the night guards who tried to grasp her reigns. Her mouth was foaming incessantly as she bucked and pulled against her would-be captors. All the while he was trying to scream to them, trying to relay his message, fulfill his oath, but his lips were frozen shut. They didn't seem to notice him lying against her neck as they fought for control of the crazed horse. Screams rang out in the dying light and his horse barged into something small and fragile.

He felt a guardsman grip him underneath his frozen arms and jerk him mercilessly off the now calming animal.

"This one's frozen. Fetch the doctor." His gruff voice was like music to his ears.

I have made it. I am here, and now they will know what has happened. I will tell them everything; the castle and its people will be safe. If only I could rest for a moment, I will regain enough strength to share my knowledge. I just need a moment to warm by the fire. He smiled to himself; he had made it, he was not too late. Death would have to wait for him as he told the guards his story. If he could just sleep.

Lonessa

"You're dead!" A small girl, wrapped in a fur cloak, stood out from behind a stack of barrels where she was hiding.

"No, I'm not." Her opponent, a freckled faced young man, contested as he strode quickly to where the girl was leaning gently on one foot. "That completely missed me! You were swinging blindly and ran away behind those." He argued while pointing to her pervious hiding place. His ginger hair bounced with every step nearly undoing the curls and covering his green eyes.

"No I felt it hit something. I felt it bounce back. You're dead, I win." She stomped her foot, turned on her heel and began walking away from her friend.

"That bail of straw, that is what you hit. Hey! Listen, don't go running off like that. It's just a game." He followed her—she was running now—but he was no match for her agile dance through the various obstacles of the busy castle streets. She just wanted to get away. For some reason she could not explain, she felt sad, horribly sad, but he was right— it was just a game. The sense of foreboding and gloom slowly prodding at her heart was a vast overreaction to the minuscule defeat of having hit a bail of straw, which she knew she did. But the tears, now creeping out of her eyes and drying softly in the warm valley breezes, were evidence of a larger fear that she could not dismantle.

The valley never got actual snow, being warmed by what the Lord Protector's scientists called 'cleansing waters' and the vast network of underground springs that started near the crest of the mountain and let out a steam that kept the winters chill and snow to the top of the hills on either side. But today felt different; the temperature was severely under-normal for early spring, and she could feel it. She had been alive thirteen summers and remembered eight of them clearly, and not once during the winter months had she felt cold underneath her mother's green and gold fur cloak. She shivered.

Seeing her escape she darted into the open door of the bakery; warm fires heated the stone walls where the baker, Mr Grahm, was hard at work tossing uncooked bread to and fro in a finely choreographed chaos. She attempted to remain unseen by scooting under a table, close to one of the wall ovens. Here she could hide from Garon and begin to regain her warmth.

The flour in the air danced with the smoke and stung her eyes causing an unwelcome tingling in her nose. Mr. Grahm got closer. Her nose was now being tormented by the smoky flour and could hardly withstand the onslaught any longer. She tried to resist the force welling inside her as best she could; knowing that if she let it go Garon would be sure to hear it. Her small hands clenched till the knuckles stood out white against the strain, and for a moment she forgot she was cold. Then it hit. Like the explosion of a thousand horses charging down the valley hillside, "Ahhh-Choo!" She screamed, and immediately covered her face and mouth, hoping that it could have gone un-noticed in the abnormally quiet bakery. She peered through a crack in her fingers to see the large round face of the baker staring down at her as she was huddled under a table.

"Lonessa, what are you doing here? Why are you on the floor? Come on out from under there and grab a slice of this fresh bread while it is still warm. You must be hungry it is nearly mid-afternoon." He grabbed her small hand in his, and beamed an approving smile down on her.

"Thanks, Mr. Grahm. I *am* hungry." She allowed him to hoist her out from under the table, swing her through the warm air of the bakery, and set her down gently on a table near a few large bowls covered with rags. His short curly brown hair bounced freely as he moved with surprising agility for a man of his girth, and the gracefulness with which he fetched Lonessa a fresh baguette fascinated her.

She sat there almost swaying with his every move as he danced about the bakery floor; the flour and smoke created a dreamlike haze in the room. She was transfixed like this for what, to her, seemed like hours. Then before her eyes a vision manifested itself out of the palpable air; two men, locked in a duel spanning centuries, their once shiny plate mail now bogged down with the dirt and grime of the ages; blow for blow they exchanged positions and tactics. Fading in and out of the vision, she saw the baguette wielding first knight land a crushing blow on the oven-like second, a sure victory. But the oven knight used tactics unknown to the aggressor; fire shot from his eyes and engulfed the baguette. He ripped off his helm and revealed long reddish-brown hair and bright brown eyes. The knight was a queen! Her mind, flitting back and forth between reality and the vision, confused the two in an amalgamation of dreamy warmth and fantastic sword play.

Snapping back to reality she noticed buttered bread on the table next to her. The rag covered bowls were gone and her ginger haired friend was seated and already digging into the soft loaf.

"What are you doing here Garon?" She jumped off the table and sat down on the bench. "I *did* win."

"Lonessa, I am telling you, you hit a bail of straw, not me. If you kept your eyes open while fighting you could be better. You are fast and fight hard, but when we play at swords you always close your eyes. I don't get it." The freckles on his face were starting to deepen while the rest of his skin stayed a fairest white.

The baker looked back from his oven, "I think the only way to decide this for certain is a rematch."

"Yeah!" Garon agreed enthusiastically.

"Fine, but I won the first time." She stubbornly insisted.

Mr. Grahm stooped down and whispered in Lonessa's ear, "Sometimes the winning is enough, not everyone has to know you won. Perhaps go easy on the boy?" He stood up and began to clear away the debris left by two hungry children devouring warm bread. "Now off with you two. Lonessa I will be seeing your mother later. It is your birthday tomorrow and she wanted to give me instructions about the cake. Is there anything special you want?"

"No, you make the best cakes already." She waved a carefree hand as she brushed the last of the airborne flour out of her eye-length bangs and bounded outside, wooden sword in hand, straight brown hair dancing in the warm valley breeze.

As she stepped outside a wooden blade missed her face by mere inches. She ducked and spun, throwing her legs out as she did, making contact with Garon's shin and sending him toppling, flailing wildly, into the mud. She darted away, "Catch me if you can! I will beat you fair and square this time!" He struggled to his feet and set off in pursuit of his younger friend. Mr. Grahm watched the two children disappear down the muddy castle streets and chucked softly to himself. Tomorrow was going to be a good day for Lonessa, but first he had a lot of preparations to make—cakes to build, rolls to brown, and most importantly a present to finish wrapping. Night was coming.

The two duelists had taken a break from their evenly matched fight to rest against the bails of straw set out for the night Guard's horses. The sun had set a few hours ago but neither child wanted to turn in just yet; they knew if they were not home in another hour the wrath of their parents would be quick and severe, but they wanted to eek out the last few minutes of fading daylight. As they picked up their play swords a bell started ringing in the thinning night air, heralding the approach of a rider. After a shared glance, both were off running with all the vim and excitement exclusive to two young children about to experience their first bit of real life to happen in their quiet little castle town for the first time. To the gate, then the bridge, they were bound to witness something interesting; no one had ever before approached this city after the sun had set.

Garon was the faster of the two and reached the gatehouse first. Lonessa was not far behind and she stopped dead in her tracks. "Garon stop!" she yelled. He did not hear. "Garon!" She darted ahead with a newfound energy and was trying her best to catch him. She had seen it coming over the bridge before he did, and she watched in horror as what she thought was a rabid steed barreled right into Garon's side. The night Guards were trying in vain to steady the horse and it flung its hooves about like a feral beast, catching Garon on the side of the head before he went down in a heap in the mud below. Lonessa screamed. The guards were yelling. The horse was bucking. A large man grabbed her by the shoulders and threw her into a stack of hay,

"Stay there!" he ordered. She obeyed.

She could not peal her eyes away from the ghastliest scene she had ever witnessed. A guard was pulling a body—presumably dead—off the horse. It looked frozen to the bone. The large man that threw her to safety was shielding Garon from the horse's flailing hooves, taking a shot to his shoulder as he did so. All was still. As soon as the rider was pried off her, the horse stopped and stood calmly nuzzling a nearby barrel of water as if she had returned from a lazy ride through the valley. The guards had managed to get the body inside and next to a fire, the large man was kneeling perfectly still over Garon, and the world seemed to stop. She had enough; a black calm took over her mind and narrowed her vision to a small pin focused on Garon's bleeding face and she remembered no more.

Aviana

With the fierceness of the southern-mountain winter, a cold wind rushed down the mountainside and swirled around Lady Aviana, her green and gold fur cloak toying with her ankles in time with the wind. Her unblinking eyes focused on the peak of Seri Umenriot, the gray mountain that loomed taller than the rest in the southern sky. Clouds bent and broke around the peak keeping the summit shrouded in mystery. No one had ever made it far enough south to see the mountain, nor did anyone even know how far away that mountain was—but still it loomed over the castle and the city of Riverspring— the final city before the expanse of the southern frozen desert. She re-wrapped the cloak against the harshness of the wind. Today was supposed to be a good day, honoring the day of her daughter's birth, but last night had altered their plans.

Taking one last glance at the far away Seri Umenriot, she turned awkwardly on her heel and slid back inside her daughter's room. Her husband was sitting in a small wooden chair by their daughter's bed; his head pressed down on his hands in grief and sadness, his face wet with recent tears. "Two dead in one night. How can such a tragedy strike my city? What god have we vexed to bring this doom upon our heads?"

"My dear sweet John, we have done nothing to displease any god. Fate and misfortune laugh down on us and we can but toil under the strain of her mirth."

"Fate, you speak to me about fate? My child's friend and one of my rangers are dead, my child has yet to awake from her unnatural slumber, and you speak to me about fate." He rose slowly and kissed the hand of his daughter. "I will be in the temple." The dull slaps of his boots echoed in the still air of Lonessa's room and in the heart of his wife as she watched him leave. Lady Aviana, feeling the weight of sorrow descend on her like a mantle, took the vacated seat next to her only child. "May the gods inhabit your dreams, and the river wash away your sorrow." A prayer past down for generations of Valley dwellers now pasted from the lips of the only member of the Lord Protectors family to have been born outside of the valley.

Her family had a difficult past and some people in the Five Kingdoms still viewed them as disloyal.

Aviana's forefathers were not traitors, nor usurpers, but they refused adamantly to be the king's yes men. For generations the Rawfields had been the governors of the coast in service of the King, but that was a long time ago. After a brutal war, the Colbralians of the Gold Coast bought the crown and restored the Rawfields to Fieldhaven, her home city and seat of the Rawfield's province. Lady Aviana was the second child of Justin Rawfield, the Lord Protector of the Midlands, and as such was married to John Bryne as soon as she came of age. She liked the vast mountain ranges of her new home, and the perpetual spring that the cleansing waters provided the valley. Two years after her marriage, on her only trip outside of the valley, she wanted to see the Seri Gorda the mountain range at the edge of the world; she nearly froze in a harsh summer storm and lost the little finger on her left hand to frostbite.

Lonessa stirred in her slumber, with a faint moan and a flickering of her eyelids. Lady Aviana leaned over her daughter, "It is safe honey. You can awaken." She brushed the light brown hair away from Lonessa's face.

"Mother?"

"Yes dear I am here. Are you all right? How do you feel?"

"Garon!" She shot up in bed and tried to rip the covers off.

"Lonessa, be still. I will tell you everything." Aviana scooted her chair closer and smoothed the folds from her dress. "I will tell you everything," She repeated, choking on the words. How was she to tell her only daughter that her friend was dead? She dreaded this conversation, the fear and nervousness that she felt earlier that day only grew now that the time had come to divulge the information to her precious child. Her mind wandered for a moment to thoughts of Garon's parents. How would they cope with the loss of a child? Could she do it? What if their places were reversed and they were the ones having to explain to their child that their friend was dead? How would they do it? How would she be able to carry on living when her only child was dead?

Her mind continued to wander to the day she gave birth to Lonessa, the day she almost did not survive; the day the doctor told her she would bare no more children. This, she knew, was a source of great pain to her husband John. His only child and heir to the seat of the south—The Valley—was a little girl, now lying in her bed, and would not carry on the family name. A wave of self-loathing and disappointment flooded over her walls of protection, and tears burst forth as she buried her face in her daughters bedding.

"Mother, what is it? What has happened?" There were tears in her voice, and she never sounded so helpless to Aviana before.

"The horse that you saw last night, the one that ran so wildly into our streets bore a rider, one of the rangers. He was patrolling with his party near the foothills of Seri Umenriot. They did not survive. He alone had enough strength to find his horse and return to us. But the journey proved too much for him and he was dead long before he passed over our bridge." Aviana sighed.

"But what of Garon? What happened to him?"

A long and torturous silence descended upon the room. With the courage only available to a child Lonessa spoke again. "Is he dead?"

A slight almost imperceptible nod from her mother told her everything she feared was true.

"Why? How? I want to see him." Tears now streaming from her eyes, left pink streaks on her small, round, dirty face.

"His funeral is set for tomorrow where he will be buried with our kinsmen on the mountain side. You can see him then." Aviana patted her hand and stood to leave the room.

"Don't go mother, please. I don't want to be alone."

"I am only sending someone to fetch your father. He will be glad you are awake."

The castle halls were cold and damp to the grieving mother. Never in her time here in the Valley had she felt so alone. Her only child lay in her bed, broken and depressed, her husband had not touched her with love in his eyes for over three months, and she missed her homeland and family. A letter had arrived from Fieldhaven two days ago with the news that her father had been taken ill and the doctors had tried everything. He was dying. *My father, my daughter, what have I done to deserve this. Please don't take my husband.*

"You there." She called to the closest guard. "Summon the Lord Protector. His daughter is awake."

"Yes my lady." The guard bowed and walked quickly down the hallway. The sound of clinking mail echoed in her heart as it echoed in the hallway.

When Aviana re-entered the room she found Lonessa dressed and tying up the last of her boot laces. *My daughter, so grown. It is hard to remember she is only thirteen.*

"Where are you going?" She asked, trying to pull together the falling pieces of her heart.

"Out. I want to find Garon. He thinks that I don't know that I hit a bale of hay yesterday and I want to make sure that he knows I lost. He was always better at swords than I was, and I need to apologize to him."

"Honey, Garon is gone."

"I can bring him back!" Lonessa yelled. "All I have to do is tell him he was right." Tears were flowing freely down her young cheeks.

"That is not how it works." Aviana could not hold back her own tears.

John Byrne, Lord Protector of the Valley flew into his daughters room. The door didn't even have time to close behind him before he fell to his knees in front of his daughter, his tears carving new wrinkles on his already careworn face.

"Lonessa, my sweet, sweet child." He embraced her.

"Father, I must go." Lonessa stood up straight.

Aviana moved behind her husband and laid her hands on his strong shoulders. Lonessa made eye contact with her and she tried to will her out of sadness.

"Go where, my darling." John asked.

"I have to go. I need to see him." Was all Lonessa could say between sobs.

"My child. He is dead." He said.

The words echoed in Aviana's ears.

"He can't be dead, father, he can't I need to make things right, I was such a brat to him yesterday, and I feel so awful." Looking into her father's caring eyes with her own, large and brown, she pleaded with him. "You are Lord Protector of the Valley, steward of the King, and High Guard of the Mountains. Please, please for my sake tell me I can see Garon today." She wept freely now.

John's heart nearly broke from the weight of the sorrow on his house and lands, "Life is the great master, Lonessa, the gods give it, and the gods take it away. Who are we to defy their will? We will go to temple and pray for the soul of your friend."

They passed by the bakers shop on their way from their large estate to the temple built to honor the mountain gods hundreds of years before the city was built around it. She looked in expecting to see Garon talking with Mr. Grahm but all she saw was the smoky flour filled air slowly swirling with the baker's deliberate movements. He noticed her and came to the door. Raising a hand he saluted the Lord Protector and his family, bowing his head in reverence and mourning for the loss the city had sustained. Not until now did Aviana remember it was her young daughter's birthday, and a new wave of tears nearly tripped her as she walked mournfully along the muddy street in the fading twilight of a moonless spring evening in the Valley.

Renyard

The fire crackled and smoked, giving off little heat in the small stone room of the gatehouse as Renyard Storm sat on a loosely tied bail of straw, trying to warm his hands by this uncooperative flame. The smoke from the dying blaze was beginning to fill the room and he wondered at how he had yet to choke on the normally suffocating fumes. He was about to open his lips and call out to whoever could hear him to alleviate the pressure on his limbs so he could stoke the fire when the door swung open and the smoke rushed out causing an audible swish as the heat escaped from the room. Two guardsmen entered, both looking very grave—one with a liter and the other carrying a shovel. He wanted to speak.

Now was his time. These two men could alert the rest of the castle to what he had seen out past the mountains end, but before he could utter a word the taller man spoke up.

"Still cold is he? This room is blazing. Put that fire out. No need for such waste during the day."

"Aye sir," obeyed the shovel-carrying soldier, sloshing water onto the dying fire.

Blazing? He thought to himself, *I must have a chill, too long out beyond the reach of warmth. A few more moments and I will have warmed back up. I still must tell them,* he thought to himself. Searching for the right words to express the horror and fear he had felt that night was difficult in this bucolic little gatehouse of the castle where he was born. He must tell them. After finally gaining the courage to bring the memories back to his mind—the effort nearly doubled him over, shaking every limb and inducing a cold sweat as the atrocities of the previous night washed over him, he attempted to speak. Nothing. No sound came from his frozen lips, but he could hear the words in his head, rattling around like the dwindling echoes of a horrible nightmare. Reaching out to grab the first guard as he leaned in to pick him up he paused. *Why is he picking me up?* He asked, confused. With the awful suddenness of death itself, the guard grabbed his body threw it on to the litter and motioned for his companion to grab the other end.

"'Ere ya go, lift that end and we will bring him to the mountain side." The first man spoke with a rough voice but there was compassion in his words.

"Aye sir." The shovel wedged between his upper

arm and chest the second man lifted the liter, and he watched in horror as they carried out his body. A sickness passed through him, causing the world to spin and whirl. The small room seemed to shrink. He needed fresh air and he was still cold. When he rushed outside the sun shone brightly almost mocking him with its golden rays, but he could not feel it on his skin. The wind toyed with his long jet-black hair, but he could not feel it. *What has happened to me? What is this magic?* Panic struck him again. His heart raced in his chest, or rather, he felt his heart should be racing in his chest yet he felt nothing—not a single beat. Reaching up to his neck he noticed his hands for the first time, blue, as blue as the pale morning sky in the valley. He was dead—frozen on his horse before he reached Riverspring, or bled out from the wound on his head. He reached up, to see how bad it was, and was not altogether surprised to find that it was not there. *How is this possible, how am I to continue?* Then the words of the Mountain Rangers came rushing back to him. At the time he did not understand the full meaning of them, and thought they were just words—an oath to scare off lesser men. But now he realized that he bound himself to the protection of this land even beyond death. *I, Renyard Storm, swear by the mountain gods to protect and defend the people of the Valley, the people of the realm, and the Lord Protector. I will forsake not my post; I will forsake not my mission. I will bear loyalty and fealty to the Lord Protector of Riverspring, my commanders, and my brothers in arms. I am a Mountain Ranger. From this moment onward even past death I will be the shield of Riverspring and the realm. So say we brothers.* Had these words bound him? When he swore them before the temple many years ago he did not believe in the mountain gods, mere shadows, and stories for the younger children. But here he was, dead, walking the streets of Riverspring, and oh so cold.

He wandered the streets of the castle town aimlessly. He had only one experience with death but was far too young to remember it. His mother had died shortly after his birth and his father never spoke of it. Every mission he undertook, save the last one with the Mountain Rangers, had been quiet. For twelve years he had roamed and ranged the mountains south of Riverspring, even approaching the foothills of Seri Umenriot itself, where giants are said to still wander the alpine forests. Never once had he lost a member of his troop. Never once had he come face to face with death, until that night. *What had happened that night?* The memories were starting to fade now. What was once so clear in his mind only a few hours before now seemed but a wisp of a dream, images of giants, and wolf-headed men, or wild men in wolf's clothing—or was that only a nightmare of his youth? He could not remember. 'Death,' he mused, 'has a way of erasing life.'

The long low bells of the temple broke his reverie. A service was starting, or ending, but it wasn't weeks end. *What was the occasion?* He wound his way slowly in the direction of the temple. Oblivious to the new found incorporeal nature, he was standing in the middle of a blacksmith's cart when a voice cried out and he looked up astonished. A small girl wearing green canvas pants and a grey pullover shirt was looking right at him—at him, not through him as everyone else had done.

"You can see me?" he spoke, or tried to speak.

"Yes, you're dead." Her dirty face showed the stains of tears and the smudges of her mother's thumb where she'd tried to clean it.

"How is it you can see and hear me?"

"I can see you, 'cuse I can see you, and I don't really hear you, I just know what you are saying. I don't know how that works. How did you die?"

"I don't remember." That scared him, but try as he might, the more he thought about his life the less he remembered.

"My best friend died, yesterday night. He was run over by a wild horse."

"Should you not be saddened by this?"

"I was, but I will bring him back. I made a promise with the mountain gods today. They spoke to me. I offered my life as their servant, and they promised he would come back."

"I do not worship the mountain gods? Or any gods..."

"Why not? They say they have power over life and death, and you are dead, so..." her voice trailed off as if he were supposed to follow her logic, but he was lost, the shock of being able to communicate with the living, even if it was this one girl, was still fresh in his mind. He felt that he had something of terrible importance to tell her but it was slipping out of his grasp.

"I have something very important to tell you, little miss."

"Lonessa Bryne."

"Miss Bryne, oh! My Lady," he bowed and for the first time realized he was in a cart, "You are the daughter of our Lord Protector," he said while side stepping out into the open. "Yes, but don't tell him. I made a bargain with the mountain gods. He would not understand."

"I do not think you need worry about that. You are the only one I can talk to."

"Well, good. Now if you will pardon me Sir Knight."

"Renyard Storm."

"Sir Renyard Storm, I need to go back to the Temple."

"By your leave, my lady." He bowed again.

Lonessa curtsied as best as she could, stuck her chin out, and all but marched back to the temple. Renyard followed at a distance, careful to keep out of her sight.

Lonessa strode deliberately into the temple's center and knelt carefully on the cold stone hearth of the fire that was in the center of the round building. The statues of the mountain gods stood silently, watching her mouth her prayer almost inaudibly.

"If you just bring him back, let me play with him again, I will be your servant." She echoed her promise from earlier. "May the mountains forever stand in peace," Adding the traditional priestly close to her prayer.

Renyard watched as tears forced their way out of her tightly closed eyes. His heart yearned to help her, to comfort her pain. *Why am I still here if not to protect the people of The Valley*. He was on the verge of kneeling beside her and offering his help when she stood.

"Why?" she screamed at the statue of a giant man holding a horn.

Mr. Grahm slowly appeared from the shadows, "I heard your prayers little one. The gods do not interfere with life and death any longer."

"They told me so. They said I could...win him back." She lost her battle, and collapsed into a heap of tears as she sobbed violently in his arms. "Let's get you back to your parents. It was kind of them to let you come back to the temple to pray for your friend. But now it is night and you should be safe in bed."

"It was my fault Mr. Grahm. I let him die, so I can bring him back."

"Hush child, no more of that talk." He lifted her in his unusually strong arms and carried her across the city to the castle.

Renyard left the temple and wandered around the dark city streets. The echoes of shops closing and people turning-in for the night dwindle away into crushing silence. There was no sign of the moon in the sky that night.

Gravous

"I have heard from my little crickets that the Broken Lands have nearly three times the amount of gold to be dug from those hills as the Gold Coast itself." He shoved another mouthful of chicken breast and spiced peppers into his mouth even though he had yet to finish his last bite. "If it were up to me, our armies would already be on the move to that untapped wasteland." Bits of his mid-afternoon meal escaped from his champing jaws as he spoke. The High Council sat around the heavy wooden table, no one daring to speak. "What of the horsemen there? What of the nomadic tribes of that barren desert? Two thousand men at arms would dispatch those vagabonds in less than a month. Do you deny this?"

His round face was turning a bright shade of red as he struggled against his massive weight. The pressure on his lungs added to the suffocating wheeze that fought through the food to form itself into words.

"Your Grace, I must advise against this." Lord Gravous Lynch, the youngest and newest member of the High Council spoke up. He arrived from Fieldhaven just two months before this meeting, taking the place of his Lord Father's uncle, who had died in his sleep a fortnight before. "For many generations the five mighty houses vied for rule of the Broken Lands, they cannot be held." His long black hair hung loosely around his studded leather jerkin. The great hall of the ancient seat of the Colbralians fell silent, Lord Robsfeld stopped his loud chewing for a moment to look at this newcomer, his face growing even redder, bordering on purple.

"For generations," Started Robsfeld, "the Great Houses, not the King, I am the King." The Colbralian's had been Lord Protectors of the Gold Coast for hundreds of years, but it was not until after the War of the Feathers did they buy the rights to the Throne. "I can draw on the might of all the kingdoms. A united army, under the royal banner, will fare better than the smaller broken raiders of the individual lords alone. Do you deny this Lord Lynch?" The King spat through his thin wispy gray beard.

"Your Grace, I apologize for our overzealous member. I will see to his education in the courtly matters personally." Lord Felter Morris cooed to the King obsequiously. "He will not speak out of turn again." Lord Morris bowed low, baring his cleanly shaven head to the room. He kept his head and face clean of all hair, including the ritual shaving of his eyebrows, and Gravous heard rumors that those were not the only things he shaved.

"No need to apologize, Lord Morris. No doubt, he wants to leave his mark on the royal court. However he does speak the truth." For a rare moment Robsfeld's mouth was empty. "How would you approach the matter?" He directed the question to Gravous.

"By your leave, Your Grace, I would not." Gravous was sitting quite still and only a slight twitch of his finely chiseled, stubble covered chin betrayed his inner fear at confronting the Lord of the Gold Coast, richest man in the realm, and king.

Back in his homeland he had heard rumors of the Colbralian's wealth, but did not believe them until he arrived in Aurorum. The city was practically built out of marble, with gold trim on nearly every building. It had been rumored that the Colbralian family had bought the crown when the five houses met to end the disputes and come together under one banner. Money like that would have been near impossible to wield—the price of a crown, paid to four other houses —but seeing the seat of their power Lord Gravous Lynch had no doubt in his mind that is exactly what they did. But that had happened many generations ago and the secrets held by the grave are the hardest to reveal. His mind came back to the matter at hand. "There are ways to expand your riches without risking the lives of so many men." He decided to appeal to the king's heart, but before the King could respond Lord Morris chimed in again.

"Your Grace, I will speak to this impetuous lord. By your leave, we will leave you to your meal." He gave a glance to the rest of the council and all four men stood and bowed to the King in unison leaving him to his feast.

When the metal door—all the doors in The Golden Hall were metal—slammed shut with an echoing boom, Lord Morris turned swiftly and grabbed Gravous by the throat. "What do you think you are doing?" He hissed through his yellow teeth. He was nearly twice as old as Gravous but a few inches shorter.

"Lords, please." Lord Potter Corbett stepped between them, dislodging Lord Morris's clinging hand. "We are the king's men. Leave the brawling for the small folk and peasants in Little Town. Up here a solution can be found in a more *civilized* manner." His gray beard was streaked with black framing his chin and his golden hair hung nearly to his eyes as he stood between the two lords.

Gravous did not much like the way Lord Corbett emphasized civilized. "I beg your pardon, lords, I am new and know very little about court. I beg your forgiveness and entreat you to discuss the matter further with me." He bowed low, not taking his eyes off of his rival.

Lord Robyn Hamstead, the oldest of the council and quite possibly the oldest man alive, leaned heavily on his cane as he hobbled up to face the two fighting men. "Many m-m-men have come and gone from c-c-court. I have served three k-k-kings myself. The only c-c-constant in this realm is the c-ccouncil." His deliberate and measured speech was dominated by a stutter. "I do not know how you wiggled into this p-p-position, but now that you are here, remind yourself daily of that fact. We are the K-k-king's men, and what the King wishes we p-p-provide." His long white hair blended into the thin wisp of a beard that outlined his wrinkled face.

Lord Morris cut the old man's speech short. "For generations we have represented the interests of the Five Kingdoms before the Royal Court. You would do well to remember where you come from boy." Gravous knew very well where he came from, but he could not let them know.

Gravous was the adopted son of Edward Lynch, the cousin of Justin Rawfield, the Lord Protector of the Midlands, and was chosen to represent them at court. But he knew his true home, and he would heed the old man's advice. He would indeed remember where he came from.

"I beg your pardon again, a momentary lapse in judgment. It will not happen again." This game of cat and mouse was worse than he had imagined. Everything these members of court had told him so far was a twisted version of the truth. "If we represent the Five Kingdoms, sir, where is the Valley? A humble question befitting a newcomer to this high honor." He added the last part quickly as Lord Morris glowered at him.

"The Valley has not sent a representative to court in generations. They are too busy fighting the earth itself to worry about what goes on in the real world." Lord Robyn chuckled these words to Gravous's relief. "The Brynes stay hidden in their mountains and care little for what happens outside their borders."

Lord Morris waved his hand in dismissal, "A Raven at court?" Gravous joined in the laughter half a beat late hoping no one noticed, but Lord Corbett's eyes were on him. Through the feigned laughing he could tell that he had aroused his suspicions.

"If you will excuse me my lords, I will retire to my chambers and contemplate my origin." Again relieved to see his joke passed well with the council. *I need to be more careful,* he thought to himself as he passed out of the royal sector and into the courtyard.

The sun shone brilliantly in the clear light blue sky, and a hot wind struck his face as it blew past him and over Little Town before it reached the sea. Aurorum was nestled between the golden bay and the Grand River with Little Town clinging to its walls. Most of the poor would live in this collection of mud huts and thatched roofs while gathering fish and other resources for the King out of the waters below. Gravous traced a path with his eyes through Little Town and out to sea, once again marveling at the bay. The water reflected the sun's rays and appeared to be made from liquid gold, bouncing and toying with the rocks on the beach. From this courtyard, high above sea level, he could see many leagues out across the inlet and all of them reflected the sun's color.

He leaned against the marble railing and mused on his homeland. Far across the bay were the 'Broken Lands' to the people of the Five Kingdoms, but to him they were home. He remembered scrambling across the rocky hill faces, catching his first wild horse, fishing in the many land locked lakes, and learning to live off what little the land provided him. But all of that was fading with time; it had been nearly fifteen summers since he last laid eyes on the land of his birth, the tribes there cared not for politics and scheming, and rarely warred amongst themselves. But on one of the rare occasions that the tribes did war he had been carried off by raiders and sold to slave traders from the Midlands at age ten. His strength and cunning had allowed him to win the favor of his Lord Master, Edward Lynch, and he was raised as one of them. But in his heart he was not one of them. He was free. He was a force of nature.

Another gust of wind whipped past him and out to sea, bringing with it the unwelcome but familiar voice of Lord Robyn Hamstead, shaky and frail. The oldest man in the kingdoms was almost upon him when he turned around. He cursed himself under his breath; there was a time no one could catch him unaware, but this old frail man was nearly close enough to knife him before he'd been detected. Vowing not to be caught off guard like this again, he put on the mask of a royal court member. "Lord Hamstead, to what do I owe this visit?"

"I wanted to speak to you without the p-p-prying ears of the other m-m-members." His voice sounded more calculated than usual and Gravous could not decide if it was a product of his age or if the old man was scheming.

"Speak with me, my good lord. You honor me with this request. Age grants wisdom, and I will gladly hear your words."

The ancient man shifted his weight and leaned

heavily on the railing. "The royal c-c-court has been around for hundreds of years." He began breathing heavily between words. "It is a remnant-"

"-Of the Senate that ruled the Ancient Lands before the sundering." Gravous interrupted. "And as the legend goes, the Great Kings of Veldoria adopted this practice but with the Lord Protectors, former Monarchs in their own right, appointed one member from their Kingdom to sit on the Council. I know my world history Lord Hamstead."

"If you k-k-knew it well enough, you would respect the s-s-seat which you hold."

"I hold this seat with-" The force with which the old man slammed his cane onto the marble pathway sent echoes tumbling around the courtyard and startled Gravous out of speech.

"You have no respect! You are a p-p-product of over breeding and under educating. Your Lord Father will be disgraced in front of the king."

"But, if history is true, he is the first among equals of the Lord Protectors." Gravous was getting nervous, but still could not hold his tongue from betraying his thoughts to the world.

"He is your *King*!" Robyn scolded him in a voice that rang clearly off the castle walls and faded out in Little Town. "His family bought that right after the War of the Feathers. Mind your tongue boy, people have d-d-died for thinking less. W-w-watch your w-w-words."

"I apologize," Gravous wheezed through clenched teeth. His whole body was screaming at him to put this old man in his place. No one spoke to him this way, but this was a different place and a different set of rules. He should be thankful this man was willing to speak with him and not cast him aside. "I am looking forward to studying seasoned members of the court such as yourself. You can provide me with a font of wisdom and knowledge." He almost choked on the words and bowed deeply, deeply enough to hide his face, which was grimacing against the spiritual turmoil he felt.

"Very g-g-good, my boy." The old man's hand descended lightly on his shoulder and Gravous blenched from the surprisingly strong grip. The foul smell of age and skin oil danced on the breeze as Lord Hamstead leaned in close to whisper in his ear. "I know w-w-where you came from boy. Do n-n-not give me cause to share my knowledge." *How could this man have figured it out. What am I to do. Deny it, he has no proof.* Gravous hoped for the wind to pick up and carry away the rotten smell that berated him each time the ancient lord stuttered out his words. But there was a long still silence; even the wind had abandoned the courtyard as the two lords faced each other.

Gravous broke away first; he needed to breathe, "My Good Lord Robyn Hamstead, I must take my leave of you and prepare for the day tomorrow. I do not wish to dishonor the Royal Council again, and would greatly desire your input on the appropriate actions for one in our position." He bowed again, hoping the old man was convinced by his contriteness.

Lord Robyn laughed causing his old frame to bend and buckle under the strain. "I will accompany you to your c-c-chambers. There are more than a few basic things that I can teach you. I do not wish you to mis-mis-misunderstand my motives. You remind me of m-myself, many ages ago. I see great potential in you, if you can overcome your bloodline," he added in a low commanding tone. "Lead the way Lord Lynch. Let an old m-m-man lean on your arm." He took Gravous's arm and leaned heavily as they walked back towards the castle.

***

He woke early the next morning after a night of restless sleep, and for many hours, wandered aimlessly about the castle, losing himself in the many halls and passages in the underbelly and sewers. This was the last place he expected to be found; after what had happened, he hoped he never was. The Royal Council would be in an uproar, and the King would be furious this had delayed his feast.

Once a year since the dawn of the great Veldorian Kingdom of old there had been a King's Feast. This year's was to take place in less than a month. The ancient ones were open to everyone; the poor and beggars and destitute would come and eat in the king's presence. But after the kingdoms split and declared their own lords, the feast at Aurorum began to change. By the time the king's great-grandfather bought back the crown, the King's Feast had already turned into a political vetting, and this King followed in the path of his fore-fathers, selling seats, like favors, to only the noblest and most respected houses of the realm.

"Lord Lynch, ho!" a steely voice rang out in the

castle hall, startling Gravous.

He snapped back to reality. "Who goes there?"

"Lord Lynch, your presence is requested in the Royal Court," a soldier bellowed, clad in the armor of the King's Guard with three interlocking gold coins all displaying the profile bust of the current King.

Gravous had always wondered how gold could serve as a house sigil, moreover, how one man would have the audacity to put his likeness on it, but he had to focus. "I went for a walk in the morning air and seem to have lost my way. If you could take me back, I do not wish to miss the council's summons."

"My, lord? You did not hear?"

"Hear what?" Gravous lied.

"Follow me, I will take you." The guard turned and clattered briskly down the passage. Gravous wondered how he could not have heard this noise coming. And once again he had opportunity to curse himself for being less aware than he should have been. He knew this kind of behavior would get him killed. He hurried after the guard, still cursing himself silently.

The great metal door stood before him, the three interlocking gold rings taunted Gravous to open them and pass within. There was nothing to do now, the guard that escorted him out of the underbelly stood behind him. Gravous thought he heard him reach around and draw his sword an inch or two out of its scabbard; he knew he had to enter that room, or die a dishonorable death from starvation in one of the many dungeon cells that comprised the majority of the underbelly. *How could they know? They cannot know, this is normal protocol. I am a*

Breaker of Worlds. He thought to himself, *a Breaker of Worlds.* He could not remember the name of his people in their native tongue—only the title the Five Kingdoms used to refer to his true family.

Disappointed, he once again donned the mantle of Lord and swung open the heavy metal doors. "Lord Gravous Lynch, about time you decided to answer your king's summons," Robsfeld roared.

"I beg all your apologies, my lords, Your Grace," bowing to hide his face as he nearly spat the last word, "I was lost in a reverie during my morning walk and found myself in the underbelly. I pray you will all forgive me for my ignorance of direction." There was a silence. All eyes were on the King, waiting to see his reaction, letting him dictate the mood of this reprimand. He roared with laughter and the other two lords joined him, not without a meaning glance from Lord Corbett.

"Lost in the underbelly, you really are green aren't you?" The King bellowed in his mirth. Relief flooded over Gravous as he took his seat at the foot of the table, much too large for the three council members that were present, and the king. "But your foolishness aside," he calmed, "What are we to do about this; doubtless you have heard of the passing of Lord Robyn Hamstead of Blackwatch in the Marsh."

Gravous gave his best effort to look surprised. "Your Grace, he has died? Only last night he was in my room assisting me with my preparations for your feast." *I need to leave the castle.* He thought as he could feel the eyes of the other two council members.

"There will be no feast; make no further mention

of it! That old man had the indecency to die so close to the day of my celebration. Now I will have to postpone for another fortnight at least. And all the nobles from the Five Kingdoms will be here. They have doubtless left their castles already. Do you know the expense of housing those blasted uncouth men for that time? I can't very well send them back and tell them to make the journey twice in a month."

"Your Grace," Lord Corbett spoke up, "We can be done with the funeral preparations by tomorrow evening. His burial can be a solemn event used to further unite the kingdoms in mourning a great servant of the realm. And as to the money for the added expense, Cor Donovan has suggested a plan which would raise enough to cover this slight inconvenience."

"What?!" The King bellowed, and even Lord Morris looked at him with surprise.

"As macabre as it is, Your Grace, we have been making arrangements for his passing for months now. He was nearly eighty-five and already ten years older than any other man alive, I felt it was my duty, our duty," he added gesturing to Gravous, including him in the funeral preparations. "To make sure Your Grace was not disturbed by such an awful ordeal."

"But Lord Lynch has only been here a few weeks?"

"Perhaps, but his actions were essential for the expediting of the funeral. Green as he is, when I came to him for help, he was more than willing to assist me in a task we deemed would free your rule from the unpleasantness of mortality." While Lord Corbett was talking, Gravous was doing his best to appear as if he knew what was going on, however his mind was racing, What *does he know? Why is he including me? How am I to handle this new horror?* His outward demeanor betrayed no sign of his inward shock.

"Your Grace, if it pleases you with but a few modifications, ones I can attend to myself, we can hold the feast as planned, and as I say use it as a celebration of an old man's victory over death." Lord Corbett concluded.

"Make it so. Lynch, I want you to oversee the modifications."

"As Your Grace commands." Gravous bowed in his chair, he had already bowed more in the two months he was in the castle than any other time in his life.

"Now to other business. Who replaces the old buzzard?" The King was looking around for something to drink. "Wine!" he bellowed when he realized the table was bare. A young boy barely ten and bald-headed ran up to him and filled a glass from a beaker and placed it in front of the king. He had many young boys running about him with food and drink and it was not uncommon to see them hovering around the council chamber.

"Two new council members in two months. Your Grace, is that wise? Perhaps we let Lord Lynch settle in before we make a new appointment." Lord Morris asked with his eyes narrowed.

"No, there are only a few times I chose to lean on tradition, but this is one of them, Lord Morris. The kingdoms would be in an uproar if we did not choose from one of them before the feast." The King responded in a rare show of cunning.

"Lord Hamstead was from the marshes. He has

many sons that could be summoned to serve the King." Lord Morris observed. "I will send a summons to the Blackwatch, they will respond."

"Your Grace, if I might make the suggestion." Gravous put his hand in the center of the table. "If as the saying is true, the Brynes care not for what happens outside their borders. Why not summon one of them? You could even force them to comply. Besides, they have more claim to a council seat than the lesser Lords of the Blackwatch, and, I am sure, would prove to be no obstacle for the conquest of the Broken Lands."

"Have you had a change of heart then? Just yesterday morning you advised against attacking." The King eyed him narrowly. "But no matter. John Bryne refuses to send an envoy, and always has."

"No, Your Grace, I still believe it would not be in your best interest to attack the Broken Lands, but if you want support from the council, why not choose from those who will not oppose you? The Marsh is sure to oppose the invasion of a land where they gather riches through trade and diplomatic relations with the savages. The Valley will surely not support a land so far from their home instead of their King." Gravous had to bite his tongue as he called his kinsman savages, but he knew a council member from the Marsh would be sure to have the same cunning and trickery as these men here. There was a chance, he felt, that a man of the Valley would not pose the same threat to his discovery.

"Agreed. Send word immediately: I, King Robsfeld Colbralian, Lord Protector of the Gold Coast and Protector of the Realm, do hereby call upon The

Valley, smallest of the kingdoms, to provide a lord to sit on the Royal Council." The King stood to leave and the other three men jumped out of their chairs in respect. "And make sure the Blackwatch sends a replacement as well."

"I will see it done." Gravous bowed and watched the large man waddle through the great metal doors.

Lord Morris turned as soon as the door slammed shut and yelled at Gravous. "How dare you disrespect me in front of the King? I am his cousin's son."

"If you will excuse me, my lord, Lord Corbett and I have much to discuss about the coming feast." Gravous bowed to him and left the chamber followed by Lord Corbett and for the first time since his arrival he felt he had succeeded.

That night, as he sat on his balcony musing over what had taken place and recounting the plan Lord Corbett had hatched, he studied the intricate patterns of the stars through the smoke of his pipe. Only somewhat surprised by the lack of a moon in the sky.

Tobin

Tobin set down his parcel on a cushiony spot of moss next to a large tree and took a seat. The sun was poking out from behind some tentative clouds and the air was thick with the humidity off the swamp; the air was always dense this far into the back country of The Marshes. He had traveled only a few miles east of his home, Blackwatch in the Marsh, on foot because no horse would be able to wade through the thick mud of the marsh. Tobin had found a hidden path of solid land leading back to his now favorite fishing hole.

He brandished his fishing rod, cutting a swath through the thick air, and attached his bait to the end of the line—a small portion of rotting chicken. After casting the bait into the depths of a nearby pool he leaned back a bit, took up his pipe, and lit it. Taking a few quick puffs he settled down on the cushion of moss and focused on the tip of his rod. Fishing relaxed Tobin, and after a stressful day of preparing to travel to Aurorum for the King's feast, he would have to leave by tomorrow morning. This afternoon was all his. He enjoyed a peaceful life, outside of the prying eyes of his father, and the misshapen chaos that polluted the capital of the Five Kingdoms. He hated going to the capital, but as a member of Lord Robyn Hamstead's family he was expected to be at the feast and he knew he would be severely punished if he did not attend.

A large bird with long legs swooped overhead and landed not very far from where Tobin was blowing smoke rings into the still air of the swamp. The rod tip jumped. He carefully set down his pipe and gripped the rod with both hands. He felt the creature on the other end jerk against the line. His heart started racing, *this has to be the biggest catch of the season*, he thought, feeling the beast pull against the tackle. Bracing against the tree and tugging hard against the unknown from the swamp, Tobin started to wrap the twine around the sturdy wooden rod to bring the fish—if that is what it was—closer to its capture. Branches snapped and broke behind him, but he did not notice because a large fish jumped out of the water and he was oblivious to all else that moved. If it were not for the tree, the shock would have felled him, but leaning harder and wrapping faster he started to bring this swamp giant closer. It was huge! He could see it was as long as a small man, or a boy, when it had jumped from the water. A hand grasped his shoulder and he jumped, on the verge of dropping his tackle.

"What are you doing, older brother?" The voice of his little sister Fallia rang clear through the swamp. She knelt down and started to pick flowers from the muddy ground. Her blonde hair bounced as she moved and Tobin wondered, not for the first time, how she was the only child not to have brown hair.

"How did you find me?" He breathed a sigh of relief, and refocused on the battle at hand. "I will always be able to find you. There are riders from Aurorum at the Blackwatch. They want you to come back and get ready to leave. It will take you a week to get there, and you need to attend that feast."

"Let me land this fish. Here, grab the net from next to the tree there." He said, bending his neck towards the tree. She grabbed it and crouched down close to the water's edge, waiting for her older brother to pull in his catch.

It jumped again and Fallia let out a small scream, "That is the largest fish I have ever seen!"

"You are only fifteen, you haven't seen anything yet. Just be ready, he is close."

"Yeah, well you are only fifteen too. Ten months isn't that long. How much could you have seen?" She argued as her blue eyes scanned down from where Tobin's line was being wrapped around the rod, to where it entered the water, zig-zagging across the surface. Then she saw it. It was silver and its tail was the size of her head. She dropped the net and backed up screaming. "No way am I getting near that, it will eat me!"

Tobin cursed her under his breath and gave one last large yank on the twine. This would either land the catch of the year or break his tackle. Realizing his eyes were closed when he did it, he knew it worked from the screams of fearful delight echoing across swamp from his little sister. He opened his eyes. The monster, flopping and gasping on the moss, was taller than his sister, nearly four feet long and two feet thick with whiskers and a large flat mouth. Tobin tried to pull his hook out of the fish's mouth but the beast had inhaled it whole.

"It must weigh a ton!" Fallia exclaimed.

"Maybe, but we still need to carry it back; this will cook up nicely!" There was no hiding the excitement in Tobin's voice. *I can't wait for father to see this,* he thought, but did not share with his sister. She was always their father's favorite and he, being the second youngest, had a hard time living up to the expectations he had of them. Havar, the oldest at twenty-six, was already captain in the Blackwatch with forty shock troops under his command. Markus, the second oldest by only a year, was away in the Broken Lands, learning their customs and language in preparation for the merchant guild. Fallia, fifteen and the apple of their father's eye, could do no wrong, and he had taken the blame for her misdeeds most of his life. He did not bear her any ill will, however. He loved his family and would do anything for them, but could not shake the feeling that he was largely unnoticed. It came as a shock to him that he was expected to attend the King's Feast this year, and was more than a little annoyed when he found out the whole family was going and he was just tagging along, as usual.

"Well," he said as he bashed the head of the great catfish to end its slow suffocation, "we better get going back to the Blackwatch. Father will be furious if you are away too long," he joked.

"Maybe, but look at the size of that. Can you carry it back alone?"

"Grab my parcel there and take this tackle. I will tie it up and strap it to my back; there is no way we are *not* going to bring this back." Tobin was busy preparing the fish for travel and after Fallia gathered the rest of his gear and they started through the marsh back to their castle home.

They were only halfway through the hidden path known only to them when the sun became completely hidden by a harsh rain that stung their skin. Thunder boomed around them, with the wind whipping and tearing at their clothes. Fallia stumbled and slipped into the swamp, soaking her pants and nearly losing Tobin's fishing tackle into the swamp. The hidden path became thick mud that grabbed at their boots and ankles but after an hour, and only a few stops later, they arrived at the back of the Blackwatch's grounds.

The Blackwatch, their family home for hundreds of years, got its name from the stones of the tower keep, turned black by gasses and moist air from the surrounding swamp. It was built on an island, the only solid ground for hundreds of miles, with a twenty-mile wooden and stone walkway leading away from the castle to firmer ground.

Tobin tightened the rope around the fish to his back, grabbed the parcel from Fallia, and tousled her hair. "You run along, I need to bring this to the larder; I hope we get to eat it tonight!"

"We will! I will tell father, but you should hurry. They have been looking for you for a while, and we are a mess!" She laughed as she tried to brush the swamp out of her clothes, "I need to change and so do you!"

"I will be there. Hurry along." He smiled as she set off towards the tower to dry and prepare for tonight's departure feast. It was not often that riders bearing the king's standard came to the Blackwatch and they were sure to bring out the best food and ale for this occasion. Tobin knew that he would be missed if he did not show up for the feast tonight, but he had a hard time convincing himself he should attend; the wrath of his father was something he dealt with on a semi-daily basis, and he could handle whatever the crazy old man could throw at him. He never knew what it was like to have a father that was proud of him. Even this fish—the largest fish that had been caught in the marsh in a long time, he knew it was at least that big but the butcher could tell him for sure —was sure to get passed over by his father. This feast tonight was going to be very trying but the smiling face of his little sister in his mind's eye convinced him he should go; she was the only member of his family that did not overtly hate him.

He found himself at the door to the larder and banged heavily. "My lord, to what do we owe this honor. Please come in out of the rain." A hunched-backed old man with thin white hair opened the door and welcomed the young man into the kitchen. "What is this here?" he said helping Tobin unstrap the large catfish from his back. "Bless the gods, I have never seen such a beast as this!" he exclaimed. "Bring it here, we can use this tonight for the departure feast. Your father will be proud of your catch." Tobin knew this was a lie but he was thankful for it. He felt closer to this old man than he did to any of his family.

"Thank you Vorlind, I will have to show you the fishing hole sometime. The path is not so difficult. We could fish when I get back after the King's Feast."

"I would like that, m'boy." Vorlind often times called him m'boy when no one was around to hear it. He would get flogged for such disrespect, but Tobin preferred it. Sometimes he dreamt that he was the butcher's son. He would spend his days fishing and hunting in the morning, and cooking and cleaning at night—a simple life, a life filled with chores, hard work, long days, but most of all love. "When you get back." Vorlind clasped him on the shoulder and Tobin thought he could see tears in his eyes before he was pulled in close for a tight embrace. "When you get back." Repeated the old man. "Now run along, we will get this prepared and have it sent to the head table. You need to dress, can't go to a formal feast with the king's men soggy and muddy." Vorlind shooed him out the door, gave one final glance and wave, and returned to the preparations for Tobin's final meal at the Blackwatch.

With a smile on his face—he always smiled after any dealings with Vorlind no matter how short—he picked his way through the back alleys and hidden passages of the Blackwatch, hoping to avoid being seen before he was dressed and ready. His father would never forgive him for dishonoring the family in such a way in front of the king's men who had arrived to take them back to Aurorum. The call for dinner was going to sound any moment and Tobin knew he could not be late; he picked up his pace and traded caution for speed as he entered the final hall before his door. Just before he was safely inside and able to clean up a voice from behind him startled the handle out of his hand.

"How did it take you this long?" It was only Fallia, clean, dry, and dressed for the feast, making her way to the receiving room.

"How are you already done?"

"If there is one thing I can do well, it's look beautiful." Tobin could not argue with that. Her long curly blonde hair and pale blue eyes captivated him; he didn't even have to see any other girl to know she was the most beautiful. In his darker moments he would wonder what it would be like to hold her, to kiss her softly, but it was forbidden by the ancient laws and he always felt ashamed of himself after battling with those thoughts.

"Run along. I need to change."

"Well, hurry up. I am so excited to see real Knights of the Realm. Father says I may marry one someday, but I don't think I would like that too much. Hurry!" she squeaked the last word as she stood on her toes and kissed his cheek then ran away downstairs. Tobin was frozen. Nothing like this had ever happened to him before. No girl had ever kissed his cheek, not even his mother. This show of emotion was more than he could understand. Suppressing the rhythmic beating of his heart and the shameful feelings, he hurried inside, dried and dressed as quickly as possible.

***

The soup that was the Marsh air hung in the great hall of the Blackwatch like a curtain hiding the true faces of the strangers. Tobin was not surprised to see that all his family was recalled to the Blackwatch for this feast, but was surprised that he was not told Markus was back from the Broken Lands. He seated between his brothers Havar and Markus with Fallia just to the left of Markus. Their Lord Father sat to the right of Havar with their mother next to him, all facing the great hall filled with the king's men, servants, and a few lesser nobles from the far corners of the Marsh. Next to his mother, although Tobin could not get a good look at him, was Jondavid Murray, the ten year old son of the Lord Protector of the Marsh, Madison Murray.

The last time a Murray broke bread in the Blackwatch was before the kingdoms united many hundreds of years before. Tobin had a suspicion that this was because the Murrays were to busy trying to impress the people outside of the Marsh that they lost touch with their own people. This had to be much more than a mere envoy to summon them to the King's Feast. He felt disconnected. The only person that would even talk to him was his little sister, and she was pontificating about how their father's sister had been married to the House Wyllallia very young and her daughter was Jondavid's mother. In some sense they were akin to the ruling family of the Marsh, but Tobin did not have a brain for following complex family trees and political alliances through marriage, so he merely champed at his food listlessly and took comfort in the soothing familiarity of her voice.

Markus was in the middle of explaining to his two younger siblings that he was to leave tomorrow morning to return to the Broken Lands when Tobin noticed it. The chefs, led by Vorlind paraded the giant catfish he had caught earlier from the kitchen to the head table. He was very pleased to see that his masterpiece was the admiration of the knights from Aurorum. Many, he noted, said it was the largest fish they had ever seen. He saw Vorlind lead the column to the head table and whisper a few words in his Lord Father's ear before bowing and leaving the great hall. Tobin knew he was telling his father that he caught the fish himself when his father glanced at him, but that was all by way of acknowledgement, a glance. No words of praise, no special mention of his efforts, but at least for a brief moment he knew, he really knew, that his father had seen him. That was enough.

Tobin turned back to Fallia and tried to engage her in a conversation he knew something about, limiting it to Marsh survival, fishing, and other common themes. Fallia too had seen the glance, and from the smile on Tobin's face and the gleam in his blue eyes, something she had rarely seen, knew he was happy and played into his joy by indulging him with conversation. Even though it bored her nearly to tears, Tobin did not notice and continued his jovial conversation throughout the meal, forgetting himself in mug after mug of a sweet-wine made from blackberries and honey until the servants had to carry him off to bed.

Before he passed out he had a vague, dreamlike memory of Fallia leaning over him, "Sleep well, older brother," she was saying. "I pray that the merriment of tonight can carry us through the long days ahead of us." He dreamt she kissed him on the cheek again and remembered no more until the door of his chambers burst open suddenly the next morning.

His head was throbbing, and his eyes refused to open. He felt for the blood but there was none, and then remembered the sweet-wine last night. "Close the door." He managed to choke out from a dry coarse throat before covering himself with a sheet in a futile attempt to keep the morning sun out of his eyes.

"Get a move on, boy. The Caravan departs in an hour and you are not even dressed. It is a blessing that I had my servants pack for you, or you would be responsible for the disgrace of our family in front of the king's eyes and ears." His father's voice rang out clear and crisp in his room and Tobin leapt from his bed kneeling before him, scared. These were the first words his father had spoken to him directly in almost a year and, harsh as they were, Tobin was gratified. He felt important. Struggling against the throbbing of his head and the coarseness of his breath he pulled on his riding britches and a loose shirt just in time to see Fallia standing outside his door. "You better hurry; I have your sword here. Strap it on and we can still make it to the stables before the knights mount up. I would have woken you earlier but I couldn't get down here without father seeing me, and we both know what he can be like." They shared a knowing glance that spoke volumes about their father's wrath and raced down the spiraling tower stairs to the livery.

The stalls were quiet. *The calm before the storm* Tobin thought, and they had no trouble brushing and tacking their horses before the stable boys descended to ready the knight's animals for the long journey. Tobin finished first, despite only being able to open one eye at a time, and went to help Fallia.

She stood abruptly, "It's ok, I can do it."

She seemed defensive to him. He was confused. "Suit yourself. I will see you on the parade grounds then." The whole departing company was to meet there for a traditional Marshland farewell.

Tobin mounted his horse and urged it forward gently. Trying not to rattle his head to much, he walked his horse carefully to where he knew servants would be preparing the caravan. Lord Rorym, his Lord Father met him as soon as he came around the corner from the stables.

"You readied quick. That will suit you well. Remember you are a man of the Marsh, and a Lord of the Blackwatch. Try to act like it." Tobin was stunned. He didn't know how to respond to the most loving thing he had ever heard from his parents. "Look after Fallia. If any harm comes to her I will have your head." Lord Rorym finished.

"Yes, Lord Father." Tobin did not try to press his luck by talking more, and his father rode off. He was musing about these words when Fallia rode up.

"We are leaving. Look." She pointed to the great

column of people leaving through the north gate. "Where is father?"

"He is not coming with us." Tobin answered. "We are the only two going to the King's Feast this year. Weren't you listening last night? He explained to Sir Barin Fairclough why he could only send us, and I am sure he only sent you to make sure I don't die." She giggled.

"He told me that. He said if anything happens to you...he would kill me." His eyes were solemn and the laughter died in his sister's throat. She silently fell in next to him and they left the Blackwatch together.

The road-bridge through the swamp was long and winding, doubling back on itself several times while following the driest ground out to the plains. When the caravan finally stopped for the night and made camp, they were only half way to the Marsh Road that would lead them to The Dam. Tobin was grateful to get out of the saddle and to lay on his back staring up through a small opening in the trees when Fallia sat down beside him.

"It is really dark tonight." She mused as she rolled out her sleeping mat.

"There is no moon tonight." Tobin answered and rolled over, facing away from her and trying to stifle his nervousness.

"Good night, Tobin." She whispered while pressing her back against his.

Tobin did not sleep that night.

Aislinn

Aislinn grabbed the small iron pitchfork from the corner of the one room house that she shared with her mother. They had spent the morning rolling dough into loaves to be cooked in the wall oven that afternoon so they and their neighbors would have something to eat tomorrow. Now finished with that work, Aislinn would walk the streets of Little Town with her small cart and pitchfork looking for anyone who would pay her two pence to remove the horse droppings from outside their front door, as she did every afternoon. It was not a good way to make money, but she never came home empty handed and always had enough to buy flour so they could eat. As she reached the door her mother called out.

"Aislinn, please." Her voice was filled with tears.

"No, I told you. You can't run my life. I am not a child any longer." Aislinn's voice was dripping with annoyance.

"Honey-"

"Enough. I won't talk about it anymore. I will see you when I get home. But I won't change my mind." Aislinn grabbed the pitchfork and stormed out of the house nearly colliding with an old man who was crossing the narrow street in front of her and pushing a small cart. The sight of it caused her to groan in frustration as she realized she forgot hers. Taking a deep breath she turned and went back inside the house.

"Listen mother," She began as she threw the pitchfork into the cart. "I love you, but you can't control me. I am old enough to live my life."

"I know," Her voice was racked with tears. "I will always do what is best for you, and I know what is best for you more than you do."

"How can you say that?" Aislinn was fighting back tears and nearly screaming.

"You can't understand. It's about your father....Just listen to me." Her mother collapsed onto the pile of straw that acted as a bed. "Please."

"We will talk more when I return." Aislinn's heart broke to see her mother like that and she wanted to hug her, but left before she gave in to that temptation.

Why is she always treating me like a child? She thought to herself as she brushed her shoulder length reddish-brown hair out of her bright brown eyes. She wandered the streets aimlessly for a while, lost in her reverie. *I need to start making my own decisions. I can't let others control my life.* She nearly bumped into a large dark-skinned man. Giving him only a cursory glance, being careful to make sure he didn't see her looking at him—she knew all too well what happened to street urchins like her who were caught staring at their betters—his whole appearance surprised her. A thin tunic hung from one of his shoulders leaving half of his chest bare; his skin was the deep red of wet clay and his bald head reflected the mid-afternoon sun as he walked slowly away from her. She compared this stranger to herself, dressed in a homespun cotton tunic and wool breeches, with no boots and hair that was matted and stained with the dirt of Little Town. She knew this man had come from very far away and was very out of place here in her home.

A breeze brought the smell of horses and sweat from around the corner near the great wall of the city and with it the sounds of a gathering crowd. Curiosity drew her closer to the sounds and she crept slowly around a broken mud hut to see a vast gathering of the dark-skinned people. They had spears, nets, horses, carriages with bars for sides, and all manner of strange animals inside some of the carts. *All those horses—I am going to be rich today,* she thought as she headed back into the heart of Little Town.

A rough hand reached out and grabbed her abruptly. "Are you clearing dung?" A large hairy man scowled down at her. "Yes, sir. Two pence for in front of your door." She tried to smile but her arm ached under the pressure he was exerting.

"Begin." He shoved her back and slammed the wooden door to his hut closed.

The echo that bounced down the narrow street filled her with a sudden and intense dread. *I should just go home.* She shuddered. *The fight with mother, and the rudeness of this man. Never has Little Town been this cruel to me.* She had never seen this man before and was nervous about staying here, so close to the city wall. The thought of all those horses kept her, and she got to work removing the debris and manure piles from in front of his door. A loud bang told her that there was more than one person inside and she could just barely hear two voices leaking out from between the panels of the door. She stopped to listen for a brief second, once again letting her curiosity get the best of her.

"...and the preparations have been made." The first voice was scratching out through a rough dry throat.

"My payment?" a musical voice inquired.

"Lord Corbett will see to that. Just see that he receives his payment when they are sold." The gruff voice answered.

There was a rustling inside the shop. Another crash interrupted her listening and the door swung open. "You missed a spot." His gruff voice boomed into the narrow street. "By the cart," he said pointing. "Can't you see anything? Why am I even paying you?" The large hairy man emerged from within with a thin willow branch and began whipping it around landing more than a couple of blows on Aislinn as she staggered away from him.

"I was not finished yet." Her voice was small but

not without a hint of defiance.

"Well finish, before I finish you. Too many little street urchins hanging about these days. If the King knew what went on in the streets of his city, he might think twice about allowing the likes of you to build your fake little town against his city walls." He gave one more flick of his wrist sending Aislinn sprawling under the sharp crack of the make-shift whip.

The tiny stones of the gravel street dug holes into the palms of her hands as she landed with considerable force only a few inches from the pile of horse dung he had pointed out. Her left ear was throbbing and after carefully removing the last of the imbedded debris from her palms and retrieving her pitchfork, she reached a tender hand to inspect it. Blood from the fresh wound begin to trickle down her cheek and past her chin, dripping to the dirt below. She knew this would not be the last time she shed blood on these city streets, and tried to hold back the tears as she watched it slowly pool up between her crossed legs. Her blood-covered hands held back her stomach as it suddenly tried to vent its contents onto the street. *I can't show weakness,* she thought to herself, *I need the money, and soon enough I will be done.* With renewed determination she set to work again clearing the street in front of his shop. Scooping and throwing fork load after fork load, the pile of round steaming mass gave off wave after wave of nauseating fumes until she was finally done.

Dust from the road and the older piles of dung settled on her clothes and face, crusting the blood on her ear and mixing with her sweat to form a thin layer of tainted mud that covered her. She timidly knocked on the door and waited, expecting to get a face-full of the willow branch when it did open.

"Well?" was all he said when the door finally swung open.

"I finished sir." Her voice mirrored the internal agonies she was feeling.

"Here's your two pence, now scurry back to your hole. I have an important visitor."

Aislinn did not know what went on inside his little shop, or who could claim to be so important if they came all the way down to Little Town; nor did she want to. It wasn't even inside the city, merely a collection of small mud houses nestled on the southeast corner of the outer wall, between the moat and the sea. No one of any importance ever visited Little Town, unless it was to burn and level it because an invading army was approaching.

She peered around his massive frame and caught a glimpse inside. It was very dark in the windowless room but she could see well enough by an oil lamp's light to distinguish the shape of another large man, dark-skinned with no hair on his head. He bore a scar across his face where his right eye should have been. All that was left was a gaping black hole he was cleaning out with a corner of his tunic. He looked familiar. The smoke from the quickly burning oil was wafting about the room causing Aislinn to squint and her eyes to start burning as she kept trying to see what was going on inside this secret house. Just as she was starting to turn away and leave the man inside called out, sending a shiver down her spine. His voice was melodic and smooth but cold as steel.

"Cor Donovan, who is that young urchin spying on me?"

"No one! She is leaving." Cor Donovan said while shoving the end of his makeshift whip sharply into her ribs.

"Not so fast, Donovan." He stood and crossed the room faster than Aislinn could have thought possible and she noticed for the first time the curved sword hanging from his waist. "This one can work for me." He smiled.

Fear wrapped its icy grip around her heart and her instincts told her to run, but she stayed. "I will not work for you." She hissed through clenched teeth while trying to bring herself to her full height—still feeling dwarfed by the two large men who now surrounded her.

"I like this one's temper and build—strong for her age, by the looks of it. She couldn't be more than twenty summers. Take her to my personal carriage." He almost sang.

"No!" Aislinn screamed and drove her heel down as hard as she could into Cor Donovan's foot. He yelped with pain and she threw her pitchfork at the dark stranger, who caught it out of mid-flight. Sending little chunks of excrement across his thin tunic and half bare chest as he spun it around. Holding the pointed tines right at Aislinn's face, he hissed in his tauntingly musical voice, "Only a fool gives up her weapon."

Aislinn avoided the spear thrust by only a few inches and tried to grab the handle of the pitchfork, feeling foolish for giving it up. *He was right, why did I throw it? What was I thinking?* She scolded herself as she dodged under a nearby cart trying to avoid the flurry of thrusts this dark-skinned stranger threw at her.

Her attacker slipped on a fresh pile of manure she had missed and nearly hit the ground face first. Induced by blind panic she fled, racing down alleys and across open roads, running almost in circles. Her sweat cut lines in the scat filled mud that covered her face and clothes, giving her a tiger like appearance as she darted from shadow to shadow in the now darkening streets of Little Town.

Hours later, after the sun had finally given way to the cool night, she stopped running. Her breath came hard and fast, and her heart beat its rhythm against her back teeth and echoed in her temples. Fires started to burn all around the city, and after making sure she was no longer being followed she took some time to compose herself and regain her bearings.

The outer wall of the city was not too far to the north. She could see it standing high over the tops of the mud huts, and the gate was not far down the wall. She knew where she was—very close to her house. Sneaking out from under the overturned cart where she hid, several dark-skinned guards ran passed her with spears and nets. As she darted between the buildings, more of Little Town seemed to come alive as if the whole of her childhood home was under attack. A haunting realization came over her; the fires in the streets were not the cooking fires of her neighbors; the lights in the homes were not the oil lamps illuminating a family's evening meal; the cracking and popping of wood nearby was not the simple wheels of an ox-pulled cart rumbling towards the city gates. Little Town was on fire.

Her mother's stories filled her head with the grim past when Little Town would be destroyed before an invading army arrived, or an evil King would take out their wrath on the small folk and peasants who called Little Town home. Nothing like this had happened here for hundreds of years. *What is going on?* She thought. *Why is this happening?* In her mother's stories someone would always swoop down from the city and save Little Town, but it was usually a hero, or a King. Aislinn knew only one King and for all her twenty years he had been just and kind, even sending food once a week into Little Town to help ease the starvation that was prevalent in the dirty dung-filled streets. A plan started to form in her mind; *I need to tell the King. He was always kind to us before,* she thought as she rounded a corner and almost walked into the back of another dark-skinned invader.

Choking back a scream she dived back behind the corner of the hut, pressing her slender body against the mud trying to push her way into it. Before she had taken up her hiding position she had seen that the invaders had her mother bound and gagged, and were leading her to a prison cart. Her lip starting throbbing and she could taste blood before she realized she was biting it. The plan she had crumbled in the emotion of seeing her mother. *I have to do something. They have her.* Her blood rushed to her face and she could feel the pressure building in her temples. A rage began to take her and she grasped around looking for anything that she could use as a weapon, cursing herself again for throwing the pitchfork. Her left ear started throbbing from where she was beaten by Cor Donovan, but she tried to ignore the pain. She had to rescue her mother.

She snatched up a small stick leaning against the mud wall of the hut and practiced swinging it. It was short but sturdy, and although she knew it would not stand up to a blow from a proper sword, all she saw was nets and spears and she could avoid those easily enough. Pulling in a few short deep breaths she leaped from behind the hut and smashed her stick into the temple of the invader standing in front of her. He crumpled to the ground without calling out and his body began twitching.

She flew to the next attacker and her face exploded in pain, nearly blinding her. The pain awoke in her an inner beast, a primal force she had never felt before. Her eyes opened to the tip of the spear speeding towards her face; she dodged the assailant's fatal blow and grabbed his spear, pulling him off balance. The narrow end of her short stick shot into the would-be captor's eye socket, killing him instantly. She kicked him off the end of her stick and he fell through a hut and into the flames that were burning within. Sparks flew from where his body landed and the fire raged anew with the additional wind and fuel. Tossing the spear aside Aislinn spun around, brandishing her stick, and now faced four captors with a renewed vigor, as if she was drawing power from the flames.

Her mother stared out from behind the bars of a prison cart. The sight of her caused Aislinn to pause, her rage fading. Her eyes filled with tears and her lip was starting to swell from where she had taken the butt end of the spear.

"Mother!" Aislinn yelled, her voice cracking from the smoke that started to fill her lungs.

"No..." her mother's voice was faint, weak and muffled by the gag. She could barely hear it over the chaos in the streets.

The four men advanced, circling to surround her. Aislinn saw a way to escape—a gap between two of the men, wide enough for her to slip through before they could reach her. She could slip passed them, back into the streets and be free. She started towards the gap when she caught her mother's eye. Something in the way the tears were flowing, something in the way she mouthed 'I love you' with a rope through her teeth made Aislinn stop. She dropped her stick and sank to her knees. Just then the one-eyed man from Cor Donovan's shop approached her.

"You have done a lot of damage." He said surveying the two dead bodies. "Lucky for you, I respect the ability to fight." His musical voice sounded out of place against the background of fire and screams. "Bring this one with me. I claim her."

"I will see you die." She said as she was kneeling in the blood filled street, ashamed and crying, longing for her mother. "I will see you die."

He bent down to look her in the face and whispered, "No, you won't." A hard object struck the side of her head and she knew no more.

***

Aislinn awoke with a throbbing headache. Blinking away the pain she tried to move her hands out from behind her but could only manage to grab hold of the bars of the prison cart. The shock of being tied up and in a mobile jail allowed fear to steal her breath away as she struggled against bindings that held her arms. Night blanketed the landscape preventing Aislinn from recognizing her surroundings, but she could tell they were traveling along the gold road next to the sea, and far away from the city by this time. The slow and rhythmic churning of the wheels of the cart bore into her mind as she struggled against the jostling effect of the uneven road.

Suddenly she jumped, her whole body convulsed at the realization that she was not with her mother. She looked around the cart again, taking careful note of the people surrounding her. There were two other girls both short and gaunt, huddled together under their mass of tangled blonde hair. They had to be twins. Sitting next to them, an old crone—whose severely hooked nose and witch-like appearance added to the fear that was consuming Aislinn—eyed her suspiciously. A large mass of blankets in the far corner of the cart shifted under the jostling of a large hole in the road the cart had struck and she saw a human form under them. Scooting as best she could across the floor over to the mass she leaned in close to where she thought the head would be.

"Mother?" she whispered. "Mother, I am sorry, I know you love me, and I love you too."

Another rut in the road sent them both flying and Aislinn's heart sank as the pile of blankets scattered around the cart, a few falling between the bars. There was no one underneath them. Leaning back on the pile she turned her face into the mass to hide it as best she could and cried. She was alone. After a few hours of fighting the jolting road, trying to avoid injury from being slammed into the side bars, and crying almost uncontrollably, Aislinn was exhausted. Despair took her and she leaned back, giving up the constant struggle and trying to count the stars.

The scruffy face of the large man they called Cor Donovan broke her view of the moonless sky.

"Shoveling dung will be easy compared to where you're going." Cor Donovan snickered at her.

"I will live to see you dead." Aislinn's voice was calm but her eyes filled with a red glow as she rolled over and pretended to go back to sleep, ignoring him completely.

Gavrill

Stars carved out tiny holes of light in the blanket of darkness. The moon had not yet risen to give full reign to night, and the world hung lost in the twilight that preceded every night since the dawn of time. A slim figure, heavily wrapped in animal skins, sat huddled next to a small fire, clinging to its faint halo of warmth. Frozen particles of moisture rhythmically exited the figures mouth as he tried in vain to ward off the chill of the mountain peaks. Here, far to the south, farther south than the city of gold, farther south than the wind swept plains, farther south even than the ground-heated valley, the mountains rose from the earth signaling the edge of the world. The slim figure sat next to his fire holding a cold rock in both hands.

> "Past the edge and over again,
> The stone will turn to flesh.
> There you'll find the Queen of Men,
> Daughter of frozen Death."

The rhyme of his tribe's shaman echoed ceaselessly in his mind, *past the edge and over again*, he thought to himself. *I have gone past the edge, but over again?* He dared not dwell on the rest. As he blew carefully on the flames, the stone fell, or jumped from his arms to land in the ashes, nearly extinguishing his life line of heat. "On you go then," he voiced to the rock, nearly kicking it out of frustration. "Damned stone will get me killed!" he bellowed into the night. "At least there are trees here; I must have gone over again. Haven't seen any living tree in weeks." He kept talking, drawing comfort from the sound of a human voice, even if it was his own.

Before gathering up the stone, he turned to marvel at the progress he had already made. Behind him loomed a seemingly endless mountain range. Above him, a single peak reaching far into the heavens, only visible in the night from where it hid the stars. He knew it all too well. First approaching it, having it loom ever in front of him unchanging in size and grandeur, the Gray Mountain, his people had called it, the northern edge of the world. Then burrowing his way through it, following cave after cave, passage after passage till he found the path through and out into the snow-covered mountains on the other side. He alone had seen the mysteries hidden beneath the Gray Mountain, and he alone would bear that burden till his death. Now traveling past the edge and over again, the mountain hung in the background, watching his departure, and watching over the other mountains. As he kept moving farther north, the Gray Mountain never seemed to shrink; it remained constant in the southern sky. In this frozen night, before the moon could crest over its foreboding and jagged peak, it merely blotted out the stars, preventing the eyes of his gods from watching over him as he continued on his mission.

He was alone.

The large oval rock was smooth to the touch and at times seemed to glow faintly gray. At other times all color seemed to be lost in the intense black sheen that covered its surface, but at all times, the cold exterior felt as if it were being heated by an inner fire. He re-wrapped his animal skins around him and pressed the stone tightly against the bare skin of his belly. The shock of the cold rock stunned him for only a moment until the inner fire began to keep him warm, the only thing that kept him warm. Farther on he pushed through the knee-deep snow and harsh winds of these frozen peaks, ever onward and ever downward. He could feel the slope now; he was going down. Soon enough the world would flatten out and even provide warmth and food again. Too long had it been since he had tasted meat, or lay in the grass of a sunlit meadow.

The madness of cold was wrapping itself slowly around his mind; he knew it. The only things preventing him from slipping peacefully into its gaping jaws were the stone he carried in his arms and the words he carried in his heart. "Past the edge and over again…"

A bolt of lightning crashed overhead and a gust of wind brought the echoing boom of thunder. A winter storm howled down from the Gray Mountain pushing him ever northwards. Night bore down on him with the storm and dark clouds blotted out the star's meager light. "There should've been a moon tonight." He scolded the blistering night. "You should've had a moon to light my path, last night the moon was full, and here, the northern mountain gods steal away the moon." He curled his arms around the rock even harder, willing the inner heat of this stone into his limbs to keep him alive. His mind wandered as he trudged ever down the mountains.

He thought of his home, a village far to the south of the Gray Mountain, farther south than even the mountain range itself. A small village of stone houses nestled next to a lazy river with fields stretching as far as the eye could see in all directions, a large forest half-a-day's ride to the west and the mountains four days to the north, with the single looming peak of the Gray Mountain watching over them like a caring god. He remembered the summer festivals, the streets lined with heather and other flowers, the summer wines, the maidens dancing to honor the gods of the upcoming harvest. Even the year the King had visited his quiet hamlet, with all his guards and men, the festival was still the same as any other year. The Peace and prosperity of his home filled his eyes with tears and he knew he would never see it again.

He thought back on the fateful day when he

started this journey. He woke that morning next to his wife, as he had for the past ten years, and set out in a horse drawn cart to the forests of the west lands to bring wood back for fires. The winter was harsher that year than it had been in a while, but it was manageable. A few of the stronger men set out every day to gather wood and returned at night with enough to keep the village warm. It was his day to help with the collection. He bundled in his animal skins and hopped into the cart. The great forest was dark, dense and massive. He set off to begin chopping when, only a few yards from a companion in the labor—and in an area that had been well traveled—he tripped on a large rock.

"Damn my curiosity!" He yelled into the moonless night. "Why did I have to dig you up? Why did you call to me as you did?" His voice broke his chain of thought and he gripped the rock closer and charged head first into the now whipping snow of the mountain storm. The earth itself was bucking against his presence, as if it knew what he carried, even if he didn't.

The shamans reeled and groveled when he brought the rock home from the forest. After explaining where he found it and how no one else seemed to know it was there, the shamans told him it was his responsibility and they would not take any part of the rock. They called it the egg of the world, birthed by the earth itself to herald a new creature entering the circle of life. Stories had been passed down from generation to generation about how the earth had given eggs before.

First the horse to the first men, then a cow and

oxen to the farmers, and the last egg given to man was a tame wolf, man's best friend. This was a new life, a new creation the earth-mother sent to bless the world, and it was his charge.

Not all blessings given by the earth were for the betterment of humans; he knew that full well. The giant lizards that stalked deep in the forest known to eat man and beast alike or the Roc, a giant flesh eating bird, that would steal away cattle and horses to its nests in the foothills of the Gray Mountains. He did not know what kind of gift this would be, but the shamans had told him he had to take it over the mountains past the edge of the world and into the wild beyond. There it could grow and survive to become what it was meant to be.

A large drift crashed down on him from the branches of a massive pine tree, burying him in a few feet of wet snow. The rock seemed to react to this influx of wet and cold and began to radiate more heat, keeping the man warm. "Whatever this is, it can't be bad." He muttered to himself. "You have been my salvation on this journey, my light under the mountain, my heat in the snow. Whatever you are I beg the gods to watch over you once I leave you where you are meant to be." He caressed the outer shell of the rock with something like loving care before he battled his way back to his feet to continue on.

Step after step he dreamt of home, his loving wife, his village. Step after step he worried about the rock, what would happen, how he could return when it was over. And step after step he dreamt of warmth and comfort. When at last he exited the thick wood he had been struggling through for an hour, he looked out below him and saw a valley stretching far to the north. Steam rose from this valley and there was no snow covering the ground. A small castle sat astride the ground heated creek that flowed out from the mountains surrounding it. This had to be what the shaman spoke of, past the edge and over again, he thought, this is over again. People lived here; the world did not end at the mountains. He sat down in the cold snow, stunned by sightings of humans, and the sight of the end of his journey overwhelmed him. He began to cry.

Suddenly an earth shattering crack rang through the alpine forest and the rock he was carrying leapt from his grasp. He felt the cold immediately as it struck him like a blow to the chest, nearly knocking the wind out of him. The rock cracked and split down the middle, sending another crash over the mountainside. A flame reached out from inside the oval shell and grasped at the nearest tree sending it into a raging inferno that spread quickly through the snow covered trees. The hissing of melting snow and the drying of wet wood sang like a chorus of snakes; the popping and cracking of burning wood joined it to fill his ears. The cacophony was punctuated throughout by the inhuman screams coming from the rock itself. Giant shattering crashes from the rock splitting, and wails from the beast within almost drowned out the sounds of the world around him burring.

The fire had a life of its own and moved about the forest with the will of a conqueror, but never coming to close to the huddled man in heavy animal skins.

The shattering had stopped but the fire blazed brighter than ever and he took a few steps closer to where his rock had landed. There in a small pool of melted snow sat a large, black, winged lizard and he knew at once that the ancient creatures of legend were alive once again, born of fire into the cold forest in the mountains on the edge of the world. The inferno raged on and this small almost helpless dragon opened his eyes for the first time to a world that was thousands of years older than his ancestors. Stretching his wings he called into the night sky, leaving thin trails of smoke rising slowly from his nostrils.

Brovo

Fog rolled down the mountainside, escaping the sun as it crested the snow-covered peaks. The valley had been farther away than he had first thought, and without his heat source—the dragon egg—he almost froze in the harsh snows of the alpine terrain. Frostbite was eating at his fingertips when he finally came face to face with the cold iron gate of the walled city; stones rose far above him and he craned his neck to see the top of this man-made structure so alien to his own experience. *This could only be past the edge and over again,* he thought as he recalled his homeland where no walls were erected to cage in humans, no walls divided peoples. *This has to be the home of giants to have a house this large.*

"Who goes there?" A voice boomed down from heavens.

"It is only I Gavrill, son of Gormond, your humble servant, Lord of the Stone." He fell to his knees and bent until his face was almost buried in the almost frozen earth.

"I'm not your lord. What's your purpose here?" Came the reply.

"I seek shelter for me and my charge. I have come past the edge and over again looking for the Queen of Men." Still not looking up at the voice that echoed down the stone wall.

"You will find no queen here. But enter and share our fire, it's not our policy to turn away pilgrims from the Frozen Plains of the south."

"South?"

"Aye, you have the pleasure of approaching Riverspring, southernmost city in all of the Five Kingdoms. If you are lost then you have great need of our hospitality. Please enter."

The gates opened as he spoke and Gavrill was awed at the size of the wooden door that parted to allow his entry. This truly was the land of giants. The roof of the archway loomed over him and he passed through feeling more like an ant than a human when the dragon, who was until this point curled around his waist asleep, stirred and poked his head through the heavy animal skins to survey the outside world. He tried to conceal the great lizard, worried about what these giants may think of a baby dragon.

The words of his shaman echoed in his ears again as he approached a small hovel nestled next to the wall. He was over again, the stone had turned to flesh, and he was sure he would find the Queen of Men in this giant laden town. Fear gripped his heart as he recited the last line: "Daughter of Frozen Death."

"What's that?" A human form emerged from the hovel.

"My lord, kindly take me to the Giant Lord I have much to discuss with him." He fell to his knees keeping his eyes fixed on the cobble stones below him.

The guard paused, eyed this strange figure who wrapped his hands around his waist as if he was fighting with his own intestines, and leaned on his spear. "Giants?"

"Aye, my lord. The giant that built this huge dwelling, and who spoke to me from over the walls of his fortress." Gavrill still did not venture to look up.

"I spoke to you from the walls." The guard shifted his weight on the spear, "Where are you from?"

"I have traveled north for many months. I cannot be specific because the moon has been inconsistent and I am confused as to the time I have been on this journey."

"You came from the south?" The guard's voice was almost mocking. "How is it you speak the common tongue of the Five Kingdoms?"

"I beg your forgiveness, my lord. I did not know this was your kingdom." He fell to his knees. "I have crossed past the edge and through the great Gray Mountain, and over again to this fortress of stone. I need rest and food." As he was talking, the dragon stuck his head out from under his many layers of animal skins.

The guard lowered his spear and took a few steps back. "What is that?" He said becoming instantly enthralled with the young dragon.

"It is my charge, born on to me not four days ago. He is mine to present to the Queen of Men." Gavrill struggled to get the creature back inside his outer layer.

"I will take it to her." The guard advanced slowly with spear still lowered. "You, sir, can warm yourself by my fire and we will bring you food."

Gavrill paused; there was something in this man's voice that warned him not to trust him. The final words of his shaman came back again, 'This creature has been given to us to present to the Queen of Men, not to anyone else.' His stomach was grinding itself into knots and he nearly fell over while debating this guard's words. Delirious from the long journey, half frozen, hungry, and still worried whether there were giants inhabiting these massive stone buildings, he consented and pulled the dragon out and presented it to the guard.

The small black beast let out an ear piercing scream, accompanied by two large jets of smoke as he changed hands. His wings beat furiously against the new owner and the guard dropped his spear in order to secure the dragon. "Follow me Gavrill." He said as he ducked back inside the stone hovel.

A fire was burning and two other guards were warming themselves by its light. "Who is this?" One jumped up as they entered bearing the dragon.

"I am Gavrill, from the summer lands, south of the Gray Mountain. This is Brovo, the only dragon, gift for the Queen of Men. Already the dragon seemed to know its name and stopped its struggle the moment Gavrill spoke, but as soon as his voice was gone from the air Brovo started again, straining all of his young muscles to get away from the guard.

"Greyvich, fetch some food for our guest," The first guard ordered. "And you, Hovin, stoke the fire, we need it warm."

"Aye, sir." Hovin replied and crossed the small room to grab an armful of firewood.

Gavrill eyed the dragon in this foreigners arms, "He seems to be upset," he paused, "I am sorry, I don't know your name?"

"My name is Kole," the guard answered as he tucked the dragon more securely under one arm and reached for a spear that was leaning against the wall.

"Kole." Gavrill repeated. "He seems upset. I can take him off your hands now while you go to tell the Queen of Men we have arrived." He reached out with both hands and tried to take back the dragon, but Kole spun away.

"I will make sure your dragon is presented to the Queen of Men. Until then, Gavrill, you have had a hard journey I am sure. No one has ever crossed the southern mountains before. Please sit by the fire and warm away your chill." He inclined his head towards an open chair. "I will have one of the men fetch you some spiced wine." He turned his back to Gavrill, shielding the dragon from the foreigner's eyes as he wrapped heavy twine around its beak and thrust it head first into a large burlap satchel.

"What are you doing?" Gavrill screamed as he leapt towards his captured dragon.

Kole was faster and the spear tip slid gently into

Gavrill's chest, parting the two ribs that protected his heart with ease. Gavrill felt his life leaking out and he prayed to the summer gods that he worshiped his whole life to be able to see his wife one more time, he prayed he would be able to smell her hair as she lay next to him in their bed, and he prayed that she would join him in the eternal sleep that followed life. Tears rolled off his cheeks as a faint wheeze escaped his lips before he crumpled to the floor splitting the spear shaft as he fell.

Hovin, surprised by the noise, spun around and tripped to his feet avoiding a spear thrust near his face. "Sir! Please!" He yelled.

Kole grabbed up another spear, ignored the cries of his soldier, and continued the onslaught. Spear tip after spear tip sparked against the stone walls of the small hovel as Kole barricaded the entrance, trapping his victim. Hovin leapt from corner to corner dodging both the deadly spear and the clutter in an attempt to stay alive.

"Why must you do this? What has taken hold of you? Please sir, think of my wife, think of my children." Hovin gasped.

He was getting fatigued from the exertion, and panic started to creep into his mind as he slowly realized he was going to die. The cold dark eyes of Kole betrayed no emotion as he methodically inched closer to him. Hovin tripped on the burlap sack containing Brovo and sprawled out in front of his attacker. With tears in his eyes he made one last plea. "Wait! Please, I will do anything; I will be your servant. Please sir, do not-" His voice faded into a gurgle as he choked on his own blood.

Kole removed the spear from Hovin's chest and watched curiously as the two bodies on the floor lay still. Greyvich backed into the room carrying two trays heavily laden with steaming plates fresh from the castle kitchens, and was met with the tip of Kole's spear when he turned around. The trays gave a loud crash when they struck the stone floor and the noise echoed sharply in the small room, but only one man was left to hear it.

Kole walked slowly over to the door and secured it. The stench of blood and death was starting to fill the room and he did not want anyone passing by to observe the catastrophe that had happened. Planting a spear in Gavrill's hand and arranging the bodies to look like a staged fight was easy for Kole. His actions were calculated and measured. The sight of his soldier's lying face down in pools of their own blood did not affect him as he dragged them into place, never once showing any emotion.

During the meticulous arranging of the bodies Kole almost forgot the dragon's burlap prison. As he approached it after his work was complete it burst into flame and the small beast, having freed itself from its makeshift bonds, advanced on him with smoke rising from its nostrils.

"Hold, young Brovo. I am your master now." Kole backed away two steps and grabbed the leg of a chair that was broken during the makeshift battle. "You *will* listen to me. I don't want to harm you." As if in response to his words, Brovo let two small jets of liquid fire spray from his mouth covering Kole's banded leggings and igniting the padding beneath them. "You will stop that!" He commanded as he brought down the improvised club on the head of this priceless animal and ripped off the burning clothes; his howls of anguish could be heard through the wooden door and across the street, attracting the attention of the sleeping town.

Smoke filled the room. Kole lay on the ground unconscious with pain. Brovo lay next to him, still steaming from his nostrils. The fire raged on, consuming the small guard hovel next to the wall. The already dead bodies of Gavrill, Hovin, and Greyvich were starting to smoke from the encroaching heat. A loud crash woke Kole, as a support beam from the ceiling fell a few feet from where he was lying, landing on the body of Hovin, driving burning embers deep inside the carcass. Kole stared at it, wondering at the way the blood on the ground around him started to boil and the flesh turned black. *I have to get the dragon,* was the only thought in his head while he lay on the floor watching the bodies of his comrades burn.

Forcing himself to stand, he felt his legs crumble beneath him, sending a fresh jolt of pain that almost rendered him unconscious again. The ground rose to meet him quickly and Kole landed face down on the stone floor, shattering his front teeth. Gathering himself for a moment, fearing the flames that were drawing ever closer, he pulled his limp body across the now steaming stones towards the body of Brovo. *I need to rescue the dragon.* He was consumed by this thought. The only thing that was in his mind was the safety of this four day old beast. The neck of the dragon was hot to the touch and Kole reeled back from it. Ripping the tunic from his chest he wrapped

Brovo in it and pulled himself towards the door. Every second he remained inside this inferno he felt closer to death; the fire raged around him causing large beams to crash down from the ceiling, flames to lick around his body, and the very ground he crawled over to burn his skin. Each excruciating pull of his arms sent jolts of pain through his upper body, as if his muscles themselves were revolting against the life he was sacrificing so much to save.

Brovo gave a shudder inside his new prison sending waves of fear washing over Kole. That fear broke his mind and he fell quickly into a panic driven madness. *I will not survive another blast from this evil creature. If I am to live, I must kill it.* The thought formed itself quietly in the back of his mind and slowly grew until he was almost chanting it audibly. "If I am to live, I must kill it." He repeated over and over trying to force each agonizing pull of his arms. He inched closer to the door and closer to freedom when Brovo clawed his way out from the tunic and grabbed Kole's throat. Kole reached out with both hands and grabbed the beast around its neck and over its eyes, pushing it away from him. The two stayed locked in combat rolling ever closer to the door and to safety from the fire. Pain racked Kole's body, and his arms felt weak. Smoke filled his lungs sending him into a fit of coughing that dislodged the dragon's teeth. He saw his opening and with the last of his waning strength he shoved the face of the cursed animal into the side of a burning chair enveloping his hand up to the elbow and the whole face and neck of the dragon. The fire took his flesh down to the bone. Tears poured from his eyes, cries of anguish boomed from his lips, and he shuddered and shook with anger. A force welled up in his chest driving out all other emotions as he pulled back his arm to see the charred remains of the hand that killed three men a few moments ago; the force filled him with renewed energy and he pulled with his left hand towards the door. Just as he reached the threshold and placed his hand on the door, risking a short moment to gather his strength for the push out, Brovo leapt from the flames of the burning chair and with one fluid movement finished the job it had started by closing its jaws on Kole's throat, ripping out all but the spine and leaving a fresh pool of blood to steam in the burning room. Brovo stared down on his victim for a moment, gave a mournful cry, and leapt back into the flames to curl up next to the now burning body of Gavrill.

***

The smoke rose steadily from the flames that consumed his recent body and Gavrill looked down on the sleeping dragon. He was confused. "Brovo, can you hear me? Brovo." His voice seemed somehow wrong to him, like it wasn't strong enough.

"He won't be able to respond."

"How do you know?" Gavrill asked the new figure that appeared in the room.

"Because we are dead, and he is not."

"Who are you?"

"I am Sir Renyard Storm, knight in the Lord Protector's service and guard of the mountains. Or as it seems now, that is who I was." Renyard moved through the burning building with the ease of a spirit. "Who are you? You seem familiar."

"I am Gavrill son of...son of..." He paused. "How can I not remember my family? I thought...." His voice trailed off.

Renyard placed his hand on Gavrill's shoulder and pulled him slowly away from his body. "Come with me, there is someone you need to meet." Renyard could not shake the feeling that this man was special.

"How did you die?" Gavrill asked.

"I can't remember. I only know that I have a mission that is keeping me from moving on and dancing with the mountain gods. I was patrolling the wilderness south of the city, near the foothills of Seri Umenriot, when something...when something happened and I awoke in the very spot I found you." Renyard explained as he led his new guest through the streets of the city—now alive with a fervor of activity—to a small bakery near the castle itself. "How did you die? And why were you watching that fire?"

"I was... Hold on. I came here by way of a long journey. I was warming by the fire, I had... I had something with me... I don't know. I know I should know but it is as if a fog covers my memory." Gavrill stopped suddenly. "I forgot something. I need to go back."

"What did you forget?"

"It was... Brovo. I forgot Brovo." He stopped and mused on all the faces of the people rushing past him with buckets to form a water line from the river to the burning guard shack. He was startled by a few that ran right through him and Renyard beckoned him to continue on their way.

Stopping in front of the bakery and motioning for Gavrill to enter Renyard asked. "What is a Brovo?"

"It is a gift. My gift." Gavrill said as he entered the bakery. "What is this place?"

"It's a safe place for us to remain until we are called. We have a purpose for remaining past our deaths, but it is still unclear to me. Here, in this place, we have an ally who is still alive."

Gavrill and Renyard entered the dark warm bakery and saw two figures who were busying themselves with cleaning the inside of the shop in preparation for the day's baking.

Lonessa

Bells rang out in the clear morning air, and the sun's light snuck over the eastern peaks to find the guard shack on the southern gate ablaze. The flames licked skyward adding their light to the sun's, illuminating the city of Riverspring. Shouts from several men at arms and concerned townsfolk echoed across the city streets, and a large crowd was gathering at the tiny wall-side guard shack. Lonessa ignored them all.

She left her room in the castle early that morning, excited to work with Mr. Grahm in his bakery. Five days had passed since she witnessed the death of her friend, and the only way to relieve the agony the memory caused was to visit with the old baker. His presence calmed her, and his voice soothed her troubled heart. She looked forward to spending time with him every day. Her parents offered little comfort, always talking about the mountain gods and the mercy found in death. Her mother cried every day, and her father would hardly leave her alone. Her time in the bakery gave her a reprieve from her over-bearing parents by muting her mind's ranting with a repetitive and monotonous activity. She enjoyed losing herself in the flour and eggs and butter of Mr. Grahm's shop. Occasionally Sir Renyard would appear; she assumed that his presence was her connection to death granted her by the mountain gods.

"Sir Renyard hasn't been around for a while." She said, smiling at Mr. Grahm as she slid into the warming bakery.

"Hush child, there is no reason to talk about the dead." Mr. Grahm rebuked her. "What would my brother in the Temple say if he could hear you now? For the last time, invoking the dead is a dangerous game, Lonessa. I have allowed you your fantasy long enough, it is time you let this go and start to heal."

"I am not *invoking* him, he was already here. It is not my fault that I can see him and you can't." She was not fully convinced of this. *Why else did he appear to me after I made a deal with them?* She often thought, but never shared this with Mr. Grahm. "Besides I don't know your bother, and Sir Renyard hasn't been here in three days anyway. I guess he moved on."

Mr. Grahm slowly set down the bowl he was holding and placed both hands on the table next to it. His head was sagging deep into his chest, and he let out a long sigh. "My dear sweet Lonessa. The mountain gods no longer deal with life and death as they did in the old stories."

"Why not?"

"They no longer... They— They just don't anymore. I don't know why." Mr. Grahm held out his arms to give her a hug, but she backed away.

"Then, if they don't, who was the man I saw standing in the cart? And why couldn't anyone else see him, and why did he say he was dead?" Her voice showed her confusion. "Anyway, it doesn't matter because he is no longer around." She said, sitting down with a thud on the table in front of her. "I miss Garon."

Mr. Grahm crossed the small room quickly and placed his hands on her shoulders, giving her a reassuring squeeze. His dark curls bounced gently, dislodging some flour that tickled Lonessa's nose. She contorted her face into the precursor of a sneeze, and jumped down from the bench to run outside into the fresh air, but it hit her first.

Rubbing her nose she laughed at herself. "I think I have an allergy to flour."

"I don't think that exists child." He smiled back.

Lonessa drew herself up to her full height, "Yes, it does. I sneeze every time I come in here. Remember the last time? That is how you found me on the day..." Her voice became small and fragile. "The day Garon died."

Rivers of tears parted her flour stained face as she ran into Mr. Grahm's waiting, open arms. She buried her face in the coarse linen of his apron, "I miss him so much." She managed to choke out between sobs.

"I would do anything to see him again."

"Hush child. *'Anything'* could be an expensive price to pay, and the mountain gods do not take promises lightly."

"What do you mean?" She pulled away and starred up at his gentle face.

Her large brown eyes, still wet with tears, melted his heart. Mr. Grahm knew Lonessa's parents would not consent to him talking about this with her, but he also knew that she was different from normal girls her age. Her parents did not understand that. "The mountain gods are gentle to their followers. Remember that." He mussed up her hair and pushed her kindly back to the table and placed a lump of dough in front of her—motioning for her to kneed it. "I heard what you said in the old temple. Lonessa, I tell you from experience that they do not forget." Tears formed in his eyes, and a deeper sadness started to take Lonessa. "I will do what I can to protect you," he continued, "but you spoke the words and now you need to pay the price."

"What price? What happened to you?"

"That is a tale for another time." He turned from her and went back to the oven.

Lonessa sat in silence trying to understand what Mr. Grahm was talking about when he said she needed to pay the price. A wave of panic threatened to consume her when a city guard pounded on the heavy doorframe.

"Grahm, come quick we need your help."

"Stay here." Commanded Mr. Grahm.

"What is going on?" She was now in the grips of her panic.

"Stay." He repeated as he hurried out of the small bakery.

I know those bells, the city is burning. How can he tell me to stay here, when my home is being destroyed? She stuck her head out of the dark bakery and squinted into the early morning light. People were rushing passed her, some she knew some she didn't, none of them paid any attention to the little girl wandering out of the bakery. She slowly crept down the street and around the corner. The fire had nearly consumed the entire guard house and some of the surrounding buildings and a wave of fear crashed into her as she caught a glimpse of a body, almost entirely consumed by the flames. Catching sight of Mr. Grahm headed her way she ran back to the bakery and tried to forget by losing herself in cleaning the small shop.

Mr. Grahm did not say a word as he re-entered his shop and took up the small wire broom to help Lonessa clean. His bowed head and slouched shoulders told Lonessa everything. *People had died in that fire,* she thought, *why are so many people dying now? What have we done to deserve this?* She quietly took up a rag and began wiping down the tables, trying not to disturb Mr. Grahm. The recent deaths seemed to affect him powerfully, and Lonessa watched him as he silently went about sweeping up the shop. *Mountain Gods, if ever there was a time we needed you most, please let me pay the price to bring back those we lost.* The words formed themselves in her mind, and she repeated them several times until it became her mantra as she cleaned the little bakery.

"M'lady." Sir Renyard announced.

"Where are you?" She said looking around for the cause of the voice that echoed in her head.

"Lonessa?" Mr. Grahm asked.

"Just entered, I have brought a friend."

The two voices clashed in her head, and she waved an impatient hand at Mr. Grahm. "Where... I don't see— Oh there you are. And who is this?"

"What is it? Are you feeling alright?" Mr. Grahm put down his broom and knelt in front of her, gently placing his hands on her shoulders.

"Please, I am fine. Sir Renyard is back, and he brought a friend." She moved quickly to one side and addressed the newcomer. "And who are you, good sir?"

"I am Gavrill; I have come from far to the south bringing a gift for the Queen of Men."

"Lonessa, we should get you home, this fantasy you have of speaking with the dead is not healthy. I will send for the priest and you should rest now."

Anger welled up in her small chest causing her to nearly scream at Mr. Grahm, "It is not a fantasy, and I am not tired. Please." Turning back to Gavrill. "How is it that you came this far? The south is nothing but mountains."

"Past the edge and over again." Began Gavrill.

"The stone will turn to flesh." She muttered in response.

"How is it that you come to know my words?"

"I don't know, I just knew what to say." She wondered out loud.

"You are truly wise beyond your years m'lady." Gavrill bowed before her.

A feeling of extreme power flooded her. She felt dizzy. "I have been blessed by the gods of the mountains. They give me the words I use and control my life." Her eyes were glossing over almost to the point of becoming pure white as she spoke. "Your gift was not meant for you, but for the Queen of Men. Please you have traveled far, rest and fear no treachery from me. I am but a humble instrument of the gods."

"Lonessa!" Mr. Grahm shook her. "What are you doing? What is going on?"

"Hold on." She apologized to the two ghosts. "For the last time, I am fine. That night you found me in the temple," she paused as she decided to let Mr. Grahm know everything. "I was praying, but not for Garon, well...not like I should have. I promised myself to the service of the mountain gods, everything I am, if only Garon could live again. It was my fault he died, and it will be my fault he lives. I know that is forbidden, and I know life and death are sacred, I listen to the priest at service, but I also know they heard me. The mountain gods spoke to me. They told me I was their servant and I would be given a task, a great mission, if I succeed then Garon would be brought back to me just as he was." She stopped here to gauge the reaction of Mr. Grahm.

He had been a close friend, and the one person that truly understood her. Both her parents seemed too busy with managing the family estate to care too much about her and she looked on him as a second father. One who cared and would do anything for her. But communicating with the gods and raising the dead were forbidden, even for the priests and acolytes of the temple. Necromancy was banished from the realm thousands of years ago, she knew this. *If it had to be banished, than it is real. If it is real then I can master it.*

A long silence permeated the room, growing ever more menacing with the passing minutes. Lonessa, staring at the flour covered floor of the bakery, shuffled her feet sending a cloud of white dust dancing about the room. Mr. Grahm never took his eyes off her, starring at her as if to see right into her soul. Breaking the tension he knelt before her and laid his hands on her shoulders.

"My lady. I will serve you in this." He bowed his head.

"You will?" She asked timidly. "Do you understand what I am asking of you?"

"I understand. I also know that I have sworn my life to the service of your family. You are the sole heir to your father's seat and the dominion of the Valley; Heiress to one of the Five Kingdoms as dictated by the Old Veldorian law. You cannot do this alone, and I will not let you. I am your man."

He sealed the promise by taking a knife from a small table next to the oven and running the blade over his palm. "With this blood I pledge to you my life. I will serve you in everything, and I will honor your house." He pressed his bleeding palm to his heart and stood up.

"I thank you." Lonessa's voice was shaking. The path they were about to tread together was going to be difficult, she knew that, but his help would make all the difference.

"I beg your pardon, m'lady," Sir Renyard

interrupted, "but I know what you asked of him, and breaking the old code does not come lightly. I caution you to be wary of his quick acceptance."

Lonessa, cursing herself for not realizing that, turned back to Mr. Grahm. "Why do you so willingly set yourself on this path with me?"

"Sir Renyard is right to warn you, but you have nothing to fear from me; I was not always a mere baker." He cleared a spot on the bench for both of them to sit. "I will tell you my tale another time, first let us see what your two friends need of you." He sat, and Lonessa saw him stare right at the two ghosts.

"You can see them too?" She was shocked.

"Please sirs, tell us your tale. How do you come to be here?" He continued almost ignoring her.

"I traveled from over the mountains to bring a gift to the Queen of Men," Gavrill recited.

"Over the mountains?" Lonessa gasped. "From the south?"

"Yes."

"The gods sent me a dream a few days ago." *The moonless night,* she realized. "A creature of great importance brought forth from the rock, born of fire, and ruler of the sky." Lonessa closed her eyes trying to remember the images. "I knew it was a seer's dream, but now I know what it was about." She turned to face Gavrill. "Where is the gift now?"

"I left it. I... I am not sure." Gavrill stuttered.

"Sir Renyard, where did you find him?" Mr. Grahm asked.

"He was in the ashes of the fire."

"Born of fire." Lonessa whispered to herself.

"I found him staring at some of the smoldering

lumber. I thought that was where he died."

"It may be, but if we are going to find the gift you brought we should start there." Mr. Grahm stood up. "Wait here. I need to retrieve an artifact from my room." He strode deliberately to the back of his shop and up the small stairs to the second level.

"Do you remember anything about where you used to live?" Lonessa inquired.

"Yes. My village is... I had a wife... Did I? There was a farm. I think." A look of fear came into Gavrill's eyes. "I can not remember." Tears began to form. "I know I should. I know that I was loved, and that I loved someone, maybe I did, but it was important." He looked to Sir Renyard for help.

"I am sorry friend. Lonessa showed me my wife and child after my death and I could not even remember their names. Almost as if my life has no effect on my death."

"I refuse to believe that. I know I was loved and I will be missed." He turned to Lonessa, "I swear that after we complete this mission, I will return to my homeland and remember. I beg you to help me."

She looked into the translucent eyes of his ghostly form and felt the pain he was fighting down. "I will do my best to help you remember. Never let your thoughts wander to far from your home. Keep trying, no matter what, never forget and I will help you return."

"You truly are an ally to the dead."

Lonessa blushed and the three fell into silence for a short while until Mr. Grahm creaked down the steps holding a small leather pouch. Just as he reached the bottom an elderly woman entered the shop.

"Why Lonessa, it is good to see you helping out here. Take your mind off things."

"Hello. Good to see you too." Was all she managed to respond.

She saw Mr. Grahm walking towards her. "I need my usual two loves and also a muffin this morning." He hid the pouch in the folds of his apron before she could see it. "Did you see the fire? They say it was from a traveler, come across the frozen plains. He lost his mind from the cold and while the guards were tending to him in their guard house he set the place a fire, yelling about he could not get warm. Such a tragedy, three guards died in that fire, and this only five days after the death of your little friend, Lonessa. Such a tragedy."

"Please, Karein, I do not have bread today. If you will excuse us?" Mr. Grahm tried to usher he out.

"No bread? A baker with no bread? I guess I can't fault you. Probably helped put the fire out. Well I will leave you to it. Good to see you m'lady. I will be back this afternoon?"

"Please, I might have your bread then. Thank you." Mr. Grahm followed her out and latched the door after her.

"We need to leave." He announced after the door was secure. "There will be more customers and we have much to do."

"But I can't leave. Father will barely let me out of his sight now. How can I get away?"

"Lonessa, dear sweet child." He knelt before her. "You have to make a choice. If you truly believe the gods have set you on this course then we will leave at first light tomorrow. Or you can remain here and live out your days in peace. The road before us will be dangerous, your life will be under attack from all sides, so if you chose to remain I understand."

She looked from his face to the faces of the two ghosts at the table with them. *How can I deal with Garon's death if I stay? The pain will never end.* "I will go." She choked out.

Mr. Grahm stood. "I will search the remains of the guard house for your gift tonight Gavrill, if you will accompany me. Lonessa run home and pack a small bag, small enough to carry. We will meet here in the pre-dawn light tomorrow. Be ready for anything." He hugged Lonessa and shoved the pouch into her hand. "Keep this with you at all times, never take it off, for if you do you will end up like me."

"Like you?" She inquired.

"I will explain later, right now run along and do as I told you. See you tomorrow."

Aislinn

Shouts punctuated the clamor of carts coming to an abrupt halt. Aislinn rubbed the crusting dust from her eyes as she rose from pretending to sleep. The sun was just cresting over the horizon and its soft light cast long shadows over the caravan in front of her. A chilly morning breeze blew off the estuary in front of them bringing with it the smell of the sea. Cooking fires dotted the beach around the makeshift camp, and the smell of bacon frying over the open flame only slightly covered the odor of human excrement that seemed to pervade her cart. Gulls called across open water before diving into the golden bay in search of their breakfast.

A pit developed in Aislinn's stomach causing her to double over in pain. It had been days since she had eaten anything other than stale bread crusts and dirty water. The shouting got closer. She saw a group of dark-skinned gruff looking men, clothed in thin rags that could have been palace curtains, moving from cart to cart and unlocking them. They gathered the inmates into a line and chained all of their legs together, creating a snake of human slaves.

The door of her cart rattled as one of her captors slowly opened it while yelling in a language she did not understand. His motions were clear enough though, and she almost fell face first into the dirt as she tripped out of the cart. Her arm caught wildly around the neck of one of the twins that shared her mobile prison.

"Watch it!" One twin shouted.

"What are you doing?" The other chimed in.

Aislinn, still recovering from the shock, brushed herself off and turned to the twins. "I didn't mean to fall on you. My leg cramped, and I tripped."

"Not my problem, just don't let it happen again." Said the first twin.

"Can you believe her, Rebecca?" The second asked, with heaps of sarcasm in her voice.

"Stupid Little Town trash, Margery."

"Where are you from then?" Aislinn asked. She had assumed that everyone that was captured had been from Little Town.

"None of your concern." Rebecca flicked dust into Aislinn's face with the toe of her ragged boot, and they both turned and walked off in the direction the guard was pointing.

Aislinn spat out the dirt and brushed it out of her eyes before nursing her way behind them. Her foot was still asleep, making the going tender and slow. The guard was constantly pushing her in the small of her back with the butt end of his spear and yelling in his foreign tongue.

Struggling up the side of a steep incline, she fell again, cracking her head hard against a stone. Stars danced before her eyes until the guard yanked her to her feet and shoved her, surprisingly gently, over the crest of the hill. When she gained her footing and the throbbing in her head became manageable she was able to take stock of her surroundings. She was standing on the top of a small sandy hill. Long dune grass waved gently in the breeze blowing in softly from across the bay. Down the hill from where she stood a large river, four times the size of the one near Little Town, cut the land in two before it ended in a maze of small islands as it emptied out into the sea. Behind her the land flattened out, and fields of wheat and grass stretched as far as the eye could see. The far bank of the river was lined with trees that hung low over the water's edge. She saw small rafts launching from up river carrying four prisoners and two guards across the strong but calm current of the mighty river.

"Where are you taking us? Where is my mother?" She demanded of the guard.

"You no talk. Beaten if talk." The guard responded without looking at her.

"Answer me." She demanded.

A guard from the base of the hill pointed at her with his whip and shouted something at the guard next to her. He leaned in close to her ear. "No talk please." He whispered and prodded her firmly but without malice to get her moving down the hill.

She consented and made her way quickly to the bank of the river where the waiting guard ushered her onto a raft with the three other members of her cart. She caught a glimpse of Cor Donovan and the bald one-eyed slaver seated at a wooden table feasting on some roast fowl and what she assumed was wine as her little raft lurched out onto the river. It joined with dozens of other rafts, and for the first time, Aislinn realized the scope of the caravan she was a part of. There had to be close to two hundred slaves being brought across this river. The old crone barely moved, the twins huddled together shooting cruel glances at Aislinn, and the two guards looked disinterested as the raft made its way diagonally across the river.

The current carried them only slightly off course, and it was a short walk through the shrubs and tree roots to get back to where the main body of the caravan was setting up camp for the evening. Aislinn realized that it would take the better part of the day to get all the carts and people across this river. The guards pushed them into a group around a tree where their ankles were shackled together with the tree trunk. She hung her head against her chest and wrapped her arms around her legs trying to be small enough to be overlooked. She shuddered against the cool breeze as the long day wore on. The old crone was coughing uncontrollably now, sending small chunks of phlegm spattering across the ground. *It's only a matter of time before she falls into the eternal slumber.* The twins were whispering together, but as they were on the far side of the tree—which was rather large—Aislinn could not hear what they were talking about.

The moon hung heavy and full in the dark purple sky—mirroring the bright orange and faded yellows of the setting sun as dusk settled on the river bank. Crickets started their nightly song, and the night birds added a melody to the approaching dark. The river quietly gurgled past, adding its voice to the symphony. Smoke from the cooking fires kept most of the insects away, and Aislinn sat back and rested against the rough bark of the tree, something other than uneven bars provided a small relief. The clean air of the sea shore was filled with the aroma of cooking meats and melting cheeses, grilled vegetables and sweet wines. Her mouth watered at the thought of digging into a hot meal, but she knew that it was going to be stale bread and dirty water, if the slaves got anything at all. She took a small comfort that the river had managed to wash most of the smell from her and her companions.

"Bring this one to my table." A musical voice intoned through the crisp night air.

She snapped her head up and found herself staring into the dark eye of the bald one-eyed man. "And if I choose not to go?" She did not break eye contact.

"You will die." He almost laughed. "Bring her." He said to the two guarding her group before he walked away.

"I refuse to leave." She said defiantly, but no one noticed and the guards hoisted her to her feet, unshackled her, and one of them carried her off in the direction the one-eyed man went.

The camp was large, and it took a few moments for her to reach the table that was set up for the leaders. Cor Donovan was there along with the one-eyed man and three other dark-skinned slavers. The table was set with rustic wooden bowls and spoons and slave girls were pouring hot rabbit stew into them as she approached.

"Please, sit." Cor Donovan waved his hand indicating an open seat in between him and the one-eyed man.

"It is our pleasure to have you for dinner. You should consider yourself honored; of all the two hundred and thirteen slaves we gathered on this journey you are the only one to eat a hot meal tonight." His melodic voice was starting to annoy Aislinn.

"I will not sit with you." She stood up to her full height and tried to make herself an intimidating figure, but the lack of food and riding in the back of a cart for the last four days hindered her attempt.

A hand hit her cheek with enough force to knock her to the ground. Blood filled her mouth, and she spat it out as she struggled back to her feet.

"Save yourself some trouble child, do as I bid you." His one eye fixed on her as he offered his hand to help her to her feet.

Ignoring the gesture she fought the urge to spit on his offering, but the thought of taking another blow to the face, or maybe worse, stopped her. "Thank you for your kindness." She managed to squeeze out between clenched teeth.

"Your graciousness, however fake, is appreciated. I have big plans for you child." They took their seats and the slave girls melted away after serving the meal.

She knew the hot soup was bland and flavorless, but it still tasted like the best soup she had ever had. "What do you mean by big plans?" She ventured conversation after she had finished her first bowl and the servant girl returned to refill it.

"Have you ever seen the world outside of Little Town?" Cor Donovan asked. "Wait. Don't answer that, of course you haven't. There is a world where the King has no power. Where the laws of the kingdoms can't touch us."

"What are you talking about?" Aislinn was confused.

"I have lived my whole life serving the King, doing his dirty work, cleaning up his messes, and what do I have to show for it?" He reached into his breast pocket. "This," throwing a golden medallion on the table, "and a heap of gold."

"Cor, please. We are miles away from your King now." The one-eyed man turned his face to Aislinn. "You are no longer a citizen of the Five Kingdoms. You belong to me."

Anger welled up in her throat, and it was all she could do to keep herself from using the wooden spoon in her hand as a makeshift weapon, but after a few moments of trembling hands and clenched teeth she responded. "I thank you sir, but I don't even know your name."

He roared with mirth. "Naveed, Prince of the Broken Men."

"Prince Naveed, I graciously thank you for your hospitality and humbly beg of you leave to rest. The journey is weary for us slaves." Aislinn was no stranger to groveling having practiced since she could talk. Her tongue found the newly loosened lower right tooth, and she stole a sideways glance at the guard standing nearby.

"You will leave when I say you can leave." Naveed looked up with an emotionless face. "Sit." He nodded at her chair.

Aislinn sat down.

"I have already had an opportunity to remind you that testing my patience is detrimental to your well-being." His eyes indicated the guard, and he pointed to his tooth. "I will remind you again if I need to, but I would rather not."

"I only asked if-" A hand quickly silenced her.

"You, a slave girl, ask nothing from the Prince." Cor Donovan explained.

Tears welled up in her eyes, but she fought them back and simply nodded understanding. The little group fell into silence as they finished the soup and the slave girls returned with crisp rabbit and steamed roots. Aislinn could no longer hear the night birds or the soft gurgle of the river. She drew no pleasure from the aroma of salted meats cooking over the fires or the fresh sea air. Blood filled her mouth and plugged her nose making the simplest breath a labor. When the perfectly cooked meat was set in front of her, she merely picked at her plate and fought down sickness as the two men wolfed down their portions. Her discomfort grew as more wine found its way into Cor Donovan and he grabbed every slave girl that served him. Their faces pleading for help. With every look, her determination to help them grew, but she was hampered by her fear.

Only after both of the men had passed out in their chairs from the wine did she work up enough courage to stand from the table. Her heart beat a frantic rhythm against her chest as she slowly tried to release herself from her chair. The creaking of the dried wood and the snapping of twigs under her shifting feet seemed to echo across the little glade where she had dined with the two leaders of the slavers. Eyeing the knife sitting next to her, she turned slightly to see if the guard was still awake or paying attention to her. He was not. Now was her opportunity to act. She could slip silently around the table and slide the knife into the hearts of the two evil men sleeping off the sweet wine. Taking the first step towards this goal a twig snapped loudly underfoot and she dropped the knife and sprinted back to where she was chained to the tree.

Aislinn found the twins huddled together with their backs against the tree; one of them, she could not tell which, was snoring loudly. The old crone was missing, but Aislinn didn't have time to wonder where she went as she heard the guards starting to raise the alarm about a runaway slave. She ducked behind the tree and ran into the woods like her life depended on it, and it did. Shrubs grabbed at her ankles and tore her simple leather shoes as she ran deeper into the small trees that lined the edge of the river. Dogs barked endlessly as they caught her scent and plunged into the underbrush after her. She knew she would have to get back to the river if she was going to retain her new found freedom. The ground suddenly fell out from underneath her, and she fell.

Tumbling down the rock-filled sandy hill, she fought off larger stones from colliding with her head. Then it happened. She crashed to a stop against a cold and soggy mass on the banks of the river, her head slamming into what she thought was a rock. A wave of nausea and dizziness swept over her, and the last thing she had remembered before the blackness took her was the bloated and water rotten face of the old crone.

Night birds chirped out their songs, the river bubbled passed peacefully, and a rotten stench woke Aislinn from her slumber. The eyeless corpse of old crone stared back at her when Aislinn rolled over. The shock of the grotesqueness sent her sprawling backwards several feet. There was a large pool of blood lying next to the head of the waterlogged corpse. The sight of it caused her to notice for the first time the pounding ache in the back of her own and the sharp throbbing pain in her side. She knew if she reached her hand back there it would come back covered in blood, so she chose not to. The footprints in the sand in front of her provided the distraction from her agony she desperately wanted.

It was difficult to see in the pale moonlight, but Aislinn could just make out two sets of large footprints imbedded into the sand around where she was lying next to the body of the crone. They seemed to come from upstream, where the camp was, and follow the river north to the bay, only after a short detour around where she was. Her heart started racing. *I was almost caught. They must have thought I was dead.* She thought to herself as she struggled against the pain in her ribs to stand. *I am lost*. The realization never fully hit her until that moment. Staring at the crow-picked corpse half in and half out of the river she feared she would end up that way. Resolution beat down her fears and, not knowing how long she had been unconscious, she drug herself up the sandy cliff face and snuck back towards the camp.

The awful sight of the deserted camp, made worse by the pale glow of the moon, chased her breath away; only a few scraps of wood and broken wheels accompanied by a vast stretch of flattened grass were all that was left of the mobile settlement. She picked her way through the remains looking for anything that she could use. A crow, catching Aislinn's eye, hopped noisily around the carcass of a wooden cart. A large hunk of bread and a smaller piece of cheese seemed to be wedged underneath a few boards where the crow had a hard time getting to it. She realized she was starving. After chasing off the horribly loud bird, she pried the board loose and sat down next to it nibbling the bread to test if it was still eatable. It was. *I have to keep moving. I have to keep moving.* She repeated over and over in her head. *I don't know how long I was lying on the beach. They could be miles away by now.*

Aislinn found a scrap of cloth from a soldier's uniform and tied the ends to a small stick to form a satchel, stuffed the remaining bread and cheese into it, and set off following the slavers. *I am lost, and if they keep dropping food along the way at least I won't die of starvation before I can find help.* It seemed as good a plan as any so she followed them further east and farther away from her home. All the while never forgetting that they still had her mother chained to a cart somewhere in that caravan of human cargo.

Lonessa

The moon hung low in the night sky, sending its light through the open window. Lonessa lay in her bed, gripping the pouch Mr. Grahm had given her, not daring to sleep. Crickets chirped their nightly hymn outside her window, and night birds called to each other across the starlight sky. She could feel a great peace sweeping through her little valley, and a wave of homesickness sweep through her. Even though she had yet to leave, the mere thought of never returning to this cozy little room where she grew up caused a fear to spread rapidly throughout her chest. Tears, her best friends over the last week, streamed down her face, finding her pillow. A realization dawned on her, that if she were to follow her heart, and honor her commitment to the mountain gods, she would have to leave home, maybe forever. For the first time since the death of Garon, she doubted her resolve. *Maybe it would be better if I learned to live with the pain. Maybe I should just stay here.* She almost had herself convinced not to leave by reciting this mantra when the night sky started to lighten over the mountains and she knew it was time.

Rising silently and dressing herself in warm traveling clothes, she snuck out of her room and down the stone steps to the door of the main hall of the castle. Voices were coming from the chamber next to her and she stopped. *No one should be awake at this hour,* she thought as she edged closer to the door.

"Lord Bryne, I understand your qualms but if you are to attend the King's Feast you need to leave today." Lonessa did not recognize the voice.

"I will not leave while my family still grieves." Her father's voice echoed around the ancient hall of the Valley, bouncing off the large mounted antlers of deer and elk that lined the walls.

"Bring your family with you. My lord, they need a break from this sadness. Lady Aviana would rejoice in seeing her homeland again, and Lonessa would do well to leave the Valley for the first time."

"Do not tell me what my family needs." His voice was cold as stone, and sent a chill through Lonessa as she huddled against the wall listening.

"Yes, my lord."

"I will not attend." Her father boomed

She could listen to no more. The pain in her

father's voice cut deep into her soul. *I can't leave him now.* She thought as she paused along the passage to the kitchens. Her hand found its way into her trouser pocket and closed around the small pouch Mr. Grahm had given her. *I am doing this for my family. If Garon comes back my parents will not be so sad.* Encouraged by the lumpy contents of the pouch she almost ran the rest of the way to the kitchens to steal a few loaves of fresh bread and some smoked meat to take with them on their journey.

Once outside the castle, and in the open morning air of the valley, she slowed to a walk and waited for her ghostly friends to find her. Still holding the pouch she passed it from hand to hand wondering what was inside it. She was to afraid to open the mysterious gift, and only toyed with the contents through the rough fabric. The city streets were dark and lonely, echoing the feelings that were growing within her. Tormented by thoughts of leaving her family, leaving the Valley for the first time, and starting a new journey was almost to much for her and once again she found her self stopped and facing back to her room.

"M'lady."

Lonessa spun around startled by the sudden disturbance of the predawn silence. "Who is there?" She whispered into the shadows.

A translucent form emerged from the stone wall of the castle. "Your humble servant Sir Renyard, m'lady."

"You startled me, Sir Renyard." She turned back around and motioned for the deceased knight to follow her. "You have been beyond the mountain walls of the Valley, what is waiting for us?"

"M'lady?"

"I have never been outside of the Valley. What is out there? What does it look like?"

Sir Renyard paused a moment and tried to remember. "I remember the vastness of the sky. When headed north to the frozen plains the mountains fall away quickly and smooth out to rolling hills stretching as far as the eye can see. The plains themselves come alive in late spring and bring forth the richest fruit and sweetest honey before refreezing in early fall. The river rushes north to meet the great dam built by the Veldorians. I have not traveled that far north but the stories tell us it is the largest structure ever built. To the south the world ends." He stopped. "We thought it ended, but Gavrill..." His voice dropped to an inaudible murmur before he stopped all together and the two walked along in silence. His revery deepened as they continued on their path to the bakery.

"Sir Renyard, what is it?" Lonessa asked, feeling she needed to break the oppressive quiet. "What is wrong?"

"Something I should remember. Something from the southern mountains. I feel Gavrill was involved."

Lonessa reached out to touch his arm then remembered that she could only pass through his incorporeal body, when her hand brushed something cold.

"M'lady!" Sir Renyard jumped. "Your hand, it burns."

"How can I touch you?" She gasped as she jerked her hand back.

"You are starting to realized the power of the gift I gave you." Mr. Grahm whispered as he emerged from his bakery. "Have you looked inside the pouch yet?"

"No, but how can I touch him."

"Look inside."

She tentatively untied the thin leather straps, and peered inside. A small gasp escaped her as she saw the mummified fingers. "What is this?" She almost yelled and threw the pouch back at Mr. Grahm.

"Death breeds death little one; this is the magic of necromancy. To be able to touch the dead, part of you has to die. Your ability to see Renyard and Gavrill is slowly draining your life. The mummified fingers come from a priest of the temple, and they are consecrated and blessed and will absorb the death that would otherwise consume you. Without them you will feel your life slip away, and eventually you will succumb to the grave, not happy and fulfilled, but gaunt and empty." He bent down and closed the pouch tied it to a string and hung it around Lonessa's slim neck. "You do not need to dwell on them, but never leave them, never take it off."

"You said if I do not wear them I will become like you. What did you mean?"

"I was given the protection amulet far to late for it to protect my soul. Before I came to the Valley I had already lost the desire to live." He choked back tears. "Lonessa, I will not let that happen to you. Let us not speak of it anymore. We have a long journey ahead of us and we must be moving quickly if we are to escape the city before the sun touches the valley floor."

After a few moments, Renyard melted away and

the two living companions secured their small parcels and set out towards the north gate of the city. Lonessa kept an eye on Mr. Grahm, trying to determine what it was about him that looked different. The vision of him provided by her memory was only a small taste of what stood before her now. The sheer massiveness of him and the strength that was so apparent seemed somehow hollow and inconsequential.

The city walls seemed to have grown taller and thicker than she remembered. Mud sucked at their footsteps like small hands grabbing them, trying to stop them from making their escape. More than twice Lonessa had to stop to retrieve her boot that had been pulled off. Every time she thought she heard laughter coming from the stone itself but brushed it away. *Am I hearing things now? Calm down, Lonessa, everything will be all right.* It was little comfort. A tightness was already growing in her chest that was impossible to ignore completely. By the time they reached the gates of city wall, the small voices that echoed along the stone-lined passages of the road were too much for Lonessa and she had to cover her ears to try to keep them out.

Mr. Grahm reached out and grabbed her shoulder. "Once you embraced your decision to follow this path, the world changed for you. I am not the man I was, the world is not as quiet as it was before." He slipped the amulet over her head and instantly the voices stopped and Mr. Grahm went back to the loved baker he was before.

"Why can't I leave it off?" Lonessa took a few steps away from him.

"The dead are all around you, even if you cannot see or hear them. They affect you." He slipped the macabre necklace back over her head and rested it on her shoulders, "They are the voices of your ancestors that died defending the Valley. They are the voices of the thousands that have died inside these city walls. The Castles of the Veldorians remember their dead, and, if left without protection, they will kill you."

"Where are we going?" Lonessa almost grabbed his hand for comfort as she looked up at him wondering.

"I don't know little one. I have a friend living in Headwater," he saw the confusion on her face. "The capital of the Riverlands, he can get us to Aurorum. My brother will be able to help us from there."

"We are going to the capital of the Five Kingdoms." Lonessa almost squealed in delight. Her dreams were often filled with magical images of the marble city and the golden bay.

Her mind wandered among fantastic visions of romantic knights and grand Kings in the capital city when she was surprised to find they were already at the north gate; it was open.

"Why is it open this early?" She asked Mr. Grahm, in a voice that betrayed her tender heart and pampered thirteen years of life.

"My dear child, there are peasants and farmers that need access to the city before most people are even awake." Mr. Grahm smiled, remembering what it was like to be so young and innocent. A cloud passed over his face as he remembered the dire importance of the journey they were starting. "Just keep your hood up and your head down and we should be able to sneak past the guards without them realizing who you are."

Lonessa did as she was told and could just barely make out anything in front of her as she walked. Her eyes focused more and more on Mr. Grahm, the large form on her left and his heavy canvas pack. It moved. *My eyes are playing tricks, or it is the amulet?* She tried to convince herself when it moved again. There was something alive inside his bag.

"You there, you two. What's your business?" A hollow voice rang down from the parapet adding to the clamor that had begun again after the amulet was back around her neck.

"We are returning to our fields after missing gate closing last night." Mr. Grahm called back.

As he called to the guards his back pack shifted. A small black head slowly emerged from the pockets and stared at Lonessa. Two streams of smoke escaped its nostrils, and Lonessa's heart raced. Its dark hollow eyes haunted her, its sharp long teeth scared her, and a feeling of dread swept over her and she stumbled into Mr. Grahm's back causing it to emit a loud scream that pierced the cold air.

The sound mixed with the voices of the dead and rocked her back. Both of her hands grabbed her head and she stumbled forward again, looking for somewhere to sit. She ripped the string off her neck and instantly felt relief from the pain in her mind, but the pressure on her chest remained. The inhuman shriek pierced the still air again. Terror pushed her to run out of the city, she felt the guards chasing her, she felt the dead following, she felt Mr.

Grahm grabbing her neck. Her breath was quick and shallow, as if she was suffocating on the fresh air of the southern mountains. Dizziness and blackness loomed around the edge of her vision, grabbing at parts of her mind until she could not handle anymore. She hit the ground head first and gave in to the pressure of unconsciousness.

Gravous

"It has been nearly a week! No other sign has presented itself." A booming voice echoed between the tall pillars of the royal throne room. The hanging tapestries and thick benches that lined the walls did little to diminish the reverberation of this man's voice. "We can ignore the moonless night as nothing more than the happenstance of nature!" A tall thin old man yelled as he quickly paced around the room. He moved quicker than his appearance suggested he could. The black wool robe of his office brushed the ground with a soft wisp, and he played with the white cord wrapped loosely around his waist. His beard betrayed his age with streaks of white running down each side, and a hunch was starting to form itself on his back.

"Magister Brundrum! We have heard your argument!" The King boomed back through a mouthful of roast duck. "I refuse to believe that on the night before the full moon was due the disappearance of it all together has no meaning."

"A wise thought, Your Grace." Lord Morris whispered into the king's ear.

The King slumped on his throne, hanging one leg over the marble-covered arm. A silver platter sat on a small side table next to him, close enough for him to reach without much effort, covered with roasted fowl and dried fruits. His hands were already sticky from the juices, even though the meeting had only just begun. The members of the Royal Council stood around him, vying for position to be close to his ear.

Three distinct groups stood on the floor of the throne room, each waiting their turn to be heard by the King and Council. The Academy, dressed in long black robes, huddled close together and whispered at almost everything that was said. The Priests, clad in brilliant white cassocks with deep purple stoles, mingled about with the rest of the crowd, made up of courtiers, nobles, and lesser lords seeking favors.

"You explained your side already, Magister. You are starting to repeat yourself." Lord Lynch bowed as he spoke, trying to reduce the tension he felt rising. The old members of the Academy had always worried Gravous, but he put aside his personal views and tried to mollify the now fuming Magister.

Brundrum looked to the fellow members of the Academy for support, but none of them dared to cross the King. They merely shifted uncomfortably in their black robes and shared worried glances.

Defeated and deflated he turned back to the King and bent his wiry frame in a painful looking bow. "By your leave, Your Grace, you have heard from the Academy." He straightened up slowly and limped noticeably back to his fellows, trying to cadge pity from the court.

"Now, by the custom of the Five Kingdoms and the old Veldorian Empire, we will hear from the Temple. Mystic Grahm, please, you have the floor." Lord Corbett waved his arm in a welcoming gesture.

A large elderly man waddled from near the back of the great hall towards the front, blessing many of the lesser lords along the way. His short curly black hair still bounced despite his age. When he finally reached the king, he bowed deeply and waved an acknowledging hand at the Royal Council. Turning to the members of the Academy he cleared his throat and began.

"Our gracious King," the old mystic began in a nasal voice, "seated on the throne of the Five Kingdoms by the grace of the gods, Lord Protector of the Gold Coast, ruler of the wild islands, and rightful King of the Barren Lands, distinguished members of the Royal Council, convened by the edict of the old kings of Veldoria, and my honored brothers of the Academy. I, humble servant of the gods and the realm, have a message for you, and your court. In the bowels of the Temple of Light, the very night the moon was hidden from us, the clergy gathered to consult the portents and pray. The gods of our forefathers have blessed us with the reason behind this sign from the heavens. This sign is no accident of nature, as our learned friends would have you believe, but an omen from the gods warning of a great and mighty event in our world."

The droning of his voice echoed around the marble pillars of the hall sending jolts through the gathered crowd every time he stressed a word. Shifting feet added a muffled hum to his long winded speech. The king's hand waved Lord Lynch closer to him, breaking the spell that had caused Gravous to drift off into thought.

"Yes, Your Grace?" He whispered nervously in the king's ear. The King muttered something so thick with food that Gravous could not understand. He only nodded approval and laughed lightly as the King seemed to think it was a joke.

"The earth, mother of all things, birthed that night a creature so great that devastation will surly ensue if it is not controlled by the monarchy. The world is changing, your royal highness. Do not listen to the false prophets that tell you nothing is wrong and the divine message sent from the gods of the people is an accident of science-"

"You said that already, Mystic." The King choked down a few small tomatoes in order to clear his throat long enough to yell at the speaker.

"Your Grace has a keen memory and it will serve you well. I humbly beg your forgiveness for my lack of verbal creativity." He bowed low and produced a small glass orb from the hidden pocket in his sleeve. "I have here, your majesty, the very relic used by the first Royal Mystic to guide the Veldorian people across the mountains thousands of years ago. A relic from the dying lands, the lands of fire and death, the lands of shadow that were destroyed by Maddi, the priestess of old. This is the very glass in which I have seen the doom of our people." He raised it for the King to inspect.

"Take it from me, Mystic. I will hear no more today." King Robsfeld Colbralian stood and waited until a hush fell on the those gathered around the great hall. Grabbing his goblet filled with wine he took a long deep swallow, wiped his mouth with the back of his hand, and cleared his throat. "I will hear no more today. Take your science and your gods and leave me."

The great hall was filled with clamor as the lesser lords scrambled to pass the King to gain his blessing as they left. Boredom and annoyance covered the king's face as the exit took longer than he wanted and by the time he was alone with the Royal Council his anger was noticeable. Lord Corbett filled the king's goblet with wine and placed it gently on his arm table. He immediately grabbed it and emptied its contents.

"Your Grace, the people desire an explanation for the mysterious occurrence." Lord Corbett nearly whispered in the now silent hall. "If it pleases Your Grace, the council will look into the matter and find a reasonable explanation. Your Grace has much on his mind with the upcoming feast and does not need this little matter polluting your days."

"Stop your obsequious words, Corbett. They pollute my days more than the wind bag Grahm."

"Mystic Grahm." Gravous corrected. Instantly regretting his choice to speak.

A terrible hush descended on the room. Gravous

bowed deeply, cursing himself silently for correcting the King.

"Your Highness, a proper respect for the clergy is most becoming in our pious new Councilor." Lord Corbett quipped. "He has devoted himself so deeply to the gods that he forgets his King."

Gravous looked to Lord Morris for assistance, but the cold lord stood aside and let the King stew in his anger.

"Leave me, Lord Lynch! Leave me and go live with the priests. If you want to respect them more than your King you can be one of them. I ban you from taking a wife. You will live the celibate life of the priesthood and your family name will die with you." The king's face was deep red, and chunks of food and spittle flew from his mouth as he roared in anger.

"As you command." Gravous bowed and hurried out.

As he stepped out of the great hall, the bright blue sky of the castle gardens greeted him with a cheer he did not feel in his heart. Song birds sang out between the trees. Wind toyed gently with his long black hair. Terror filled his quickly beating heart. *Why did I say that? What was I thinking?* Cursing himself he looked around, desperate to find anything that could help him. The wind shifted, bringing with it a faint whisper.

"I know your secret."

"Who's there?" He spun around frantically not seeing anyone, straining his ears to hear more but the soft breeze melted away into the background once more. "I heard you. Show yourself." He ordered the unseen voice. *Am I going crazy? That explains why I corrected the King. It was such a small offense, he will soon forget it.* He hoped. *At least he won't let the other lord remind him.* He knew, when taken to anger, the King would forbid anyone to speak about the offense.

Gravous started to wander aimlessly around the castle gardens, allowing his feet to take him wherever they would go. The marble lined paths through the fresh tilled earth of the garden offered little resistance as he lost himself deeper and deeper in thought. The gardeners, planting small purple flowers, or pouring measured buckets of river water onto small freshly planted trees, paid him little attention as they hurried about with their duties for the upcoming feast. Taking a small turn between two larger buildings he finally realized where he was. The temple door.

He had avoided the temple to the golden gods, the gods of the Veldorians. They were the gods of his captors not his. Some unseen force seemed to draw him towards the heavy wooden doors. As his hand reached out and touched the well-worn handle, the door swung open. Before him stood a long black robe and white cassock two sizes to big for its occupant. Gravous recognized the boy from the court earlier but was still surprised at how *small* this future Mystic was.

The acolyte bowed deeply almost losing himself in his robes and motioned for Gravous to enter the dark smoking temple.

"I was not expecting you to greet me here." Gravous said as he tentatively crossed the threshold.

The acolyte merely bowed in response and silently

led him through the winding halls of the vestibule of the temple until he stopped suddenly and pointed at a large room. Motioning for Gravous to enter.

He did so, but not without fear growing in his heart. *What if my gods see me here? I should never have entered.* The strong aroma of burning incense hung heavy in the still stale air.

"Your gods are not so far away as you might think, young Lord Lynch, adopted son of Lord Edward Lynch of the Midlands. I know who you are and how you came to be here, but unlike my friend and confidant Lord Hamstead I will not be poised in my sleep." Mystic Grahm struggled against his weight to stand from an oversized chair that was facing a large wooden desk with relics and papers scattered about it. "And before you refute my claim, gracious Lord of the Midlands, I humbly ask you to consider your position. The King may not be so disposed to accept you back into his graces and—"

"How do you know about this?" Gravous stammered, almost choking on the thick smoke of the incense.

"I have my ways. The King is not the only one with eyes outside of his own." He squeezed his large frame around the desk and motioned for Gravous to sit. "As I was saying, however, you might not be in the position you once were. A choice has presented itself to you in this hour of great need. The ancient gods have dire need of a champion in the coming doom. This blackening of the moon is but a start to the peril we are about to face. I beg you, Lord Lynch, Gravous of the Broken Lands, put aside your fear and mistrust of my office and my gods and be what you are meant to be."

"Who am I meant to be, Mystic?" Gravous did not sit, but took a few steps backward toward the door. His left hand started to shake and his heart sped up, and jumped into his throat. *What does he know about Hamstead? He needs me though, he won't kill me? Will he?*

Mystic Grahm rested his large frame against the sturdy wood of his desk "You must excuse me Lord Lynch. I fear I am being over zealous. I must explain. Please sit, let me get you some wine." He picked up and rang a bell from his desk and the tiny acolyte reappeared only to have the word wine yelled at him and he scurried off again. Gravous sat.

"On this moonless night I was in conference with the fathers of the faith, praying to the gods to illuminate the mysteries of this cosmic event. I was taken by a vision at that point. I saw the fiery wings of a great beast beating back a vast army of death, death in all shades. Rotten corpses eating the living. Dark shadows of souls possessing the innocent. The bones of those killed rising to serve the Lord of Death. I saw the dread beasts of the mountains run down and destroy the land of our fathers, yours and mine alike, the evil made no distinction between races but savaged all lands equally.

"Against this wanton and mindless destruction stood but one person, on the back of a winged terror breathing flame like the dragons of old. You are to be that barrier. You can take a stand against the coming evil and fight to keep your people, and mine, free from the tyranny."

Gravous's face lost color as the Mystic was talking,

and the beating of his heart greatly increased. "What are you saying? The dead will walk and I will fly a dragon to meet them? That is absurd."

Shuffling feet and the whoosh of a robe dragging on the ground announced the presence of the acolyte with the wine and Mystic Grahm took the tray, placed it on the table, and served Gravous a goblet.

"The visions of the gods are never wrong Lord Lynch." He continued after taking a long draught from his own goblet. "They might be shrouded in allegory, however. Legends speak to us in many ways. As we have interpreted this vision, a great evil will arise from within the Five Kingdoms that will threaten the lives of everyone, and against this the gods need a hero to lead their army. A hero to stand for good. That hero can be you, Lord Lynch."

"Why do you keep saying *Lord Lynch* like that?" He nearly screamed.

"I am merely addressing you by the title of your office." Mystic Grahm smiled.

"I refuse to hear any more of your tale of doom." He swallowed the last few drops of his wine and tried to stand. "What have you done to me." He bellowed, falling back into his chair.

"My dear Lord Lynch," Mystic Grahm soothed, "I have only offered you wine, if you recall I drank from the same vessel as you."

"What is happening to me?" His voice seemed weak and far away, as he stared into his now empty goblet.

"The wine has gone to your head. Let us get you out into the fresh air."

A fog started to envelope Gravous's vision and he

did not notice the two other people that entered the room, but he felt himself being carried out into the light of the mid-afternoon sun. The wind had shifted and a cool breeze was now blowing in from off the bay, revitalizing him with every gust. After a few moments of leaning against the cool stonework of the outer wall of the temple, he felt well enough to stand. The round face of Mystic Grahm greeted him with a smile as Gravous rubbed the last of the fog from his eyes.

"I beg your forgiveness m'lord, and I humbly beg you to think on the things I have told you today. Let your thoughts dwell on them, you have an important choice ahead of you and I pray to the gods that you will make the right decision. Do not forget what you have heard." Mystic Grahm bowed, kissed Gravous's hand, and returned inside the Temple.

The recovering Lord Lynch was left on the spotless walkway in the heart of the city. The fog that took him inside the temple was all but gone and it was replaced by the setting spring sun and a gentle salty wind from the ocean. A dark figure rounded a corner and waved as it saw Gravous.

"Lord Lynch. Magister Brundrum has been looking for you. He sends his condolences on today's missteps and wishes you to dine with him tonight in hopes of restoring your position." The Academy Brother almost whispered as he got closer, his eyes darting around to see if they were being overheard.

"Who is it who addresses me?" Gravous tried to retain the dignity of his office. *The whole world must know about it by now. And how long was I inside the Temple?*

"I am Brother Adicus. Please come with me to dine with the Magister."

Gravous allowed himself to be led across the darkening streets of the city to the Academy. The towering spires and vastness of the facade was rivaled only by that of the Palace itself. Legends say three buildings in Aurorum were built by the Veldorians and survived the ages: the Palace, the Academy, and the Temple. He felt the history of the ages as he passed under its doors. They were greeted by a young servant and led quickly to the dining hall, being informed that the Magister had already sat down to eat.

"Lord Gravous Lynch of the Midlands, and member of the Royal Council." Announced the servant as they entered the hall.

"Please, Lord Lynch, dine with me." Magister Brundrum stood as his guest was announced and indicated a chair at his left arm. "We have much to discuss."

The table in front of him was copiously adorned with breads and cheeses, bowls of fresh fruit, a roast pig and several other trimmings. There was a time when Gravous was startled with the amount of food that was consumed or wasted in the capital city of the Five Kingdoms but it hardly affected him now.

"What do you know?" Gravous sat in the chair indicated and traded goblets with an empty spot next to him. "I have had a trying day and I do not wish to bandy words with another would-be well wisher."

"I respect your directness, my lord, and I will honor your request. I know the King has been in foul mood all day. Caused by your words no doubt. I know he is inebriated on wine and will forget your offense by the morning. And, it may interest you to know that I know you spent the majority of this day in the Temple."

"What does that have to do with anything?" Gravous took a roll from the center tray and tried to sound unimpressed. *Does everyone know everything?*

"Nothing, nothing. I mention it in passing by means of answering your question as precisely as possible." The Magister spent a few moments carving a side of the roast pig and serving himself a large portion. "When I heard what took place today I sent out the Brothers to find you, simply because I was of the mind you would need to dine with company this evening. To ease your mind, my lord, I have known the King for a long time and while he is quick to anger he is quicker to forgive, or at least forget. Please eat, think no more of the disagreeable occurrences of today, tomorrow will dawn bright and new and bring with it the promise of a new beginning."

Gravous served himself from each of the many bowls at the table, careful to only take food after it had been served to the Magister, and refused any wine that was brought to him, but he did feel better and near the end of dinner allowed himself to fall into a friendly debate, with the Magister, about the history of the Midlands after the time of the second King of Veldoria.

The mysteries of the Temple—and the vision that the old Mystic had—all but faded from his mind as he was escorted to his apartments by Brother Adicus.

"Lord Lynch, I thank you on behalf of the Academy for your presence tonight. I hear, from the Magister, that the King has taken a liking to you because of your strong will. Heed the words of our wise teacher and cast off the religious curses of the past."

"Thank you, Brother." Gravous bowed and let himself into his bed chamber.

The warm covers of his inviting bed wrapped around him and comforted him into a pleasant slumber. What seemed like only moments later a hushed voice whispered in the darkness, startling the young lord awake.

"It is coming, the beast has already been born." A thin delicate figure emerged from the shadows and stepped into the pale moonlight shining in from an open window. Even though he had traded the cassock and robes of the Temple for riding pants and a loose shirt, Gravous had no problem recognizing the stunted form of the Acolyte from the Temple.

"I will not be bothered this late." Gravous scolded the young boy for interrupting his sleep. "Away with you."

"So you have made your choice." The acolyte responded.

"My choice?" Gravous sat up. "What choice?"

The only answer to his question was a sharp crack and a blinding flash of light as a blunt object collided with the side of his head. He fell back against the sturdy wooden headboard and into a dreamless sleep.

Tobin

The cliffs surrounding the dam were almost as impressive as the massive structure itself. The land dropped slowly from the southern mountains until this point where it seemed to fall away into nothing. Many times during the journey Fallia had asked him why they didn't head for the river without climbing to the dam but Tobin had no real answer for it, and the king's men refused to speak with them. Only Sir Barin Fairclough, whose family hailed from a region of the Riverlands close to the border of the Marsh, would share any information with them. He silenced the constant questions from Fallia by telling her that the road to the castle passed through the dam, he mentioned that the banks of the west coast of the river were steep and treacherous for a very long way downstream.

He still took Tobin aside every night and tried to teach him about the route they were taking, the lands outside of the Marsh, and what to expect at Aurorum. Tobin enjoyed the nightly attention of this powerful Knight of the Realm; he had never seen anyone choose him over his sister before.

"Tobin, attend me for a while." Sir Fairclough waved a beckoning hand to where Tobin had just dismounted from an uncomfortable seat of his palomino. "Walk with me. Have you ever looked over the top of the world?"

Barin Fairclough was a tall man with a large barrel chest and a full beard hiding most of his face. His surcoat was dirty but still showed the two large green oaks with a red fox dancing between them. Tobin had liked his sigil from the first moment he had seen it back in Blackwatch on the Marsh. There was something about him that the young Tobin was drawn to and yet scared of.

"No, my lord." Tobin kept his eyes on the ground as Sir Fairclough led him to the middle of the dam.

Water rushed over the smooth stones in a roar of awesome power that Tobin had never seen before. Standing on the top of the Great Dam of the Midlands over the Dirgo River, he was mesmerized by the torrent plunging hundreds of feet to the rock face below. The calm waters of reservoir behind him stood out peaceful and serene in stark contrast to the turmoil happening far below him. He squinted passed the glare of the sun and strained his eyes to see the far side of the lake, but he could not. Never before in his life had he seen a body of water so large, and a sense of awe and grandeur passed over him. Turning away from the lake and back to the controlled chaos of water tumbling from small slits in the rock, he lost himself in the mist and turbulence he could just barely see below.

"My lord, why did we come to the dam and not follow the river north?" Tobin asked tentatively.

"I see you have been talking to your sister." The way Sir Fairclough emphasized sister made Tobin slightly uncomfortable. He sighed before continuing, "We came here so you could see this." The young knight gestured over the edge of the dam. "I wanted you to see the power of old Veldoria, and besides it is the closest crossing from where we left the Marshes."

"Old Veldoria, my lord?"

"I am not a lord, Tobin, remember that. You are the son of Lord Rorym Hamstead, and by that right alone you, young Tobin, are a lord. You would do well to remember that once you reach the capital. A mistake like that will not bode well for you. Especially if made in reverse." The young knight's voice was soothing and powerful to Tobin.

"The power of your people, Tobin. This is what I wanted you to see. In your veins runs the blood of ancient people. Veldorians. I wanted you to see the majesty of what your people accomplished."

"But Sir, the people of the marshes were never ruled by the Veldorian Empire, or so my Lord Father has taught me."

"There is much you do not yet understand." Sir Fairclough rested his arm on Tobin's shoulder. "In time I will teach you everything you need to know, and a few things you do not." He smiled and left Tobin staring out over the massive cascade plunging over the cliff.

The old stories of the Veldorians building the dam to create farmland in the Midlands filled his head, and he tried to imagine what this land would have looked like before the massive structure was erected.

His reverie broke when a small hand slipped inside of his, twining their fingers together. His heart leapt into his throat as he turned and saw Fallia standing next to him. She stood silently, staring out past the falls, and gently squeezed his hand in affection. His thoughts raced. Never before had he been in a situation where any woman had shown affection for him. The feelings of shame that accompanied any joy he might find in her hit him like a wave causing his knees to buckle slightly.

"Tobin, are you feeling all right?" Fallia asked as she squeezed his hand one more time.

"Yes, just dizzy from the height."

"Dizzy." She giggled, not letting go of his hand.

"Fallia, what do you know of the old Empire?"

"The Veldorians? Nothing. My governess was too busy teaching me how to stitch and how to sing and how to do other boring things to teach me anything interesting." She leaned her head against his shoulder. "Why?"

"Oh, no reason. Just something Sir π was talking about."

"I don't like him, Tobin. I don't like him at all." Her voice had a hint of poison to it that Tobin had never heard before.

"Why? He is nothing but kind to me." Tobin

almost pleaded with her.

"No, he is evil."

He pulled his hand away from her and walked quickly along the damp stone of the dam.

"Wait, where are you going?" She called after him. Following slower along the treacherous rocks.

"I don't know. I need to think." *How is it that my sister thinks he is evil? I mean, she is my sister, but Sir Fairclough is so kind to me.*

All of his feelings seemed to be swallowed by the shame and fear of the love he had been developing for his sister. It scared him, and she scared him, and the new world scared him. His earliest memories were of the two of them playing in the swamp or hiding from their father; he felt as if the feelings she sparked in him were a betrayal of, not only himself and his heritage, but his family.

Fallia was close to the cliff face and all but running to catch him when her foot slipped and he watched her thin body disappear over the edge. His world shrunk in that moment. Nothing existed outside of the few feet between where Tobin stood and where his sister had fallen. He could hear his voice calling out to her and feel his legs carrying him back to where she went over the edge. *She's dead and it's my fault,* was the only thing running through his mind as he almost watched his body slide to a halt at the edge of the dam and peer over. The mist and rocks prevented him from seeing anything farther than a few feet down the cliff face.

"Tobin, come here." A booming voice rang out over the thunder of the falls.

Sir Fairclough was calling him. *He will help me.*

Tobin reached down trying to feel anything. *Help me*. He did not quite know who he was trying to invoke, but he kept repeating it over and over in his head as he groped over the edge for his sister.

"Tobin!" Sir Fairclough's voice was closer and laced with sever anger.

The massive body of the knight reached the dam and was only a few feet away from where Tobin lay reaching over the edge. Then it happened. Tobin spotted a tuft of blonde hair standing out against the grayish-green of the mossy rocks and slid over the edge himself, grabbing for anything to prevent his fall. She managed to clasp onto a little ledge fifteen feet down, and was holding on for her life.

"Tobin!" Sir Fairclough called out again but this time the anger was gone from his voice and it was replaced by fear.

Climbing down the rock face was difficult for Tobin, and he slipped several times, coming within a few inches of falling the hundreds of feet himself. He focused only on the blonde tuft of hair he could see every time he looked down; it was the only thing that kept him moving. Inch by inch he climbed down to where he knew his sister was clinging to the slippery moss-covered rocks.

"Tobin." A faint whisper reached his ears through the constant and oppressive crashing of water pouring angrily over the edge.

"Fallia, I'm here!" He screamed in joy.

"Tobin, I'm slipping! I can't hold on much longer!"

He rushed his pace and after what seemed like an eternity, he had her. She wrapped her arms around him and buried her face in his shoulder. "Tobin, save me," was all she was able to choke out between sobs.

Tobin could not speak while he concentrated on the rock face, but drew strength from the heat of her body pressing against his back. The climb was long and arduous. His arms felt like jelly by the time he neared the top of the cliff. With one last massive effort of will he threw his right arm over the ledge and tried to grab anything that could help him pull up.

His fingers curled securely around a semi-thick plant and he released his other arm to swing it up and begin the last stage of the climb over the lip and onto safety. He felt Fallia shift suddenly on his back, heard a small scream as she dug her fingers into his sides, and saw the worried face of Sir Fairclough peering down at him. The plant he was grabbing gave way and his body plunged towards the bottom of the falls and certain death. Fallia squeezed tighter. The world turned sky-blue as he fell backwards.

I am going to die. Fear followed his thoughts and he reached out for Fallia grabbing her around the waist and pulling her close. Nothing matters now, we will die together. He clutched at her, bringing her even closer to him than ever before. The cloth of his tunic jerked upward. Choking him. Pulling him. Dropping him. The two landed safely on the top of the cliff; Fallia laying on top of her brother. Their eyes locked and the adrenaline of death mixed with Tobin's burgeoning love got the best of them and their lips locked together. Both ignoring the stray strand of Fallia's hair that got mixed between them, they kissed. Gently at first, brushing together with the care and grace of the nervous couple, until her tongue slipped quickly into his mouth. Neither one noticed the shadow of Sir Fairclough standing over them until he wrenched the two apart and nearly threw Fallia back over the edge in his furry.

"Tobin! You will accompany me." Sir Fairclough bellowed. "You, girl, will see to the horses." The inhuman hiss with which he spat the last words scared both Tobin and Fallia. The two did as they were instructed.

Aislinn

The unforgiving red dust stretched out before her in all directions. Aislinn heard stories about the Broken Lands, how they were terrible and hot, filled with savages who were rumored to eat the flesh of their enemies, and a maze of large rocks that could swallow people whole. Her only guide for this perilous journey was the large scar left by the slavers' massive caravan. The voices of the souls this land had claimed pressed hard against reality, giving the silence of this red desert a heavy feel. Not even the wind chanced to move through the Broken Lands. Scraps of food left by the slavers were becoming more scarce and she had not tasted water since the night by the river, three days ago. Pushing herself to keep moving, she stumbled repeatedly over the small rocks hidden by the shifting sand.

As the miles slowly passed, she could see large hills rising in the distance. Giants of earth, stripped bare by the years of wind and rain carving a new face on the countryside. The sun beat down with a nearly suffocating heat, and without the reprieve of shade or wind Aislinn fought the urge to give up. Her skin was tight and dry, her mind was foggy, and her stomach was upheaving. Food, what little she found, revolted in her and she had to stop several times to be sick in the dirt. Nights were cold. Days were hot. The lack of water caused the skin on Aislinn's lips to become cracked and dry. Her feet were blistered and bled most of the day; new wounds filled with sand as soon as they were created. Images floated through her vision, leaving her unable to determine what was real and what was imaginary. For days she wandered around this inhospitable land trying to follow what she thought were the tracks of the slavers. Increasingly her mind doubted if she was even on the right path, or headed the right direction.

The ground was hard and the stones sharp, as she tried to find a comfortable position to sleep for a few moments before she continued her never-ending journey towards her mother. She rolled to her right and felt a sharp pain shoot into her forearm. The needle-like sting raged with a burning fire that quickly consumed her entire arm and was working into her chest. A small black scorpion still hung from her forearm, and she tried to shake it off by blindly flailing her arms in fear and pain. Panic quickened her movements and terror aided her steps as she tried to run down the slavers trail. Tears streamed down her face, mixing with snot and a thin foam that was bubbling out of her mouth. Choking and coughing she tried to scream out for her mother, wishing she was back in Little Town safe and asleep in their house. Violently, she shook her head trying to rouse herself from this painful nightmare, feeling any minute she would snap awake, see the comforting form of her mother, and feel the warmth from the coals in their home. An unseen rock impeded her run and smashed against her foot causing a new pain to rock her frail, starved body. Her face slammed into the ground and the agony was too much for her to handle. She slipped into unconsciousness.

All hurt was gone. Her hunger was gone. The longing for home was gone. She slowly opened her eyes. There before her, in this red abandoned world, sat her mother, preparing vegetables for a stew that was boiling over a small camp fire. Waves of heat caused the ground to move and sway around the happy little scene. Aislinn could not believe her eyes. She was home, it was all a dream.

"Mother!" She called out into the desert sand, and began running to her. "Mother, I am here."

"Aislinn, dear child, what are you doing here?" Her mother's voice called out across the sand, ringing joyously in the tired ears of her daughter.

Reaching her mother, she found a chair close by and took a seat near the hearth. The cooking fire was hot and glowing; the smell of fresh potato and onion soup filled her one-room childhood home. Steam rose quietly from the boiling pot, her mother's chair creaked rhythmically while she rocked, and a feeling of peace and calm filled Aislinn's heart bringing tears to her eyes.

"Mother, I missed you so much." Aislinn did not try to stop the tears but embraced them and clung to the feeling they brought. "I am so sorry for how I treated you. You are right, I should never have left you that day."

"Dear child, there is much to say."

Before her mother could finish, the world shifted and changed before her eyes. The sand consumed her little home and the aroma of soup faded into the stale smell of sand. From the desolate landscape, a giant lake spread out before her, the product of an equally giant dam. Old pines lined the banks of the calm waters that reflected the large puffy clouds floating peacefully overhead. Two figures stood out black against the mist of the falling water behind the dam. They were kissing. Aislinn stared at the scene, trying to memorize every detail. The vision before her was so peaceful and wonderful that she pictured herself there, kissing this tall stranger. A rock tripped her, sending her sprawling in the red sand.

Why is there sand in the forest? She thought as she picked herself up and darted between the trees, trying to move closer to the dam. The lake was huge, and as she inched around the shoreline she kept seeing a shadow flutter between the tops of the pines. A beating of wings and the rustle of the pine needles betrayed the immense size of the creature flying above her. The trees swayed and shook with each flap of its mighty wings, and sand blew around her in the torrent of wind.

The world changed again, the trees melted away into the lake and the dam crumbled into a pile of sand. Pillars of fire rose from the ruins of the last vision, stretching from the earth to the heavens, which had turned black with clouds of soot and ash. Legions of people marched over the earth while winged beasts flew across the sky. It was an invasion. Aislinn felt the fear of hundreds of thousands of people as she saw the world succumb to this onslaught. As they approached, she noticed the legion was an army of the dead. Skeletons with rotting flesh dripping from their almost-clean bones. Zombies, wights, ghosts, and every manner of terrible creature that filled her nightmares as a child crawled out of the fire. Letting out a scream and turning from the impending doom, she saw the largest black-scaled leg she had ever seen.

A dragon screamed into the darkness sending flames shooting across the evil army. Taking flight, the beast screamed again adding another jet of fire to the conflagration right in front of her.

Fire consumed everything in her vision. She felt herself stumble forward again. The desert reappeared and vague memories of reality played with her mind. *Mother. Where is my mother?* A fog had wrapped itself around her mind forcing coherent thought to become an exercise in concentration. She saw the desert before her again, the large wide scar caused by the massive slave trade, scraps rotting in the sun and waves of heat distorting her vision. The scorpion. She fell to her knees. *I am dying, the poison...*her mind could not focus. I can't die out here. She struggled to her feet, and tried to focus on the path before her.

"I will find you...mother...I will...." She fell onto the red sand, her eyes staring blankly at the night sky. A large oval-shaped shadow descended from the stars and she knew no more.

Her eyes opened to a small hut. A fire burned quietly in the corner while the sun shone cheerfully through the only window in the tiny shack. Aislinn folded back the down comforter and sat up. She quickly realized that the room was very small. She banged her head before she was completely out of the bed and had to kneel to keep from repeating the injury. Next to the hearth there sat a small wooden chair and an equally small table. A vase held wild flowers on the window sill and Aislinn could hear the faint chirping from a far off song bird drifting into the room on the slight breeze. She blinked, half expecting the vision before her eyes to dissolve back into the terrifying fire of the underworld, but nothing changed. The stark contrast to the horror that she just witnessed caused her to be sick in the corner.

"I will get that cleaned up in a moment." A small voice startled her.

"Who...?"

"My lady, please, you have had a trying day."

"What is happening, and what are you?" The question was prompted in her mind when he slowly backed into the room carrying a tray. Aislinn was not a tall woman but this man was not even her height while she was on her knees in this cramped room. He had long pointed ears and a beak-like nose.

"I am your servant, of course." He placed the tray on the table and waddled over to the bed. Spreading out the sheets, he turned back to Aislinn, "I see you have awoken. That is good. We were getting worried about you."

"We?"

"My brother and I found you in the Broken Lands a few days ago."

"A few days ago? What do you mean? Where am I?"

"In my house, of course." His irritation was becoming apparent. "Taking up quite a bit of space, which I will shortly require of other purposes."

"Are you telling me to leave?" She crawled on her knees towards the door, now starting to accept the hallucinations as they appeared.

"My lady, I would never presume so much as to ask one such as yourself to vacate my property. I am at your service." A small awkward bow accompanied his words but his eyes betrayed the truth of what he was feeling. "You seem to have had a nasty sting by the looks of things." He motioned to Aislinn's arm. "A few more hours and you might have died."

"I- I will leave once I know what is going on. The last thing I remember was the pain in the desert and being consumed by...I don't know, visions, or something." She paused, the haunting images of the destruction and the winged beast rose before her mind's eye and she decided to trust this disfigured little man. "The last thing I remember clearly was laying down to sleep in the red desert. A pain in my arm woke me, I assume it was the sting, and many visions or hallucinations and I am here."

"Is she trying to brazen it out?" Another small man entered the room carrying a small dagger.

"She claims she is seeing visions." The first man answered.

"I did not."

"See, I told you she would brazen it out. Slaves are slaves and we never should have brought her back here." His thinning, gray beard made him obviously older than the first man by several years.

Both of their skinny legs were bowed outward and their feet turned inward, giving them an awkward unbalanced look. *Only my crazy mind would dream up these bizarre creatures.* She thought, still convinced that this was another hallucination.

"Brought me back where?" Aislinn interjected.

"My dear Mr. Hoppbottom, how can we leave a young lady in those treacherous sands?"

"If she is however seeing visions, as she claims, then it stands to reason that we are a vision she is seeing. This being true, we do not exist, and if we do not exist then she is still on the desert sands of the Broken Lands. And if she is still on the sands of the Broken Lands then, it stands to reason, that she is not here." Hoppbottom concluded.

"True, but one flaw I have noticed is the following: she is here. The Queen told us to be on guard for something strange. I would assume you agree this is strange?"

"Mr. Bottomhopp, I never agreed with you more. You are wise beyond your years." He turned to the now throughly confused Aislinn. "Come on then, this way." Both of the miniature men left the small room leaving her perplexed.

She grabbed her head and rested it against the wall. *This is not real, I must have fallen asleep in the desert and this is all a dream, or I am dead.* The thought scared her and she left the room in a vain attempt to leave her doubt and fear behind. *I do not feel dead.*

The world outside the room was a shock. She was used to the smell of the sea filling the air, but that was as far as the similarities went. The trees stretched into the heavens, dwarfing any city wall Aislinn was used to. The soft crunch of dead leaves and twigs underfoot added to the pleasant woodland symphony of chirping crickets and song birds. The sun peaked through the green canopy almost creating a path that the two men were waddling down. Aislinn followed, not knowing what would come next in this dream.

"This way." Bottomhopp waved his arm at her.

Having no choice but to follow, the three of them walked deeper into the woods and up a large hill. Halfway up, her escorts stopped.

"There you go. Just on up the hill." Hoppbottom pointed. "She is up there, or will be, depending on if she is or not."

"Well put, Hoppbottom. If she is there, she is. If she is not there, she will eventually be. I could not agree more."

"Thank you Bottomhopp."

Aislinn was only to glad to leave the two little men behind, still chattering away about the location of this Queen of theirs. She picked her way carefully through the close knit trees and tried to follow the path, but the farther up she went the more she felt the path had disappeared. No birds chirped and no crickets echoed as she wandered farther up the hill. Completely lost in the ever thickening underbrush, Aislinn could do nothing but push onward. The rush of events over the past few hours had her reeling. She did not know what was real and what was a dream. Half of her believed that she would wake up on the floor of the red desert, dehydrated and dying. Or worse, she was already dead and this was going to be her afterlife.

After hours of carefully picking her way around the hill several times, she reached the top. The trees broke and the underbrush disappeared and the grass of the meadow waved gently in a mild breeze. Large puffy white clouds floated peacefully overhead, and Aislinn lost herself in the calm of this secluded mountain when a twig snapped across the clearing. A large white horse walked slowly through the grass. The horse had a single horn protruding majestically from its forehead and a rider, clothed all in white with platinum blonde hair.

The gracefulness with with the rider dismounted was only rivaled by her fluid movements as she approached Aislinn. She had never seen a women so adorned and graceful this close before. Every fiber of her being told her to kneel; she had to be royalty. The breeze toyed with her silken white robe and Aislinn realized how slender this mysterious woman was.

"It is good to see you awake." Her voice was magical and soft but somehow old. "Please stand."

"Who are you?" Aislinn felt herself stand up, but didn't remember ordering her legs to work.

"I am Princess, but more importantly you need to

know who you are." Her crystal blue eyes looked down slightly at the young girl from Little Town.

"I know who I am. I am Aislinn."

"You know who you appear to be, but not who you are. Have you been told about the old stories, the tales of the Veldorians and the settling of this land?"

"My mother would tell me about them at night, but I don't remember much."

"Aislinn, there is something coming. A war is upon us and you will play a pivotal role." Princess knelt beside her. "The prophecies of the ancients are coming true."

"What do you mean a war is coming? How can I be involved in any war?" The hallucinations were becoming too much for her. "I wish I could just wake up. I need to get back to following my mother."

"Aislinn, you are not asleep, and your mother is on her way here." Her voice lowered to just above a whisper. "But you won't save her."

"How do you know all this? I refuse to believe that. There is no way that you know about my mother and the slavers. This is a dream."

"Listen to me. The slavers are on their way here because this is their island. They train the able-bodied here to become gladiators, and the rest they sell or starve depending on age and strength."

"I don't understand what you are talking about. When will my mother get here?"

"Aislinn, throughout history there have been prophecies, ancient portents that have foretold the doom of mankind. A war is coming and you are a key part in it. The first of the signs happened a little over a week ago. The moonless night. There will be others.

You need to be cautious and be prepared for anything." Princess stretched out her hand and grabbed Aislinn's shoulder. The unicorn was chewing loudly on the lush grass of the sunlit meadow. A warm gentle wind passed over the two of them and down the hillside. "This is our home, your home now if you so choose. The slavers know nothing of us."

Aislinn felt warmth spreading from Princess's hands into her body. A power welled up in her chest and she stood. "You are telling me that my mother will die, I will be in a war, and if I want I can stay here with you?"

"I am telling you what you need to hear, my child."

'My child,' how can she say that, she can't be much older than I am now. Aislinn was confused and her muscles still ached from the venom in her arm. Her vision narrowed until there was just a point of light above her. She fell to her knees and found herself staring into a puddle of her own sick. Blackness took her again and she fell to the grass remembering no more.

Gravous

"Why have you captured me?" Gravous stood before the incredibly large form of the Mystic. "What is the meaning of this?" It was still four hours before the dawn and Gravous was furious over being woken in the middle of the night and abducted in the name of gods he did not worship to meet with a fat man he did not like or trust. The anger in his voice was far from concealed. "Speak up!" He yelled in response to the inaudible murmur of the Mystic.

He met Gravous outside the side entrance to the temple in a dark ally that was hidden from the stars. Even the light from the third quarter moon did not penetrate down into this hidden street. The walls were lined with rags and other garments set out by the peasants to dry in the evening breeze that was considerable as the wind from the bay funneled passed the temple on its way across Aurorum. It brought with it the smell of the city, nearly choking Gravous with horse dung and human excrement. The King may have had his sights set on conquering new lands and expanding his rule, but the capital of his would-be empire was in disrepair, and the people inhabiting it were filthy and despondent.

"I say, my lord, please lower your voice. The walls have ears. You need to follow me to my chambers as I have much to show you."

"I will follow you." Gravous continued in his previous timbre. "Of my own accord." He raised his still bound hands.

"Please, your lordship, I beg you." Mystic Grahm's eyes darted about nervously and he half backed into the temple, preparing to shut the door at the first sound.

Gravous lowered his voice almost involuntarily. "I will follow you if you tell me what this is concerning. But first tell me why I am here, Mystic Grahm?"

"Lord Lynch, we spoke earlier about my vision. Please, I have seen more after you left us yesterday." His voice was shaking. "We have much to discuss.

Gravous detected a small hint of something in the Mystic's voice. Something that made him wary. "Release me." He snarled.

Instead, he was dragged down a dimly lit hallway of the temple. Murals that Gravous did not remember from his first visit lined the hallway, telling stories about the mystics of past years. Gravous remembered a few of them from his schooling back in the Midlands. There was Bethora the First, founder of the temple and oracle to the first King of the Veldorians. Mystic Grotham who built this building with his own hands starting when he was only ten and working long into his eighties. His sacrifice and service was touted far and wide as true devotion to the gods. More pictures of men he did not recognize and actions he could not decipher as they wound their way through the heart of the temple. Gravous realized he did not know where they were. This was not the way to Grahm's office.

"Where are you taking me?" He inquired.

"To the roof, Lord Lynch, what I have to show you can only be seen in the stars, and the wind muffles our voices up there."

Turning a corner Gravous saw a narrow door leading to a narrow staircase that wound its way up in narrow circles. *How could he possible fit through here.* A smile crossed his face as he pictured the feat, but was quickly wiped from him as he remembered what was happening. Grahm stepped into the tiny room, and with the force of a great oxen, pushed his way up the stones and around the staircase. Gasps and puffs echoed loudly in the tight enclosure and Gravous was on the verge of claustrophobia when the Mystic stumbled onto the roof and out into the cool night air.

The roof of the temple was a slender walkway around the large dome with a smaller flat section near the back of the building. It was to this flat section that Mystic Grahm took Gravous. A few chairs and one table were set out with several scrolls, star charts and mugs littering the area. He positioned himself in front of a chair; with the help of the table he thumped down so heavily that Gravous was surprised the chair didn't break.

"Now that we are here, we can speak more freely, Lord Lynch." Grahm unclasped the heavy wool cloak from around his neck, and motioned for the acolyte to deposit the prisoner in the chair next to him.

"Once again, Mystic Grahm, I ask you, why am I here? I have played your game," He indicated the rope binding his wrists. "I have followed you up here, tell me what I what to know."

"You are here, Lord Lynch, because I had a vision. I saw the winged beast." He pulled out a long pipe from a hidden pocket in his sleeve and grabbed a pouch of tobacco from the table. "The beast has been born. Through fire and snow the creature will come to you."

"That is it? You disturb my slumber and drag me across the city in the dead of night to bring me to the roof of your temple and tell me that I have to do nothing and the creature, that may or may not exist, will find me and all I have to do is live?" Gravous stood and raised his hands to knock the pipe from between the lips of the fat mystic.

"No! Sit down!" Mystic Grahm yelled. "You will not speak to the oracle of the gods in that tone. It matters not if you believe or if you doubt. My gods have all the power here."

Gravous sat down with a thump, causing his chair to groan under the pressure. He felt an unseen force latch onto his upper arms with the pressure of a blacksmith's vice. He could not see his attacker but he did not need to, the Mystic was chanting and every time he raised his eyes to Gravous a new pressure would manifest itself on him. *I am being cursed by the gods of the Veldorians. What have I done to deserve this?*

"It is not what you have done, it is what you failed to do." Mystic Grahm stopped chanting under his breath and struck a match to light his pipe. Rising, he puffed freely and stared at Gravous. "You are not from the Five Kingdoms, this much I know. You were raised by the Lynches of Midlands as a charge given to your Lord Father by the son of Lord Murray of the Marshes. You were brought to him after you were captured from your village in the Broken Lands." Mystic Grahm's smoke-filled words bounced off of Gravous's face. "Whether by some misfortune or by a deliberate act, you were captured and carted off from your homeland to become a slave. Once you arrived, however, your Lord Father had compassion on you. He raised you as a son, and even sent you to take his place at court, knowing full well that the honor you have now is one of the highest in this land. You serve on the Royal Council, an advisor to the King of the Five Kingdoms and steward of old Veldoria. Yet how do you repay this honor? How do you act in the company of the people that raised you as their own?"

Gravous struggled against the unseen hands that held him down. "I have done nothing!" He shouted. "You have no right-"

"And you have the right to murder? You have the right to sell hundreds of the peasantry into slavery?" Mystic Grahm cut him off. "You made your choice. The gods called you and you did not answer."

"What are you talking about?" Panic entered

Gravous's voice.

Grahm leaned close to his victim's ear. "Lead the way, Lord Lynch. Let an old m-m-man lean on your arm." A chill went down Gravous's spine as all he heard were the last words Lord Hamstead spoke to him. "I w-w-will not let you get away with this."

Gravous tried to defend himself but speech was wiped from his lips.

This has to be a trick. His gods are attacking my mind. Stay strong, you are a force of nature, you are a child of the earth. He struggled against the words of the Mystic and forced himself to focus inward. *This is a dream, nothing more. He cannot harm me.*

"Lord Lynch, I can do as I please." Mystic Grahm answered his thoughts as if he spoke them aloud. "But you are right, I will not harm you. It is more than you deserve. You murdered Lord Robyn Hamstead, and conspired with Lord Corbett to sell hundreds of citizens of Little Town into slavery. Not the same slavery that you suffered, but sent them to their deaths. And for that Lord Lynch, your part in the coming battle is over. The honor you would have had is no longer yours." Mystic Grahm was on the verge of tears. "I have seen it. I have seen their deaths, from your sin comes the one that will kill you, I have seen your death Lord Lynch.

"Now that I have your attention, we come to the real reason why I have brought you here tonight. For all the evil you have caused you could have still made up for it, but when the summons came, it found you wanting. My acolyte told you it was coming and you ignored him."

Gravous found he was able to speak again. "You will pay for this, Mystic. You cannot hold a member of the Royal Council like this. You better kill me where I sit or I swear by the gods you-" His voice failed him again, and his throat felt like he swallowed a burning ember.

"You swear by gods you do not worship, to harm their devout servant." Mystic Grahm laughed. "No, Lord Lynch, I will not pay for this. You have a lot to learn. This very night, 'ere the sun rises, you will be so far from this city no one will find you. I have word from my brother that he has the creature foretold by the moonless night, and I will be sending you to him. He can handle a spoiled lordling from the Midlands as well as any. The gods still have a plan for you Gravous, but that does not mean you will not pay for your sins." Two more acolytes appeared while Mystic Grahm was talking. "Take him. You have your orders."

A large solid object descend rapidly on the crown of his head and Gravous knew no more.

***

When he opened his eyes again the world was very different. The sun was blazing in the sandy desert, the cart beneath him rattled with every small bump, and his legs and arms were bound. Struggling against the cordage that held him, he shouted to his captors. No one listened to him. He recognized the small form of the acolyte that met him at the door when he first entered the temple.

"You, where am I being taken?" He called.

No response.

"I demand to know what is happening. I am Lord Gravous Lynch of the Midlands, a member of the Royal Council, and your superior. Where are you taking me?" *Maybe I shouldn't have tipped my hand like that, but they have to know who I am. The temple is behind this....* He fumed and banged against the stout metal bars of his mobile prison.

"Lord Lynch." A voice from behind him shouted against the rattle of the cage. "You have offended both gods and man. Your punishment is exile."

"Under what charges?" Gravous was furious. "I demand to know."

The voice's owner rode into view on a brown gelding. He was wearing the colors of the King and he flew the banner of the royal court. "Lord Gravous Lynch of the Midlands, you have been tried and found guilty of the murder of Lord Robyn Hamstead of Blackwatch in the Marsh, conspiracy to commit murder of a member of the Royal Council, and impersonation of a noble."

"Impersonation of a noble? Under what grounds. My father-"

"Your adopted father." The man corrected. "Even now a tribunal has been dispatched to arrest the man you call 'father' and bring him to the King's Justice for sending you to the council. For his crime of wanton and deliberate deceiving of the King and his court he will most likely receive death. You, '*Lord Lynch*,' I imagine will be left alone to live out your days in exile."

"Where are you taking me?" He demanded again. His face was flush and a strange heat burned behind his ears. Tingling began in his hands and arms. *They will kill my father, and I am powerless to defeat them. I must do something. I am a force of nature. I will overcome this.*

"You do not need to know that." The man galloped forward passed Gravous's field of vision.

"Tell me!"

After hours of traveling in this dry expanse he saw the river. *I am not so far away from the castle, or Fieldhaven. If we have not yet crossed the river I might be able to make my escape.*

"Gravous." The man was back. "Prepare yourself."

Two armed guards opened the back gate to his cell-on-wheels and pulled him out. His legs were rubber and his head swam with the motion.

"Stand." The man commanded. "Stand!"

Gravous found he could not stand on his own. *What has happened to me? What is wrong with my legs?*

"Hold him up." He spat at the guards. "I, Lord Bortlin Grendel, by Royal decree from the King, Robsfeld Colbralian, Lord Protector of the Gold Coast, ruler of the wild islands and rightful King of the Broken Lands, do herby declare you banished from the old empire. You are not permitted to cross this river again. Nor are you permitted in any city of the Veldorians. Make your life from rock and field but do not show yourself in any city. This is the will of the King." Lord Grendel bent down. "My advice for you, *Lord Lynch*, is simple; run back to the Broken Lands. Go back to where you belong. Do not show your face in the Five Kingdoms again." He stood, and with once swift movement sliced the rope that bound his wrists. "Be gone."

With that the two guards threw him into the rushing waters of the Dirgo River. Gravous's useless legs pulled him down under the current and he flailed his hands around him looking for anything to save him. Pushing and thrashing he succumbed to the river's current and gave himself up to death. *I can't fight this, let the waters take me, and I shall return greater than before. I will be water, and I will reap my revenge.*

A small arm grabbed him around the throat and hauled him onto shore. Gravous coughed and choked for several minutes before he realized who it was who had saved him. The young acolyte.

"Lord Lynch, the mystic sends his regards," He began. "And he tells me to relay to you his good will on your journey."

"What are you talking about?" He spat out more river water with the question.

"Here take this. It will help." The acolyte handed him a water-skin, and Gravous drank deeply. "I am taking you to Headwater. Or at least just outside Headwater, as you are not allowed in any city."

Gravous stared at the water-skin. "What have you done to me?" His face was numb, his fingers would not bend. His lips swelled. *Why does this happen to me?*

"I am but a weak man, my lord, I cannot hope to subdue you and allow escape. No, the mystic needs you alive and within reach; he will not abide your flight to the Broken Lands. As you are banished, no one will come looking for you either." The acolyte rested his hand on Gravous's shoulder. "No, Lord

Lynch, you are at the mercy of the Temple now." His insidious smile haunted Gravous as he felt the all to familiar rope wrap around his wrists once again.

Tobin

A large black bug buzzed noisily around Tobin's ear. He waved his hand trying to rid the world of this particular nuisance. "I thought being on the water would limit the amount of bugs." He mumbled to himself as he rewrapped the brown canvas cloak around him.

He had been traveling down the river in a large barge for three days. After one night at the dam, the whole company had risen early and loaded onto three large barges. They were simple boats with two levels and a small room near the back. The lower level was used for cargo and the peasantry to help row when going up stream while the main deck had straw mats and a few benches. The room was for the boat's captain and any ranking lords that used the ferry. Tobin was bunked in the room with Sir Barin Fairclough and two other knights that were traveling down river.

Sir Fairclough had not let him out of his sight or talked to him since the incident on top of the dam. He also forced Fallia onto a different barge. The monotony of floating silently down the river and the irritation of having everyone on his barge ignore him weighed heavily on his mind. His dreams were filled with haunting images of his sister, and his bedroom back in Blackwatch, causing him to wake in a cold sweat fearing that Sir Fairclough would know what he was dreaming.

The shame and horror he felt every time he thought about his sister never fully left after the incident, but the time alone had helped him to regain some control over his thoughts. After a short battle with what turned out to be some sort of wasp, he scurried belowdecks to find the feed for his horse. The lower deck was near pitch black and he was not allowed to light any of the lamps because it was full of grain and hay for the horses. After a few moments of picking through the stacks to find a bail that had not been broken open, he found one and grabbed it. Dragging the awkward bundle up the stairs proved to be more difficult than he anticipated; he only fell once and was fortunate enough to land on the bundle, averting any major injury.

After dropping the feed in the makeshift stables he absentmindedly strolled along the deck.

"Tobin," Sir Barin Fairclough strode up behind him. "We will be docking by the sea tomorrow. I want you to make sure the horses are ready to go."

They were the first words that Sir Fairclough had spoke to him after the dam, and Tobin's heart leapt at the sound of his voice. Over the past week Tobin had grown fond of this young knight, looking on him as a father he never had and the devastation that came from being ignored was worse than the years of never being noticed by his real father. To have lost the attention because of his actions with Fallia festered in him like an infected wound.

"Yes, my lord."

"I am not a lord, I am a knight." Sir Fairclough reminded him again.

"Yes, Sir."

"Tobin, you are the son of the Lord of the Blackwatch. When we reach the Capital, you will be expected to act the part. With Lord Hamstead, your grandfather, dead, the council needs representation from the Marsh. Lord Murray refuses to send his only son Jondavid, so the role falls to you."

"What do you mean?"

"I have told you this before." The disappointment in his voice wounded Tobin. "Your father has chosen you to sit on the council to represent the Marsh in Aurorum." Sir Fairclough rested his hand on Tobin's shoulder.

Tobin stood up to his full height, drawing comfort and strength from the warm clasp of this knight. "Why would my father choose me? He barely speaks to me. Why was I chosen for this honor?"

"It is not an honor. The King has a wicked temper, and no respect for the council. You will be the most junior member of a group of lords that lives on treachery and deceit. The odds of you surviving your first session with any modicum of authority are slim at best." He turned his back to the river and stared back onto the deck of their barge. "You need to take great care in your actions or you might end up a waif on the streets of Little Town."

"How?" Tobin paused. *He is trying to shake me. This is some kind of punishment.* "How could I become a waif? Could I not just return home to Blackwatch?"

Sir Fairclough stared at the young lord from the marsh with something that looked like pity in his eyes. "Fallia will be returning to the Blackwatch after the King's Feast. Your father's wishes." He said as he walked back into the cabin.

Does my father know? Is that why he is sending me away? "Sir Fairclough!" He called after him but the knight did not respond.

A dark cloud of doubt and fear griped him. His stomach knotted and jumped to his throat while his heart beat a furious rhythm against his ribs. Trying to regain control over his fears he moved along the railing towards the back of the barge. He found a bench attached to the back wall of the small room and sat, staring at the other barges, following them, hoping to catch a glimpse of his sister. Every time a figure would find its way into his view his heart would skip a beat, while still battering his chest with a wild vigor. *What is wrong with me?* Tobin held his head in his hands and did not try to hold back the tears that were forming in his eyes.

A sudden splash accompanied by shouting from the boat closest to him broke his trance. Several men were now leaning over the railing and shouting; one of them was pointing.

***

Fallia sat in the small section of the only cabin on her barge, waiting. Three days had passed since she had seen Tobin, and she was furious. Strange men would bring her food, but she would barely eat and was starting to feel very weak. Never in her life had she been away from her brother for so long. A deep longing grew in her heart every day causing her to slip further into comatose state, barely aware of what was happening around her.

She wrapped her arms around herself as she lay on the reed mat that acted as her bed. Pulling her knees up to her chin she slowly counted the cracks in the wall in front of her, knowing full well that she would reach twenty-four and then have to start over. A small hole near where the wall met the floor was growing slowly; with every count she would pull a small sliver of rotten wood out and press it into the now tender skin of her left forearm. Some of the wood would break off and remain under the skin, causing large red sores, but most would fall off harmlessly.

After the first day of her self-imposed solitude on the vessel, the captain, after seeing her wounded forearm, discovered her carving small but deep cuts into the soft flesh of her inner thighs. She found the pain comforting, a familiar experience in this unfamiliar place. He had taken her dagger from her and tried to comfort her, but she hardly heard anything he said, except that he would disclose this information to her father unless she cooperated. Not understanding fully what he meant and fearing her father she agreed, and at least twice a day after that moment he would force her cooperation as she lay on her back counting the planks of the wooden ceiling.

The slamming of a heavy wooden door startled her out of this haunting memory. Sunlight was filtering through the woodwork, casting ominous shadows on the far wall. Rubbing her eyes, she saw the shape of a large man with a wool cloth draped over his head. He edged slowly towards her with his hands rubbing together and a hideous smile that struck fear in her young heart. Her mind was racing, but she could not move. Any commands she gave to her body to flee from this strange man were met with a cold refusal from her limbs. He crept closer. His breathing was loud and irregular as he sucked in through his nose and blow out though his mouth in a rough staccato.

She could smell him. The horrible odor of the unwashed deckhand mixed with the ripe smell of horses nearly suffocated her; she could not move. She could feel him, the rough skin of his brutish hands brushing her hair away from her face. Her eyelids squeezed together, wishing not to see the face of the man that was attacking her. Screams died in her throat as he rubbed his hands down her neck and over her young breasts. She wanted to kick and yell and swing her arms to get away from this barbarian, but she could not move. His hands parted her legs and rolled her over, jarring her head into the side wall. That broke the hold fear had on her, she would submit no longer.

Leaping to her feet and swinging wildly she felt her hand connect to a solid object.

"Watch it, wench." His voice was as horrible as she knew it would be. He grabbed her shoulder and pulled her back towards him. His tongue traced the outline of her ear then he spun her around to face him. "You remind me of my own daughter."

She screamed, filling the small room with the echoes of her terror. The door flung open.

"Banger!" Fallia recognized the captain's voice.

His arms fell away and she seized the opportunity. Pushing hard against her attacker she made a dash for freedom. The sun blinded her as she crossed the threshold, but not enough to prevent her from seeing her brother sitting on the barge in front of her holding his head in his hands. The distance from where she stood to the edge of the boat was only a few yards, and she ran as fast as she could, away from the evil that attacked her, away from the loneliness of this river, and towards her brother.

***

"Fallia!" Tobin yelled, rushing to the edge of the barge. "Fallia!" *She is coming to me.*

The swirling water around the hull of the boat pulled her under. Tobin's heart leapt. *She is going to drown.* Frantically looking around the deck for anything useful, Tobin saw a crew member running up the railway holding a large rope. He grabbed it and shoved one end into the hands of the startled crew member.

"Hold this!" Tobin ordered and jumped over the side.

Water crashed around him in a torrent of noise and chaos. As he submerged, the outside world seemed to melt away. He saw her. Floating freely in the undertow of the barge, blood leaking from a large wound on the top of her head. She was not moving. He surged towards her, battling the current and the undertow. The hull tried to suck Tobin into it, doing to him what it had done to his sister. His lungs were burning and he had to fight to keep his eyes open. Trying to fight down the urge to breathe in a lungful of cold water, he reached out and grabbed Fallia's hand. Tugging on the rope, he accidentally sucked in some of the angry river. He could not hold his breath any longer. His vision narrowed. He felt her limp body slipping away from his. In his last moment of clarity he wrapped the thick rope around both of them, under their arms and tried to tie the end.

The sun slowly crept passed his loosely closed eyelids. His head throbbed against his temples. "What happened? Where is Fallia?"

"Try not to talk. You swallowed a lot of water." Sir Barin Fairclough leaned over him.

"Fallia?" Tobin's voice was weak and he erupted into a fit of coughing.

"She is alive, resting on shore."

Tobin sat up. Fighting back the urge to succumb to the blackness again, he tried to stand. The bank of the river was lined with a large wooded dock, complete with landings for up to ten large river barges. A wooden staircase led the way up the steep bank to the ridge above. Tobin struggled up the many steps, and when he finally found himself on top, he saw her. Fallia was lying on a bench with several people standing nearby. She had bandages wrapped around her head, left arm, and both thighs.

"What happened to her? Why are her legs and arm bandaged?"

"Tobin?" It was his sister's voice.

He threw himself on his knees by her side. "Yes, Fallia, I am here."

"I need to speak to you." She opened her eyes and saw the crowd around them. "Alone. Please."

"Leave us." Tobin commanded. Everyone except Sir Fairclough wandered away slowly.

Tobin grabbed her hand and waited silently for her to speak again. The sun was already falling quickly behind the large trees on the western bank. The faint wind that accompanied them down the river had all but disappeared and the world seemed to pause. Not even the insects moved through the stillness. Tobin waited.

"Tobin, he...he raped me." She opened her eyes and stared right into his.

"What?"

"He came into the cabin and raped me. The captain. All because you would not let us be together." She hissed the last words when she saw Sir Fairclough standing behind her brother.

"My sweet sister. I love you." He bent down to hug her and she flinched. "Fallia?" He pulled back, confused. "Fallia, I will take care of this."

Standing and wheeling around on Sir Fairclough, Tobin drew his sword. "You will stand here and protect her with your life. No one touches my sister.

Is that understood?"

"Tobin, you-"

"Lord Hamstead. I will not have you be to familiar with me now. You may be a Knight of the Realm but I am your lord."

"As you command, my lord." Sir Fairclough bowed, but not without obvious disappointment.

Tobin turned back to where the riverboat crew was standing. "Captain!" He bellowed. "Captain, come here."

The short, round man cowered at the sound of the young lord's voice. He shoved a large scruffy man in front of him. "He did it. He is the one that assaulted your sister."

Tobin leapt forward and slashed the throat of the makeshift bodyguard. A bloody gurgle escaped from the wound and his body crumpled to the sandy ground. A pool of blood started to form between Tobin and the Captain.

"Face me, bastard."

"My lord, forgive me. My lord, I did not mean offense, my crew are brutes and seldom know how to treat a lady. If I had but known my guest was your sister-"

"Enough!" Tobin roared. "I have it from her own lips that you...you." Tobin could not bring himself to say it. "Draw your sword."

"My lord, I will not assault a noble from the Marsh. I give you my word I did not touch her. She caused the wounds herself, I tried to help her." He fell to his knees causing the blood to splash onto Tobin's boots.

The fear in his voice was like a sweet wine to the

now enraged Lord Hamstead. Without a word, he crossed the blood lake and drove the point of his sword deep into the soft flesh of the captain's exposed throat.

"Fairclough, clean this up. Fallia and I will ride ahead to the Inn, meet us there for further instructions." The authority in his voice did not leave room for argument. Sir Fairclough did as he was ordered.

Tobin cleaned the blood from his blade on the clothes of his victim and walked back to his sister.

"Fallia, can you ride? The Inn is less than a mile from here."

"I will follow you anywhere, my brother." She whispered faintly as Tobin helped her onto a nearby horse.

Lonessa

A growing resentment for the dragon festered in Lonessa's heart. Always the dragon was there, screaming, hissing, haunting her dreams. She had faint images in her memory about Gavrill and Renyard coming and going, Mr. Grahm teaching her ways to communicate with the dead spirits that did not manifest themselves, certain incantations that were meant to shield her from the icy fingers of death itself, but the only thing she could remember clearly was the dragon. Its inhuman cries when Mr. Grahm attached a chain around its neck, or how it moved, or rather slithered around the camp looking for anything to kill and eat. The way it moved terrified Lonessa, like it was sliding gently out of some horrid nightmare that she could not escape. She had seen it stalk a large beetle and when it pounced and crunched through the exoskeleton, Lonessa thought she was going to be sick.

The journey itself was smooth enough. They acquired horses from a small village about a mile outside of Riverspring, or so she had been told. Mr. Grahm said that he had to carry her that distance because of her panic attack. She had not yet decided if she could trust him anymore. He had been the baker in the city for as long as she could remember, always jovial and willing to talk. He was kind and thoughtful; she would often spend time in his bakery eating the leftover dough or tasting a fresh muffin, all the while he had this pouch hidden away upstairs. This pouch of dried human fingers. *What else does he have hidden away? What other secrets is he keeping from me?* She repeated night after night as the long journey wore on.

Then there was the voice. The ever present voice. It haunted her mind and listened to her thoughts. She could feel it at all times, even late at night when Mr. Grahm was asleep and she would slip the amulet off and enjoy the solitude.

It started shortly after the first night on the road. She slept with the fingers around her neck and her dreams were filled with images of a dark land ruled by fire and lightning. Ghouls crawled over the burnt rocks, and wights picked over the bones of once human corpses. The voice called to her then, through the death and smoke, comforting her. She believed it, or him, but now his voice never went away. It was all she could do to deal with this and live in the world.

She did manage to push it aside enough to faintly follow the journey.

They were traveling northwest away from the Valley to a city Mr. Grahm called Headwater. After clearing the mountains, the land spread out before them as far as the eye could see. Lush tall grasses and wildflowers seemed to dance in the stiff breeze coming down from behind them.

The first night in the open plains it rained, and Brovo had escaped from Mr. Grahm's chain to bury itself in Lonessa's backpack, ruining everything she had brought with her except for one change of clothes that she was forced to keep tied up in a roll and use for a pillow. After the rains, the world exploded with color. All the wildflowers bloomed over night and Lonessa was shocked by the aroma. It would have been her dream to see such sights, but the voice would not let her enjoy it.

For the past few days of the journey they had been following a small stream, and the ground was nearly impossible to traverse. Small dense shrubs lined the banks of the stream, creating an almost impenetrable barrier; fetching water for meals was an unbearable task. Once clear of the shrubs and on the top of the bank, the ground turned into a mud pit five inches deep. The horses were worn out, Lonessa was agitated, and Mr. Grahm was growing more silent with each passing hour. The journey away from her childhood home turned out much worse than she had imagined.

Her whole short life, she had imagined leaving the castle walls, leaving the protective boundary placed around her by her loving parents. In her mind it had been a joyous occasion, filled with songs and flowers. Her mother and father leading her down the river to the giant Dam of the Veldorians, even traveling as far as Aurorum. To visit the capital of the Five Kingdoms would be magical. Many dreams were wasted on this fantasy, and they only seemed to intensify now that she was finally outside. In the back of her mind, however, the voice was always there, turning to ash any moment of happiness she found. *I have all that I need. I am safe with Mr. Grahm, even though he is not telling me everything.* She tried to convince herself.

"Lonessa. Fetch the water, I will start boiling the stew." Mr. Grahm called to her from near the small fire he was building.

Fearing the treacherous slide down the side of the mud hill into the river she gripped the rope handle of the small bucket he had brought with them and stood at the summit looking down. The river flowed slowly and peacefully on its way to Headwater. At only a few inches deep she hardly thought it was worthy of the name, the one that ran through Riverspring was deep and moved quickly. This sad excuse was close to six times as wide as her river, but as far as she could tell only six inches deep all the way across.

"Lonessa, water!" Mr. Grahm shouted again.

"Going." She called over her shoulder. *Is he growing angry with me? Why?*

"He fears you."

"What do you mean?" *Was it audible that time? I am going crazy.*

"He fears you. You must do as I ask if you want to

survive, and if you want Garon back."

Lonessa smiled to herself. For the first time she felt that having this voice inside her might not be as terrible as she thought.

Just as she feared, the first step onto the downward slope caused her to slip, and she performed a rolling slide all the way down to the water's edge. It was freezing. The icy waves lapped at her ankles and she stood and dipped the bucket into the river. *This water is much colder than my river.*

Having filled the bucket, she hung it from her neck so she could use her hands to help climb out of the muddy pit. Panting and covered with mud, she crested the hill and could walk more freely. She removed the bucket from around her neck, and walked slowly to where Mr. Grahm set up their camp.

It was on the top of a small incline of land, just enough room for the two of them to lay down. He had already started the fire, but because there were no real large branches out here to keep a fire burning for a long time, the glance he shot Lonessa when she returned told her he was worried about there not being enough to boil the water. Once the small black kettle was hung gently over the flames, he unfastened his backpack and laid out his gear for the evening. He had shoved his sword into the ground near where he prepared his bedroll, and to it attached two ropes, long enough for their horses to graze.

"Won't they be happy when they reach a stable?" Lonessa wondered aloud. "I mean, it can't be fun having to be tied so short all the time."

"They are means to an end, child. Do not focus on them. We have much to do tonight." Mr. Grahm's voice seemed to be changing.

"More studies?" She asked sullenly. Studies were what he called it when he forced her to communicate with the dead.

"You don't need to study." She ignored the voice when she saw Mr. Grahm did not hear it.

"Yes. I urge you to focus on what I teach you. Feel the power that you have and learn to harness it, or it will soon consume you." He had spoken of nothing other than this consuming power of the dead since they left the city.

"I have done as you asked every night, I spread my thoughts, I touch the underworld, I speak with the dead, and yet you still push me. I am sick of this. I don't want this." She grabbed the small pouch from around her neck, and just as her fingers closed on the cool leather, her hand exploded with pain. "Ouch!" She yelled. Her hand now throbbing. "What have you done?"

"I have done nothing. The pouch protects you from the dead." A look of fear crossed his eyes for a moment, she was sure of it. "Leave it alone and let it protect you." He said regaining himself and turning away from her.

She looked at her hand. It was red, and blisters were starting to form on her palm and between the first and second knuckles on her two middle fingers. She surveyed the camp. The two horses were at the near extent of their ropes, the dragon was sleeping quietly next to Mr. Grahm, he was stirring the soup as it simmered over the fire. The whole scene was the picture of peace, but her hand was burning, and he was hiding something.

"You say that if I train I will gain power over the dead?" Seeking relief from the pain, she shoved her hand into the muddy ground.

"Lonessa, child, these questions are too dark. Please join me for some dinner and we will skip your lessons for the day."

I'm on to something. He never let me skip before.

"You are right, child. He is hiding something from you."

I knew it.

"You know what needs to be done. He has been lying to you this whole time. Do it and I will teach you more than you ever dreamed."

"Do what?" She whispered.

"Send him to me. It will be the first step to returning Garon to you." The voice that escaped her lips terrified her. It was old and raspy but powerful beyond measure. *It's taking my voice now. It...is ...taking me.*

Mr. Grahm's head shot up. He looked at her with horror.

"Send him to me." She repeated, her eyes large and filled with tears. "What is happening to me?" She pleaded with Mr. Grahm.

"Fear not, child, I am your guardian now. You have no need of this." She choked out the words, trying to keep her mouth closed.

As she hissed these words, the rope that held the pouch around her neck bust into flame and fell to the ground, leaving a thin line of burned flesh behind. *I don't want it anymore. I don't want you anymore.*

"Help me." She screamed. "Too late." She was forced to say.

Mr. Grahm stood quickly. Pulled a small book from inside his shirt and held it before him. "I know you, I have heard your voice. You will not take this child as you tried to take me."

"You are wrong old man. I am this child." The thing that had taken over her body retorted.

Lonessa pulled herself to the surface again. "Mr. Grahm, I know who it is." She smiled. "All your teaching has reaped a reward. I know what is happening."

"My dear child, are you back? Are you hurt? Please let us pray to your gods." There was now unmistakable fear in his voice. Lonessa enjoyed that.

"Mr. Grahm. I am unhurt. Your fingers," She pointed to the ashes of the mummified hand. "That was not protection, it was a summon. You summoned us. You will be rewarded for your service." She stood and walked deliberately to where he was now kneeling, shaking with fear.

"Rewarded? I don't understand."

"For your service." She smiled. *You were right. We are one now.* In one quick stroke she pulled the sword from the earth, and removed his head.

She knelt next to his body, blood was pulsing into the ground from the terrible gaping pit that was his neck. She grabbed the head and lifted it to her lips.

"Please say hello to Garon for me." A lonely tear rolled down her cheek. "Tell him I will save him soon." She placed the head backwards on the body and poured the now boiling water over it.

"Why did you do that?" A voice asked from behind

her.

"Sir Renyard Storm, that will be the last time you question her. Is that understood?" Lonessa's voice melded with the raspy hiss to form a new sound for the young girl. "I will not suffer to be questioned by my subjects. Bring me Gavrill."

"Yes, my lady." He bowed and vanished.

"Now we must complete the ritual." She spoke to the twitching body of Mr. Grahm.

It took her small hands six hours to create two human forms out of mud. The fire died. The rain started. Both ghosts watched as she meticulously formed each person. First the feet, ankles to knees, then hips, torso, and finally the head, spending extra time on the eyes and mouth of each form. After she finished both she stood and admired her handiwork.

"I am finished." She announced. "Which one do you want, Sir Renyard?" She asked, her voice returning to the sweet sound of the thirteen year old girl.

"Lonessa?" He inquired.

"Yes," She laughed. "I am here. Don't you understand, we are one now. I am death. But need I remind you never to question us? Please, you were with me first, you get to pick your new form."

He studied the two, and pointed to the one closest to him.

"Lay down. Gavrill you take the other." She pulled the body of Mr. Grahm in between the two mud forms. Each ghost now laying inside the mud she used her small knife and sliced deep cuts into both wrists of the dead man. She sat on his chest to force some of his blood to start oozing out. When it touched the mud forms it oozed faster, like the earth was pulling the blood from the fresh corpse. Lonessa stood and slit her own wrists, although not as deep, just enough to bleed, and hung her arms over the forms as well.

"Blood of our enemy and blood of our heart." She started. "It pulls the death from us, and brings the dead to life. Rise my first, rise from the blood we shed and the work of our hands."

She stood there repeating the incantation until she was too weak to carry on, and fell to her knees. Her arms fell into the mud, causing mud to fill her self-inflicted wounds stopping the flow of her blood.

At that moment Gavrill and Sir Renyard Storm both sat up. The mud figures rose and carried her back to Mr. Grahm's bedroll. Renyard laid a blanket over her shaking little frame while Gavrill started the fire which seemed to burn hot and furious from nothing. Then they both sat beside her, watching.

Just before she lost herself to the call of sleep, she grabbed Sir Renyard's arm. "Be sure to keep that dragon away from us while we sleep. I do not like that evil beast, it is filled with...with... Life. We need to end it, and find our horses."

"As my lady commands." He smiled and pulled the wool blanket over her arms and up to her neck.

"You heard her. I will find the horses, you keep that dragon quiet." He said to Gavrill.

"Aye, sir." He responded holding the creature in his lap as he sat cross-legged by the flame.

Aislinn

"Here, try this one." Bottomhopp handed Aislinn a new bow.

"I like the length on this one." She said, as she gently took it from the little gnome and pulled the sting back to her cheek.

"That one is with milkweed and dogbane, it should hold even in wet conditions." The gnome stared lovingly at the bow he crafted.

"It is slightly heavier too."

"Well, you have grown in strength since you came to us, m'lady." He smiled, the sight of his teeth still slightly unsettling to Aislinn.

It had been five days since Aislinn had first arrived on the island. She had not seen Princess since their meeting on the hilltop, but had spent most of her time in the company of the two brothers, learning. The two gnomes taught her how to survive in the wilderness of these forgotten islands, what plants were edible, what ones would kill her, how to stalk prey, and how to shoot a bow. They had made new clothes for her as well, four different sets of brown trousers with a white long-sleeved shirt she always tucked above her elbows, and a blue vest with several pockets. 'You never know when you need a pocket.' The gnomes would laugh at each-other like an inside joke while they were making it.

The cottage was small, about half as big as Aislinn needed, but it suited the brothers well. Two small beds, a small dresser, work bench and a back work area that had a kiln. Aislinn had been forced to sleep outside under a tarp they had tied up to some nearby trees. Privacy was scarce out here on this island but she had been enjoying herself. Her mother was coming here, and she was training to rescue her, although she would not tell the gnomes that.

"I am going to try it out right now." She left the small cottage.

Halfway across the clearing to the wood line she realized in her excitement she had forgotten the quiver of arrows that was usually around her waist. Doubling back, she heard voices coming from inside the small room.

"Did you tell her yet?" Hoppbottom was asking.

"No, should I have?"

Aislinn nestled under the window of the tiny cottage. Using all her skill to remain silent.

"No! We will keep it a secret until we are ready."

"I am finished in my task. The bow is being tested and I have completed the sword." Bottomhopp had more pride in his voice than normal.

"Good. I too am almost finished with my project. I should be able to have it completed by supper. The real difficulty was gathering the measurements."

"I can imagine."

"Despite the hardships I will be done by supper." Hoppbottom shuffled out the back door.

What are they talking about? If they are planning some plot against me... What do I really know about them? Her heart started to beat faster as fear nudged into her conscience. *No, they talked about the bow, and I am holding it now. It is a good bow. A sword, and something else.* She pondered for a moment. Doing her best to be quiet and out of sight. *No, whatever they have planned I will let it be. Supper is not that far away and I like a good surprise.* Aislinn smiled.

She retreated a few yards from the door and called out. "Bottomhopp. I have forgotten my quiver." Making sure to announce her presence before she got too close, so they would not suspect she heard them talking.

"Not a lot of good you would be as a hunter without your arrows." Bottomhopp replied.

"I don't need arrows to be a good hunter." She joked.

"Every hunter, no matter the skill, needs arrows, and these are good arrows."

"How do you know they are good arrows? Isn't an arrow the same everywhere?"

Bottomhopp took a few steps back and shuddered.

"I made them."

"Than they are the finest arrows in all of the Five Kingdoms."

"There are not many things that can claim to be gnomish made." Hoppbottom appeared in the doorway to the back room.

"Where do you come from?" Aislinn had been dying to ask this question since she first arrived on this island. "I mean, I have never heard of gnomes before."

"We were both born in what you would call The Midlands."

"Then how did you come to be here?"

"When the Veldorians first arrived on this land they met us. Our people were there to help them establish themselves. We partnered with the Veldorians, to create the Dam and build the cities. Aurorum, Headwater, and even Fieldhaven were gnomish built. The Veldorian Empire spread and they ruled everything north of the mountains. Even the King in the Broken Lands bent the knee.

"Around the time of Vorlian the Great, their first king. The dam was commissioned to replace the waterfall that divided the river in half. Trade routs were created and travel along the river was expanded. We gnomes loved to build and create and invent, so being hired by the Veldorians to help them establish a kingdom was second nature to us." Hoppbottom found a stool and pulled it close to the now seated Aislinn.

"For thousands of years we gnomes served the Veldorian kings in creating and building anything they needed. But as the years went on the bloodline of Old Veldoria was polluted by the indigenous peoples. The wisdom and glory that was, faded into obscurity."

"There are rumors, brother." Bottomhopp added hopefully.

"Rumors and secrets, a story for another time." Hoppbottom shushed him with the wave of an imperious hand. "As I was saying, the new rulers eventually stopped paying us for our service. We became the slaves of the empire. They collected our people from their native homes and forced us into labor camps in the cities. We created their roads, their river boats, even their castles in the capital cities. All these are of gnomish make, under slave conditions.

"There came a day, young Aislinn, when we as a people would not stand for being treated as we were. We," He indicated his brother and himself with a waggle of his crooked and boney finger, "Were only little children at the time, but three hundred years ago there was a revolt. A revolt that showed our captors that we would not submit to them any longer."

Hoppbottom paused. His brother pulled over a stool and sat next to him.

"The elders had been planning this revolt for many years, and when the time was right they enacted their plan. All the women and children fled the cities through secret tunnels that only the builders knew about. Then men stayed behind to fight, and we found an ally in the Posli People. After many months of combat, we were cornered on the north coast of the Broken Lands. Several of our people were already building boats and sailing out to sea, but the warriors stayed. The Veldorian army closed down upon them. As the story is told the Posli Tribes fell upon our enemies allowing us to escape to the relative safety of these islands."

"I don't understand." Aislinn started. "Why didn't they follow you? How old are you two? And how many gnomes are left?"

"The war that ensued after the Posli tribes attacked the Veldorians raged for almost a hundred years. It is the war that eventually split the empire."

"The War of the Feathers?"

"Yes, you know this story?" Hoppbottom looked pleased. "Good, I will not have to explain much. You see, the Veldorians all had different tribal heads. Veldoria was always a nation of united tribes, and when the King declared war on an indigenous people, some of the other tribal leaders would not support him. Leaving us free to inhabit these islands."

"How many gnomes are left?" She asked.

"Thousands, hundreds of thousands. We have prospered here, protecting our secrets and honing our trade. There are few craftsmen in this world that could rival a gnome."

"How did the slavers take this island from you?"

"This is the smallest of all the islands, m'lady, and my brother and I were the only ones to settle here with our family. When the slavers arrived there were only two of us left and we lacked the heart to remove them all from our land." Bottomhopp explained.

"Thank you for your history." Aislinn felt awkward leaving after they shared so much with her. "I feel I should test out this fine bow before the sun sets."

"As you wish m'lady." Bottomhopp jumped down from his stool and bowed.

Aislinn escaped into the woods. She wandered aimlessly through the trees, practicing everything they taught her about being a hunter. *'Move everything that needs to be moved. Never break anything. Make only as much noise as the wind.'* She mused over the story the two gnomes told her. They certainly were good at crafting and forging things. This bow she held was an example of how their skill was put to use since she arrived. *I don't know much about bows, but this is nicer than all the bows the slavers had.*

The sound of a twig breaking disrupted her concentration. Her head snapped to her left. There, not thirty yards from where she stood, as silent as the trees, was a large deer. Its antlers spread wide and reaching to heaven. *This is the biggest animal I have seen on this island.* She tried to regulate her heart, *I can't let my emotions control me. Stay calm.* Her left foot rose slowly and found a resting place on a downed tree a few inches from where she stood. Her right foot followed. Soon she was crouched on the makeshift bridge over the underbrush.

The deer stood in the small clearing sniffing at the grass. Aislinn silently removed an arrow from her quiver and notched the bow. Pulling back on the sting, she had to regain her balance. The strength was more than she had used before. *I can do this. I only need to have it back long enough to- damn!* The deer had laid down, and began rolling in the grass. Aislinn could not see the shot. Her right arm started burning. Her left arm started shaking. I won't be able to hold this much longer. *If I let it go I won't get the chance to pull it again.* A loud cracking startled the deer. It raised its head.

Once she saw its neck she knew where to take the shot—down slightly and to the left. Twang; the new bow sang out into the forest. It was a clean shot. The young buck rolled over and thrashed its legs around for a few moments before giving in to the arrow's call.

Aislinn almost shouted as she leaped off the log and ran to her kill. The arrow had pierced its spine and pinned it to the ground. *I can't wait to show this to Bottomhopp.* She thought as she carefully removed the arrow. *Can I drag this back to the cottage?*

She was saved from having to answer that question by an arrow that flew passed her face and embedded itself into a tree behind her.

"Get her." A man's voice filled the forest.

"You missed." A second man taunted.

"I won't miss again." The third man's voice sounded familiar.

Instinct kicked in. The inner beast that first manifested itself in Little Town reared its head again. She felt the power of its anger pumping through her veins, and it clouded her thoughts. Aislinn knew her best chance at survival was to lose them in the woods and run back to the cottage for help, but something deep down inside her prevented her from doing it. Notching the arrow that she just pulled from the deer she drew and released. A scream and a gurgle told her that she had found home in the neck of one of the assailants.

"Gods! Circle 'round her." The first voice yelled.

She spirited through the underbrush, breaking nothing and flowing like the wind through the leaves.

"Where did she go?"

That voice. Where do I know it? Distracted for only a moment she lost the inner rage, and her footing on some dead leaves, and came to rest a foot away from the man with the bow. Both of them drew their weapons and started at each other. *This was the slaver guard that was nice to me!* She realized. *I can't kill him.* She tried to lower her bow but her arm snagged on a sapling and she lost her grip. The arrow flew right though the unarmored body of the slaver. His eyes grew with the pain and he fell to one knee, loosing his arrow harmlessly into the sky.

"Forgive me, my lady." He whispered as he fell forward, gushing blood over the forest floor.

What have I done? She gained her feet and took off again. *I can't lead this man back to the gnomes. I need to kill him.* She spun around only to come face to face with Prince Naveed. Fear pushed the last of the rage from her mind.

"Now, how is it that you have come to be here?" His musical voice filled her with dread.

"I was waiting for you." She spat as she pulled the small knife from her waist and slid it quickly into his exposed belly. His grip on her shoulders loosened, but only for a second.

"If I were that easy to kill, I would have been dead already." He threw her to the ground. "Take her." He shouted as he turned a left.

A large blunt object landed squarely on Aislinn's

right temple and she remembered no more.

***

"Honey." Her mother swooned over her. "Honey, are you ok? You look like you have been badly hurt."

"I'm ok, mother." Aislinn feared this hallucination would end like the last one. "I looked for you."

"I know you did. We are together now, that's all that matters. Honey, your head." Her voice betrayed how she was feeling.

"Mother?" Aislinn sat up quickly, instantly regretting that decision. "Are you real?"

"Am I...what?" She wrapped her arms around her child. "Yes, honey, I am real."

"Where are we?" Aislinn said, standing, slowly this time.

It took a minute for her eyes to adjust to the dim fire light that danced along the stone walls. The cold iron bars on the thick wooden door, along with the growing mold on the damp stone, told her they were in a dungeon cell.

"Mother, we need to get out of here. I know people on the island. We can be safe." Desperation flooded Aislinn's voice, breaking her mother's heart.

"Honey, there is no escape."

"Lies!" Aislinn screamed and grabbed her head. The throbbing would not subside. "Guard! Guard!" She shouted.

"I was told you would need something." The raspy voice of the guard added a new level of fear to what Aislinn was already feeling. "What does the little rat need?"

"Take me to Prince Naveed." She tried to hide her fear with confidence.

"Why?"

"Tell him I am willing to negotiate." She was hoping this would work.

A shuffling from the hallway let them know the guard had moved on, hopefully to tell Naveed.

"Honey, what are you doing?" The weakness in her mother's voice scared her more.

"Trust me. Just lie back."

Aislinn found some discarded clothes and a few rags laying about the room, and use them to create some insulation for her mother. The temperature in the cell dropped significantly since the guard left them, and Aislinn was worried her mother would feel the effects.

"Mother, just...I will be back for you."

She knelt next to the fragile and cold body of her mother. *She looks worse than I have ever seen her.* A cold hand gripped her heart. *No! Don't think that.* She scolded her mind for the flash of despair. *I will talk to Naveed, he will let my mom go, or at least let her get better before-*

Her thoughts were interrupted by a voice yelling through the wooden door.

"Oy! Little rat, he will see you now." The door screamed in protest as it slowly opened.

Two large men, armed with short swords and small shields, escorted her out of the room, and wrapped a thick cord around her wrists.

"I will be back, mother, I will be back."

"Shut your mouth, little rat." One of her guards shoved the hilt of his blade into her back. "Move faster."

She followed in silence as they pulled her up a long flight of stairs. Once they reached the top, she saw that they were now at ground level. Her cell has to be thirty feet underground. *That is why it was so cold.*

The sun forced her brown eyes closed for the first fifteen or so feet out of the cave mouth. She stumbled over rocks and tree roots until the guards were all but dragging her across the dirt, forcing her to squeeze her eyes shut, protecting her from the attacking dust.

"Enough of this!" His musical voice rang out.

Naveed. Aislinn thought as she kept her eyes closed.

"Stand up, little rat!" A guard spat on her. She could feel it land heavily on her shoulder.

Open your eyes. Remember his face. She slowly gained her feet and stared right into the eyes of the offending guard. *Remember him.* They were not far from the beach and Aislinn could hear the waves rolling into shore. The trees here had formed a large clearing and a rocky cliff face was the back drop to the Slaver Prince.

"I see your spirit has not been broken. That is good."

"I have come to beg for my mother's life." Aislinn felt her voice betray her.

"Oh, have you?" He smiled through his golden teeth and patched eye. "What do I get in exchange?

A feeling of great courage started to over take Aislinn's body. Her feet and hands were first, then her arms. Next her chest began to swell with this warm bravery. When the feeling reached her head, she nearly shouted. "Your life. Whatever happens to my mother will happen to you."

Her words were met with a heavy jolt to the back of her head. "Shut up, little rat." The spitting guard yelled.

Through the gathering fog in her mind she turned to him. "You will die for that."

He raised his sword high above her head and was about to lower it with killing force when Naveed stopped him.

"Enough!" He choked on his laughter. "You are a spirited young thing. Bring her to my chambers. I will have this one tonight."

"No! My mother!" Aislinn let her emotions out, tears poured down her cheeks. "She needs me."

"Your mother is already dead."

After a long pause Aislinn yelled. "No, you lie!"

"Take her to see the body then bring her to me." He dismissed them all with a wave of his hand. "I am looking forward to seeing you soon, *little rat.*"

The stumbling walk back into the cave and down the long flight of steps might have taken a few moments or it might have taken a year; Aislinn had lost track of time. Step after step the echoes of their footsteps resounded in her head. Her wrists hurt from the friction with the rope. *It is cold down here, but I gave her those blankets. She is alright, he is lying to me.* She repeated this last phrase like a prayer with each step. *She is alright. He is lying to me. She is alright, he is lying to me.* With each echo her heart grew colder until they were standing in front of her mother's cell.

"Go in." He shoved her in the back.

"Mother?" She tripped and ran to the pile of rags.

Her mother lay underneath the soiled garments, curled up in a ball like she was trying to stay warm. Her eyes were closed and her lips were smiling. Aislinn knew when she saw her. She was dead; the stillness of death is unmistakeable. Aislinn broke.

Tears flowed freely down her cheeks, rage filled her heart, she lay on top of the corpse trying to will it back to life.

"Move, little rat." The guard yelled.

Her mother's hands were tucked under her chin and Aislinn grabbed them right before being jerked away. There was something there. Working quickly, before she was pulled too far, she opened the dead hands and pulled out the small statue that was hidden inside. Shoving it deep inside the recesses of her vest, she thought *Thanks for the pockets.*

"Let's go. You are gonna see the Prince now, I just hope he is nicer to you than his last whore." The sound of gurgling laughter filled the dungeon as they climbed the long staircase.

Tobin

Tobin beat his clothes with his gloves in a vain attempt to remove the dust from the road. He and his sister had been traveling for three days at the head of a small column of knights and men-at-arms. Sir Barin Fairclough retreated from riding with them, but still rode at the head of the knights. This inn was much like the others: dark, rich with the smell of wine and smoke, over crowded, and loud. Fallia enjoyed the noise. Something, anything, to distract her from what happened. Tobin found himself thinking. This inn, being closer to the capital, was much larger than the others. A giant chandelier, made from antlers, swung gently near the ceiling. The booths sat six men comfortably and the long tables running down the middle were packed with travelers. Every one of them posed a threat to his sister, Tobin knew that now.

"Fallia, I will get us a room, come." He helped her down from the saddle and all but carried her into the inn.

A whisper passed through the room before a hush fell on the patrons as the two entered. *Clearly my reputation proceeds me.* He thought. *Perhaps I should not have killed the riverboat captain,* but then he saw his sister's face and remembered why he did. The bags that had grown under her brown eyes, the way her hair was never brushed right, no matter how hard they tried in the morning, and, worst of all, the way she pulled away from him at night. *How dare these low-life patrons gawk at us. I am Lord of the Marshes.*

"Innkeep, I need one room for me and my companion." He shouted so the entire common area could hear. *If they will talk, I will give them something to talk about.* "I do not wish us to be disturbed. Fifty gold coins for the first two knights to volunteer to serve me this evening."

"Aye, my lord." A feeble voice spoke from the back of the room. "Aye my lord, you have my services. What do you ask of me?" The old knight who owned the voice emerged from the crowd, broken and limping. His tiny limbs were barely large enough to support his wasting body, and his back had given way to a degenerative disease leaving him hunched and crippled.

"Your name?" Tobin asked genially. *If this does not endear them to me, commissioning this poor knight into my service, I do not know what will.*

"Sir Rodrick Garrows, my lord, of the Midlands."

"Sir Rodrick, pick your second and bar the door, the only thing that passes the threshold is myself and my dinner. Is that understood?" He took the key from the Inn keeper.

"Yes, my lord."

Tobin took Fallia's hand and led her up the narrow wooden steps to the rooms on the second level. With his hand gently on the small of her back, he opened their room and ushered her in. As he closed the door behind him, he saw Sir Rodrick and a very large man come up the stairs. *Good, I won't have to worry about Fairclough's pestering tonight.*

The room was small, but lavish. The inn keeper knew his craft. The bed was large and filled with feathers, the pillows were plush. Thick black curtains sealed the window from prying eyes outside, and a small fireplace housed a cozy flame on the back wall. There was enough wood to keep the flame through the night, but the farther north they had traveled the warmer the nights were becoming. Several candles dotted the room, leaving strange shadows on the wooden walls as he led her to the bed.

"Here, my angel. We have guards at the door to prevent us from being disturbed. I will lock it. You are safe."

She smiled.

"Brother, you have been more than generous with me." Tears formed in her eyes. "Those nights on the riverboats... I feel like I have betrayed you."

"No, no, honey, no. Don't think like that. What happened is not your fault. It will never be your fault.

I have killed the men who did it to you, and will kill any man who tries to do it again." Tobin sat next to her, placing his arm around her shoulders.

"Any man?" She asked.

"Any man."

"Even the King?" She smiled and rested her hand on his knee.

"Even the King." He agreed.

"Even the strongest warriors?"

"Honey, you know I would. I love you. No power on this earth can keep us from being together."

"What about yourself? Would you kill yourself if you were with me?" Her eyes were bright, and her mouth was smiling.

Despite the roaring fire in the hearth and the many candles dotted about the room, Tobin shivered.

"No, my love. I would not kill myself. For I am rightfully yours, and no man can take me away from you, or you away from me."

"But what of the ancient laws. What of the gods," she whispered. "What we do is a slight against them."

"To hell with gods. The Valley has their gods, the Broken Land theirs, and the kingdoms worship their own gods. It is even said that the Veldorians had only one, but I have no need for a god. I have a goddess."

Her hand slipped up his thigh. "And I will be your goddess." She whispered as she grabbed him and pulled him close to her.

***

The next morning found Tobin and Fallia asleep in each other's arms. Lying there with large smiles shining through their dreams; the siblings slept well into midmorning. The black heavy curtains blocked the sun from their room, and the candles had long since been snuffed or burnt out.

A loud bag on the door startled Tobin out of his slumber.

"Sir Rodrick, who is it that disturbs me at this hour?"

"Begging your pardon, my lord, but Sir Barin Fairclough bid me wake you."

"Allow him entry." Tobin called through the door as he pulled the top blanket over the naked body of his sister, covering her bare chest.

Tobin crawled from the bed, careful not to wake her. Sir Fairclough stood at the threshold surveying the scene. The young lord pulled up his trousers and was buttoning his shirt before the captain of his guard spoke.

"Lord Hamstead. We are less than a day's ride to Aurorum. If we leave before midday we can reach the city by dinner."

Tobin smiled. The first time he had smiled since the dam. "As long as my sister sleeps," he whispered. "We are going nowhere."

"My lord?"

"Did you not hear me? To hell with your timelines, and your dates. I am too far beyond my father's reach, and these men are sworn to serve my house. Me. Not you Sir Knight, you would do well to remember that." He kept his voice quiet but stern, and chose to leave out the anger. "Sir Barin, I have wronged you. Please join me for breakfast. We will discuss the final leg of our journey." *This way Fallia can sleep.* "Allow me to leave a short note for my sister."

"As you wish, my lord. I will await your presence downstairs." With that Sir Fairclough left the room.

"Sir Rodrick." Tobin called. "Here is your money, you are relieved of your duties to me. You have proven the honor of your house, Sir Garrows."

"Thank you, my lord." The broken knight bowed and limped down the hallway.

Tobin slowly closed the door and turned around. Fallia had woken and was sitting up in the bed. Her chest bare for him to see.

"I love you, brother." She whispered.

"And I you, little sister." He was taken aback by her beauty.

"Go, I heard all. Meet with Sir Barin. Leave the key and I will lock the door."

"Are you sure? You do not have to be left alone?" He could feel his love for her start to well up again. *She is perfect.*

"Yes. Go." She covered her chest as if to release him from her spell.

"As you wish." Tobin crossed to the bed in two quick strides. "I love you." He whispered as he kissed her hand.

"Go." She smiled back.

Tobin left the room smiling, and was greeted by Sir Fairclough, who was still waiting in the hall.

"My lord, I thought I would escort you to breakfast."

"Very well, I thought you would wait for me

downstairs, but as you wish." Tobin beamed. "Lead the way, young Sir Knight."

"Need I remind you I was appointed by your father to be your guardian. Young though I may be, I am still ten years your senior."

Tobin laughed at the jest, even though Sir Fairclough wasn't laughing, and passed him on the stairs to find a table in the main room of the Inn. The inn at morning was very different than Tobin remembered last night. The smoke had cleared, the smell of wine faded into the background, and all the tables were empty.

Tobin found a seat at the closest booth and motioned for Sir Fairclough to join him.

"It has been a while since we have spoken." The young lord began, "What updates do you have of my men? How goes the journey?"

Sir Fairclough sat silent for several moments, causing Tobin to shift uncomfortably in his seat. "Your *father's* men are well, my lord. The journey is as anticipated. That is not why I wish to speak with you."

Anger flashed behind Tobin's eyes, but he controlled himself. "Then what *do* you want to talk about?"

"My lord, what you are doing is wrong." He lowered his voice. "With your sister, my lord. Please listen to reason, the gods despise your actions."

"And yet," Tobin started, matching the knight's tone, "You say nothing to anyone, I find that these people do not know she is my sister, why? If it was so heinous a crime in your eyes, why not arrest us?"

"Your father sent me to protect you. How can I go

back to him and tell him I was the cause of your execution? The testimony of a knight carries weight here in the capital, and it could carry you to your death."

Tobin sat back in the bench. "My good lady," he addressed the large, out-of-breath woman that was standing at the head of their table. "I want coffee, two slices of toast, and three eggs scrambled. If you have any meat that was not served last night, a portion of that as well. You, Sir Knight?" He smiled.

"The same. Thank you." Sir Fairclough watched her leave.

"That sounded to me like a threat, Sir Barin."

"My lord forgive me, it was not meant as such. I was interrupted by the serving maid."

"If you cannot stop me, and will not arrest me, then, as a knight, what good are you? Sent to protect me, but you cannot protect me from myself. I know what I am doing is wrong, my whole body screams of it. I cry myself to sleep when I am not with her, I cut my arms to feel, I need her in my life Sir Knight." Tobin slowly broke, he was shouting now. He launched his coffee mug at the wall, nearly missing the back of the serving maid who just set it on the table. "Save me, Sir Barin! Protect me!" He shouted.

Sir Fairclough rose and grabbed the hilt of his sword. The serving maid cowered behind a far table, and Tobin seethed.

"You, fat-woman, bring my food to my room. You, knight, make sure I am not disturbed." Tobin stormed up the stairs and slammed the door to his sanctuary.

The room was black. All the candles had burnt

out, the heavy curtains hid any light, and the fire was now just a pile of smokeless embers. Tobin tried to remember the layout and shuffled around the room looking for the bed. His anger clouding any reason that tried to sneak into his mind.

"Tobin?" A faint voice from his left whispered.

"My love, yes."

"Why were you shouting?" Fallia grabbed his arm and pulled him onto the bed.

"I was not, Sir Barin is angry that we have not left yet."

"I don't want to leave." She whispered in his ear before she pulled it into her mouth.

"And...I...don't want..." His voice was lost in pleasure when she slid her hand underneath his waistband.

***

"We are a day behind." Sir Fairclough brought his horse alongside Tobin's. "That is not a slight, my lord, I am merely informing you of what will happen when we arrive in the capital."

"Good, Sir Knight-" Tobin started with anger in his voice.

"Let him finish, please, I am curious." Fallia laid a hand on his arm.

Sir Fairclough watched her hand as she withdrew it from her brother. "The King may not be pleased at your delay, he may, however, not notice. Pray it is the latter."

"So what if he is not pleased? Tell him the riverboats were slow. Blame our tardiness on the swine of the Dirgo. Besides, if what I hear is true, then he has not left the castle walls in over ten years." He laughed and gazed at Fallia, anxious to have her see him laughing.

"That may be true, my lord, but he has a network of spies that see and hear for him." Sir Fairclough looked from Tobin to Fallia and back. "He sees and hears much."

"Enough of this." Tobin bellowed. "Thank you, Sir Barin. I can see the city, let us arrive in good humor."

The hard packed dirt and dusty ground gave way to lush grasses as they climbed a small incline and looked down on a river. On the far bank, the walls of the capital rested on the top of a small hill, staring out to sea. The midday sun reflected off the water and gave the walls a golden hue, like the whole city was built from the gold it is said to contain. A small town on the near bank was dotted with banners and sigils that Tobin had never seen or heard of before. Music wafted on the warm gentle breeze and the smell of cooking meats greeted their noses. Fallia gasped at the sight, Tobin gawked and Sir Fairclough started down the hill.

"I will lead us into the city." He said as he raised a black tower on a field of blue, sigil for the Hamsteads. "Follow me, my lord. We will, at least, enter the city with dignity."

The siblings trotted after him, and their one hundred and fifty men-at-arms followed them. The column was an impressive sight for the peasantry of the small town. Even some of the lesser knights gawked as they saw the Lord of Blackwatch in the Marsh cross the long wooden bridge into the castle walls.

"Ho there, Sirs." A guard, dressed in chain mail and the three interlocking gold rings of the King carrying a spear and small shield approached. "What is your business in Aurorum."

"I am Sir Barin Fairclough, grand nephew of Riven Noristrall, of the Riverlands. I escort my charge. Lord Tobin Hamstead, of Blackwatch in the Marsh, grandson of Robyn Hamstead of the King's council. We have arrived for the feast and to present ourselves before the King."

"Sir Barin, well met again." The guard clasped hands with the knight. "Lord Tobin?"

"I am." He responded, more nervous than he anticipated.

"The King waits for you, he bid us greet you with his condolences in regards to the treatment you received on the riverboats."

My gods, he knows. "I thank you. Lead us to him." Tobin jumped down off his horse and helped his sister. "My-" he paused. "My betrothed will accompany us."

"Very good, my lord." The guard motioned for a little squire in the gate house. "Peter, take them to the King."

They passed through the massive stone archway that allowed them entry into the capital. Escorted by the small squire, they left their horses at the stables and walked quickly towards the main gate of the castle. Tobin never saw anything like the marketplace they were crossing. The city streets were clean and busy. People darted between the crowded buildings and into small huts where vendors sold everything from fruits to exotic animals he had never seen before. One shop was filled with nothing but small vials of multi-colored potions, another had a large cage in the middle, it was empty, but Tobin's favorite was the armory; swords lined three walls and the forth was nothing but shields, he made a mental note to return to this shop. Peering into a large stone building, Tobin saw a massive forge, almost two stories high, radiating heat so that even in the street Tobin felt the increase in temperature. A few yards from the forge, there was a small hut with hanging cages and large crates. Fallia ran ahead of them and knelt by the first cage in a stack of three.

"Tobin, look."

Inside the cage a large dark purple cat lay staring with green eyes at Fallia.

"I want it." She demanded, standing up again.

"Sir Fairclough!" Tobin shouted to the knight that was following them. "Make sure this finds its way to my lady's room."

"Yes, my lord."

"Lead on, Peter." Tobin's voice was genial.

Inside the castle, carvings and tapestries greeted them at every turn, a stark contrast to the Blackwatch, where the stone walls were bare and always slightly damp. Torches illuminated the halls, but without need. There were arrow slits every few feet and small angled holes in the ceilings that allowed the sun to reflect off the marble floor, giving the castle a sense of being lit from the ground up.

"His Royal Highness's chambers." Peter bowed.

"Thank you, squire. You may leave us." Tobin reached into his vest to bestow a coin on the young man but he disappeared before Tobin's hand was halfway in. "Skittish little boy." He laughed very aware that he was only a few years younger than himself.

He swung open the heavy metal doors and escorted Fallia across the threshold. *He will be the largest one in the room.* He could hear Sir Fairclough's voice echoing in his memory.

Finding the King, Tobin lowered himself to one knee. "Your Royal Majesty, King Robsfeld Colbralian, I am Lord Tobin Hamstead of Blackwatch in the Marsh, grandson to Robyn Hamstead. I am here to take my grandfather's place on your Royal Council.

"Stand, Lord Hamstead." The King spat through a thick layer of gravy. Only then did Tobin notice the large platter of biscuits, sausage-gravy, eggs, toast and every other breakfast food he could think of sitting next to the King. "Who is this fair maiden?"

"She is my wife." Tobin lied smoothly. "May I introduce you to Lady Fallia Black Hamstead."

Fallia curtsied, her nervousness readily apparent.

"Show them to their chambers." He swallowed hard. "When you are settled, we will convene. I will see you in two hours, Lord Hamstead." The King dismissed them with a wave of his hand.

"I told you it would be all right." Tobin smoothed out the back of Fallia's riding dress as they sat on the bed of their new apartments. "The King thinks we are married, Sir Barin is the only person who knows otherwise, and I will have him watched at all times. He will not betray us, if he does our father will have him killed." He kissed her gently on the cheek. "We are safe."

Fallia smiled. She scanned the bedroom. It was the largest of the five rooms they were given but also the least well adorned. It was, however, more pleasant than anything they had in the Blackwatch. The feather pillows were full, the mattress firm. Carpet lined the entire apartment, and everything was made of oak or cherry. Silver dishes, gold framed paintings, beeswax candles and handwoven quilts filled their rooms.

"I want more, my love."

Gravous

Dust, grime, mud, grass, and all other manner of dirtiness penetrated into Gravous's soul. Living in the dirt was nothing new to him, but he had almost forgotten how to do it. Ten years of living a free and wild life in the Broken Lands had been erased by ten years of being pampered as a lord. The river, always on their left, flowed continuously away from where they were heading. Washing everything he knew and everything he was back down towards the Golden Bay. Ten days of trudging through the soggy ground of the river bank ended at a small wooden shack near the base of the great Dam.

Gravous eyed the building with contempt. *Even my forefathers would shudder at staying in a place like this. When I get free from them I will go back to my homeland and live free, live like I ought to have lived.* The door slowly opened and a small hunchback limped out of the room.

"This way." He waved his arms awkwardly. "We have been expecting you." His voice was high and tight.

"Lead on, Bumblebutter." His captor responded.

If I had not lost myself in the luxury of the city, I would have been able to take on this small acolyte. I vow to never let myself get this soft again. Gravous promised as the chain that was around his neck jerked him forward.

The door slowly closed behind him, creaking the whole way. The floor boards echoed the door's pain as they bent and warped under the pressure of the larger men. Gravous could not take his eyes off the hunchback, *this little half man is no taller than my waist,* he mused while following him the twenty feet to the back of the building. When they reached the far wall, Bumblebutter picked up a large iron rod from an unseen crack in the floor—more like he brushed the floor with his fingertips and a large iron rod appeared—and shoved one end into a large opening that Gravous had not seen before. *Pay more attention to your surroundings!* He scolded himself, not for the first time.

The grinding of metal on metal filled the small wooden shack, and before their eyes the far wall slid back slowly to reveal a stairwell that led upwards into the side of the cliff face next to The Dam.

"What is this place?" Gravous could not help but wonder out loud.

"This is The Underground." Bumblebutter announced, with a hint of pride in his voice.

"Surely you have heard of the gnomes, Lord Lynch?" The acolyte inquired.

"No, I have heard nothing of this."

Bumblebutter nearly dropped the torch he had retrieved from what looked like a sheer stone face and swooned in his spot. "You explain it, Justin." He managed to gasp.

"Thousands of years ago, when the Veldorians first came to these lands, there were people already living here. Your people, the Posli, and the gnomes. We lived together, you and I, spreading far out on this land, from marsh to sea and from mountains to golden bay, but when the Veldorians came they fought their way across our home and settled in Aurorum, which was called Veldoria. They turned on your people right away, forcing them into the inhospitable north, and they valued our friendship just so long as we served them. Before they turned on us, the expert craftsmen built The Underground, it is a series of tunnels and passages that covers most of the old Empire. While this will not take you northeast of the Dam, it does spread out into the Marshes and Riverlands, even the Frozen Plains before ending just shy of the Valley.

"Our legacy runs deep, Lord Lynch." He continued. "We were once a proud race, of staunch and hearty people, laid waste by the Veldorians."

"I am saddened to hear this." Gravous saw an opening. "I will help you avenge your ancestors and bring justice to your race. I will help you create a world for your people. I will spend the rest of my life pulling down the ruling class to leave an opening for the gnomes." Gravous extended his bound hands to the hunchback gnome.

His only response was a roar of laugher from the small man. Echoes of his mirth bounced off the stone walls and rang up the stairwell. "You, a banished false lord from the Broken Lands? Justin, you didn't say your captive would be a jester." Bumblebutter almost tripped on the stairs as he wiped the tears from his eyes. "Lord Lynch." He muttered under his breath.

"I will not be disrespected!" Gravous yelled.

"What you will not be doing, you insolent fool, is giving anyone here orders or back talk." Justin jerked the chain around his neck sending him sprawling on the hard stone. "You will do exactly what I tell you to do, when I tell you to do it. I thought the stout chain around your neck would have been enough of a reminder you are not a guest here."

Bumblebutter burst out into another fit of laughter. "How does he not understand? He is chained to the youngest son of a lesser noble, one who took the cloth of all things. No offense Acolyte Wallin."

"I live to serve Brother."

"And here he is giving demands and ordering us to not disrespect him." The gnome had a difficult time finishing his comment through the laughter.

I will find these two when I am free. They can't watch me every minute. He pursed his lips and pulled back against the chain, in a weak attempt to show defiance. *Wallin? Why does that name sound familiar?*

Cresting the stairs, a long dark passage through the rock stretched out before them, ready to swallow them whole. Gravous felt the weight of the earth crushing down on him, almost suffocating him. Hours of silence passed slowly for the three figures wandering below the earth. A slight but noticeable upward angle started taking over the passages as they moved further up into the cliff. The further they went, the more Gravous felt he would never see the light of day again.

"There it is, up ahead. I knew it was around here somewhere." Bumblebutter pointed with his torch, but Gravous could not see anything.

"I was beginning to think you were lost." Justin laughed.

"A gnome, lost in The Underground, ha!" He took a few steps and faced a flat rock wall. "Let me show you what we have done."

Tracing an unrecognizable pattern on the rock, Bumblebutter took a few steps back and watched as the rock folded back to reveal a small mine cart on a system of rails.

"What is this?" Gravous asked.

"Silence, you will not speak to me." Bumblebutter roared. "Murderers and traitors…"

"Get in."Justin pulled his chain. "We are riding the rest of the way."

The small mine cart was made of rotting wood and cracked boards. It was obvious to Gravous that it had not moved in years, perhaps decades. The metal banding along its sides rusted and warped, giving the cart more of a coffin look than Gravous felt comfortable with. He slowly lifted himself over the rusted top and into the mold-ridden center. Justin and Bumblebutter followed close behind and the old gnome pulled a lever that Gravous could not see and the cart started rolling along the tracks.

Creaking and churning filled the small underground tunnel. Gravous tried to cover his ears against the terrible grinding that was sending jolts of pain through his spine. The backs of his teeth rattled and ached. Mile after mile the cart slowly rolled along the slight downgrade farther south.

"We are about here." Bumblebutter slid a metal lever into a hidden slot and pulled back.

Gradually the cart began to scream its resistance to the newly added friction, but it slowed down nonetheless.

"Out." Shouted Justin as he climbed over the wall and gave a sharp yank on Gravous's chain. "I will not wait all day for you."

I will have my revenge. The young man from the Broken Lands vowed as he stared right into Justin's face. *Wallin, I know his family.* "Your Aunt was like a mother to me, Justin." Gravous hissed through the pain in his neck. "How can you treat me this way?"

"I will treat you how I will treat you, and do *not* speak to me like we are equals. I am sick of your constant babble." Justin jerked the chain with anger, pulling Gravous to his knees in front of him. "Those were the last words you will ever speak, *Lord Lynch.*"

Before Gravous could respond, Justin had reached in his mouth and pulled his tongue nearly to breaking point. A quick flutter before Gravous's eyes and his face erupted in a pain he never knew existed. All the cuts and bruises of his youth, even the shattering of his left arm when he was twelve, could not compare to this. Fire leapt from his mouth to his head and back. Blood poured down his throat, gagging him and sending him into a coughing fit. Justin wrenched the chain again, ripping large chunks of flesh from Gravous's neck, but he didn't notice amid the pain in his mouth.

Spitting blood on the ground and at his captors Gravous yelled a terrible wet yell and tried to curse them. *My gods! The pain is too much, take me!* He kept screaming in his mind. *Give me the strength to kill my captors and then take my life!* He continued to scream and writhe on the ground for several minutes before the chain once again dug itself into the raw and bleeding skin of his neck.

"Get up, you slag. We have pampered the lordling, long enough." Bumblebutter grunted.

"Move!" Ordered Justin, throwing the hunk of meat that used to be Gravous's tongue on the floor next to him.

Pain circled itself around his head, blocking out everything else until the world was reduced to a single point of light and he fell to the cold stony floor of the underground.

***

Gravous woke to a throbbing in his mouth and teeth. He could feel a warm sticky liquid in his mouth but it had no flavor. Rolling over he noticed he was on a patch of soft grass, the sun was shining high in the heavens, and a warm breeze gently caressed his cheeks. He spat. Blood stained the dark green grass and started pooling in the dirt beneath it.

"Ghaaalrgle." He bellowed. *They took my tongue. They took it.... I don't need it. I am a force of nature. I will survive without speech. I will reap upon my foes' vengeance seven fold.*

"Looks like the bleeder has woken up." Justin pulled the chain, sending Gravous into a convulsion of pain.

"We best be moving, now that he is awake you won't have to drag him." Bumblebutter stood to his full height and stretched his arms. "They should be fairly close to the city."

"*What city, where am I?*" Gravous tried to speak again, sending only echoes of grunts and hisses bouncing between the trees.

"It would be better if you tried not to speak. I thought that removing your tongue would have convinced you of that, but I can see that you are more ignorant than I previously imagined." Justin's tone of arrogance and haughty disdain had only increased since he mutilated his captive. *The pleasure of slitting his soft young throat will be almost too much.* Gravous thought to himself.

The three stood from the soft ground and picked their way across the meadows of brilliant flowers and tall grasses. Climbing the side of a small hill left Gravous panting for breath and coughing through the thickening blood in his throat. He fell to his knees and tried to pull the clotted blood from his mouth. His fingers only caused more obstruction and his lungs were screaming against his ribs for more air. Just as he was about to suck the blood into his lungs with one last desperate cling to life, his nail caught something and he pulled out a large gooey mass. He felt it drag along the inside of his chest. After he cleared the obstruction, his stomach revolted and he spent the following moments being sick on the hillside, only vaguely aware of the sounds of fighting going on around him.

"By the gods! What is that creature?" Justin's words echoed in Gravous's ears.

An inhuman cry filled the air as a response to the acolyte's question. Gravous covered his ears to block out the sound. Fire shot passed him, burning the edges of his clothes and singeing half of his hair.

"Gavrill, Renyard, control that beast." A female's voice shouted above the screams.

"My Lady, I cannot..."

Gravous lifted his head off the grass where he had pressed himself into the dirt. There were four bodies lying on the ground, three men and the gnome. A young girl, no older than fourteen, knelt over them with her eyes closed and her hands shoved deep into the earth beside them.

When Gravous stood, her eyes snapped up and she stared right at him.

"You must have been looking for Mr. Grahm. I was told there would be people coming." Her voice sounded thick, like there were many voices, and only one of them belonged to this small girl. "You have cost me a dragon," she smiled. "but no matter, not even a dragon will be able to stop me soon. You serve me now."

He nodded in agreement. *I don't know what she did or who she is, but if she is the only survivor of this melee, she has to be more than she seems.*

"Speak." She shouted. "Do not stand there silent before your new mistress." Her eyes flashed in an anger he had rarely seen.

He stuck out his tongue trying to show her the reason for his silence.

"I see. Judging from the freshness of this wound I gather they did it to you?"

He nodded.

"And they are dead now."

He nodded.

She sat back from her kneeling position and rested herself on Justin's chest. "I suppose you wanted to do it?"

He nodded again, with more vigor this time. *Who is this? How is she still alive?*

"And if there was a way for me to allow you to kill them?"

He cocked his head and inquired with his eyebrows.

In response she leaned forward and chanted a few words. Shoving her hands deep into the mud beside Justin's face, she breathed into his mouth. His eyes opened.

"Kill him. Kill him for me, as your first act of loyalty and fidelity to me." She smiled. He felt a warmth in that smile, like his soul was being warmed by the face of an angel. *I will kill him. She has given me this opportunity. Through witchcraft or divine power she has given me the chance to slay my enemies.* He smiled.

She stood and handed him a sword. The light touch of her soft skin on his hand sent a shock through him, and in that moment he would do anything she asked of him.

"Kill him. My sweet speechless man. Kill him."

I will do this. I will do this for my queen. Thank the gods, I will be able to reap my revenge. The nagging feeling in his chest slowly disappeared as he stared into her large brown eyes. Gravous carried out her wishes with a smile on his face.

When it was complete he knelt before her, his face smiling up at hers. He felt her teeth penetrate the raw and scabbed flesh of his neck. *Thank you.*

Tobin

"We have been here over a week and he has said nothing to you about it?" Fallia inquired, firmly holding Tobin's hand. "Where has he been?"

"I don't know. He is acting strangely." Tobin mused, his mind elsewhere. "I never knew it would be like this." He almost whispered.

"Like what?"

"So peaceful. This city, the ocean, the golden sun all day long, every day." He pulled her around to face him. "You in my arms every night. Back at the Blackwatch I would dream of this, but even in my dreams, father would ruin everything."

Fallia lowered her voice to a barely audible whisper. "Keep such things quiet. We are never alone here."

"As you wish." He kissed her gently, deliberately feeling her tongue with his, and taking pleasure in her lips' moisture.

They continued walking along the marble flower-lined pathway. The different kinds of flowers were lost on Tobin and Fallia, but the brilliant reds, deep purples, and bright yellows on a background of rich deep brown from the tilled earth still spoke to them. While there was little grass here on the gold coast, and whatever grass managed to grow was long, course and unseemly, the royal gardeners had worked a wondrous feat in coaxing the plants here to grow, and grow so beautifully.

A warm breeze pressed gently against their backs as they headed towards the sea. Marble railings separated them from a large drop straight into the golden bay. Tobin hung his head over the edge while Fallia leaned against the railing.

"Do you ever miss it?" She mused

"Miss what?" Tobin was counting the rocks in the bay below.

"The Marshes. You were born there, lived your whole life there, do you ever miss it?" Fallia's eyes glistened with a new dampness.

She is talking about herself now. Tobin knew almost instantly. "No, I don't miss it, for the most part. Vorlind was kind to me, but he was the only one." He spoke nonchalantly. "Besides you," he added in a whisper. "Do you miss your home?"

"I do. I miss father."

"Come, let us speak of this no more. Let me take you inside." Tobin grabbed her arm and escorted her back into the winding halls of the castle tower that had been set up for them.

Before they could reach the door to their private chambers, a man in chain mail and wearing the tabard of the King ran up to him.

"Lord Hamstead, your presence is needed." He managed to convey between gasps. "Follow me, my lord."

"Fallia wait for me, my dear. I will return to you." Tobin kissed her hand and followed the guard.

"I love you." She called after him.

The guard led him around the city center and back towards where the Academy had their sector. Large roads and busy traffic gave way to twisting streets and back alleys. Before long, the massive structure that was the center of Veldorian learning, loomed massively overhead. The ancient bricks were stained by the sea and the ragged bushes that clung to the base seemed to be holding the building down.

"Why have you taken me here?" he demanded.

"My lord," the guard said bowing, "The King requested it." He ran off before Tobin could question him further.

There is nothing for it then. Tobin pulled open the heavy wooden door and crossed the threshold. The interior of this massive hall was not unexpected but still surprising. Cobwebs hung from every corner and some even clung to the wall. A thin layer of dust covered the floor and easily betrayed the footsteps of the many members of the Academy. The door swung shut on its own behind him, sending a reverberating boom down the long hallway and dislodging a few of the cobwebs. He took a few tentative steps forward.

How is this the great center of Veldorian Knowledge I have heard so much about? The hallway was long, longer than appeared from the outside, with many doors lining the expanse of it. *Which door? Where am I supposed to go?*

"Hello?" He called down the hallway.

"Lord Hamstead." A deep voiced whispered from behind him.

"Ho there!" Tobin shouted, jumping around.

"Forgive me, Lord Hamstead." The tall thin man bowed. "I did not mean to startle you."

"And you are?" Tobin demanded.

"Magister Brundrum. I am at your service Lord Hamstead. Please, follow me we have much to discuss." He pointed to the closest door.

"The King is here?" Tobin did not move.

"No," Magister Brundrum conceded. "No, he is not, however, he bade me to educate you in the matter of the moonless night." He motioned again down the hallway. "First door on your right."

Tobin braved the dilapidated hallway and pushed his way into the indicated door. The vision that greeted him when he crossed the threshold took his breath away. The room was huge, twice the size of how the building looked from the outside. In the center was a gigantic globe, with several metal arms spinning around it. Each arm holding up a globe, some small, some large, but all of them spinning. Grinding gears filled the air with a faint but persistent hum. The vaulted ceiling echoed down the slightest noise, making it necessary to whisper. Narrow windows lit the room evenly with the reflected light of the sun.

"What is all this?" For a moment Tobin was the fifteen year old boy from the Marshes standing in wonder of what he saw. Memories of fishing in the swamp, and frying up the catch in the larder with Vorlind, nearly brought tears to his eyes. "Why am I here, Magister?" He coughed and reassumed Lord Hamstead again.

"You, my lord, were recommended by the King himself to be the new liaison between the Royal Academy and the Council." The Magister walked quickly through the spinning globes, jumping over the metal bars as they scraped along the floor on their continuing journey around the room. "Come, I will show you what we have discovered."

Tobin followed the old man through the winding and spinning of the giant globes, and into a small open area near the back, separated from the rest of the room by several large tables. Beakers and racks of tubes, journals and broken quills, and several pages of parchment covered these tables, making it impossible to see the top.

"Lord Hamstead, we have found that this lunar eclipse, this darkening of the night that happened on the moonless night was not, as our colleges in the temple would have us believe, a sign of the divine. It was an alignment of heavenly bodies that caused this anomaly. And, sparing you the knowledge we have found in the interim, this anomaly has happened once before." Magister Brundrum handed Tobin a large stack of parchment.

"When?"

"Considering the calculations we have made, over three thousand years ago."

"What does this have to do with the King, or me, or the Royal Council?" Tobin asked trying to make sense of the parchments in front of him.

"The people of the Five Kingdoms are superstitious. They look for the divine in the mundane, they beg for meaning from the ordinary. We have given the King his palliative for the masses. This eclipse is a reoccurring phenomenon that will happen at certain prescribed times during the natural progression of our world."

Tobin did not understand, but made no indication that he could not follow the Magister.

"Go back, to the Council, and tell the King this information. Here is our report." He handed Tobin a slim leather-bound volume. "Lord Hamstead, I truly hope that this will be the beginning of a mutually beneficial partnership between us."

"I am sure it will be."

"That is excellent to hear. One last thing before you depart. I would like a vial of your blood. Brother Adicus."

A short round young man bustled up to Tobin with a small knife and a large vial.

Tobin almost leapt backwards. "What is this?" He shouted.

"My Good Lord of the Blackwatch in the Marsh. I assure you it is for knowledge. We don't get many people from the Marsh here in Aurorum. Your grand father, Lord Robyn Hamstead, submitted to us and gave us blood. As you well know, Lord Tobin Hamstead, we are a people descended from the Veldorians, however, the course of time has hidden their secrets from us. It is the hypothesis of the

Academy that the power of the ancients lives in the blood of the true decedents of our forefathers."

"I am not sure I quite follow the particular knowledge that you have just bestowed upon me," Tobin did his best to portray intelligence in order to hide his insecurities about not understanding anything that was just explained to him. "But I will submit to your tests, Magister." He held out his arm.

Brother Adicus set the vial down on the table, grabbed Tobin's arm, and slit his wrist. Blood poured from the open wound into the vial, filling it. Tobin had never in his life felt this kind of pain. The childhood injuries he received in the Marsh never prepared him for this. *Do not let them see the pain. What would father say if he could see you now?* He thought as he watched his blood fill the vial on the table.

Magister Brundrum handed him a large white cloth when the vial could not hold anymore blood. "We greatly appreciate your sacrifice and offering Lord Hamstead. This will indeed help us grow our knowledge."

"Good. I will take my leave of you now." Tobin said weakly, while holding the cloth to his wound.

The sun blinded him momentarily as he left the Academy. His head was spinning and he felt nauseated. *What is wrong? Did they have poison on that knife?* He stumbled across the gardens and back to his tower. The stairs up to his room proved to be more formidable in his current state than Tobin anticipated, and he was out of breath and dizzy when he finally opened the door.

Fallia was on the bed with her face to the window

and her eyes closed. Her arms were spread and there was a bandage on her right wrist, blood was starting to dye it red.

"Fallia!" Tobin shouted rushing to her side. "Fallia, what happened?"

"Tobin?" Her faint voice scared him even more.

"I swear to any god that listens I will repay whoever did this to you."

"Tobin, peace." Fallia rolled over and cupped his face in her hands. "There were two men from the Academy. They came in talking about Grandfather, and people from the Marshes. All they wanted was some blood. I didn't understand why, they gave me something for the pain." She smiled and rubbed her lips on his. He was frozen. *What are they up to?*

"I have to leave." He tried to shake the cobwebs from his head. "Sleep well, I will return."

***

"Your Royal Highness, I have come from the Academy, as you have ordered."

"I did not order anything. What are you talking about?" The King bellowed.

Does he only have one volume? What I wouldn't do to have him not yell one sentence. "Your highness? I was told by Magister Brundrum that you ordered me to be the liaison between you and the Academy. They gave me information on the moonless night."

"What information?" The king's voice lowered.

I only had to wish it. Tobin smiled, seeing his opportunity. "Would it not be wise to give you this information in confidence?"

"It would not be wise." Lord Morris stepped between the King and Tobin.

"I agree, you need to disclose this information to the Council." Lord Corbett joined his colleague.

"I would gladly share with you the information, if my King allows it." Tobin smiled at the two older lords. *This is easier than I thought. The King just needs food and ego.*

"I do not." The King brushed crumbs off his thin beard and motioned for Tobin to follow. "To my private chambers, Lord Hamstead."

Tobin followed the large frame of his King into a small antechamber off the main hall, the other members of the council stared holes through his back as he left.

"Lord Hamstead, you have been on my council for less than week."

"Eight days, Your Grace."

"You correct me?" Fire flashed behind his eyes.

"Your Grace, I am but a young man trying to live up to my Grandfather's legacy here in your Council. I only wish that you have all the facts for every situation." He smiled.

"You remind me of myself when I was your age." The King smiled. "Eight days. In that time you have already managed to anger both of the other sitting members of this council, acquire information pertaining to the moonless night—something both of the other two could not do—and find the killer of your Grandfather. And that one even before you arrived. You are a marvel."

Find my grandfather's killer? He was killed? His

face flushed red and the back of his neck and ears tingled. "Yes, Your Grace. I live to serve you, and the realm."

"Tell me what you know."

"The Academy informed me that the moonless night, or eclipse as they call it, has happened before, during the time of the Veldorians. This is nothing more than a random occurrence that happens to take place during your reign. It won't happen again and it is a natural anomaly."

"Lord Hamstead, thank you. Spread the word throughout the Five Kingdoms, there is nothing to fear and no magic at foot."

"Your Grace, there is one more thing, I would ask of you."

"Speak your mind."

"Your council, this practice is an archaic tradition handed down from a time before your family united the kingdoms to form this *empire*. Do you not think it is time that you shed the limiting mantle of King and don the supreme power of Emperor?" *For all his faults Sir Barin did prepare me well.* "This council does nothing that you could not do yourself."

"Lord Hamstead, not a day goes by when I do not think about that." He rang a bell that was on a small table near his chair. "The council is powerful. Those men, however much we dislike them, are powerful men."

"But Your Grace. You are The King." Tobin stepped aside as a young bald boy rushed into the room carrying a covered tray.

"I am The King. Leave me. I would be alone."

"Your Grace," Tobin bowed. "Or should I say your

Imperial Majesty?" He turned and walked out of the king's private chambers into the menacing glares of the council members.

"Do not think for a moment that you can survive here on this Council without our cooperations."

I was warned about this. "My lords, please do not mis-understand my actions. I serve the Empire and the King. I do not serve you. I have no need of you. You, my lords, are a burden on the people of this Empire." He smiled and strode out.

He found Fallia still asleep on the bed facing out the window. "My love," he gently woke her. "My love. You will get more, I promise."

She smiled and pulled him to her. "My brother." She kissed his neck. "More what?"

"Everything." Tobin returned her kisses with a growing vigor. "The King will be easy enough to manipulate." The two entwining more and more under the thin sheet of their bed.

"Where did you learn this?" She asked quietly. While they were wrapped in each other's naked bodies.

"I spent my whole life trying to get anything for myself, and it never worked. Here it is different. I behave the same way, and the King smiles at me. I think he might..." His voice trailed off.

"He might what?" Fallia asked after a moment of quiet kissing.

Before Tobin could answer a few loud blows on the door broke the spell and infuriated him.

Not moving from his position on top of Fallia, he called out. "Who is there?"

"Lord Tobin, I wish to speak with you." It was the condescending voice of Sir Barin Fairclough.

It's like he knows. He tries to ruin me.

Tobin stood from the bed, seething. The anger that welled in him was near bursting point. Ripping open the door, he saw the knight about to strike the door again.

"You, Sir Barin are interrupting me. What do you want?"

"My lord, I would be remiss if I did not remind you that your father sent me to-"

"Speak not about my father!" He roared.

"As the Captain of your household guard, it is my duty to protect your house. All of your house." He looked passed Tobin right at Fallia, lying half naked on the bed.

Tobin stepped into his line of vision, putting himself between Sir Fairclough and Fallia.

"You are relieved of your duties as *Captain*." Tobin shouted.

"As you wish, my lord." Sir Fairclough bowed and left the apartments.

Sir Barin

"You are relieved of your duties as *Captain*." Tobin shouted.

"As you wish, my lord." Sir Fairclough bowed and left the apartments.

How can anyone be so vile? It was but a month ago that he was running around the Marshes, an innocent boy. When he learned he had power here, the corruption grew deeper than I could have ever imagined. The stone steps took longer than usual to traverse as he walked away from the Lord of the Blackwatch. *Insufferable little boy!* He struck the gray stone of the tower walls, instantly regretting his anger. The knuckles on his hand were shredded, and spots of blood began welling up. He wiped it on his tunic. The last dying rays of the sun shone through the arrow slits and regular windows, casting a bizarre pattern of squares and lines on the opposite wall. Barin was so entranced by these patterns he collided with a large body, sending both of them to the ground.

"Beggin' your pardon me'lord—"

"I am no lord." Sir Fairclough stood and brushed the dust from his tabard, the stinging in his hand growing.

Taking off his hat and daring a glance, the nervous servant started over. "Beggin' your pardon Sir, I did not mean to 'arm you. I am just 'ere to light the torches."

"Take care to not allow this behavior again."

"Yes, Sir. And Sir, a moment if you please, sir. I was also bidden to give this to the Lord of the Marshes. This 'ere." He produced a folded letter, sealed with the two gold coins of the Colbralians. "Might'en I beg your forgiveness, sir, to pass you, sir, and finish me master's wishes?"

"Give that to me." Barin almost snatched it away.

"As you wish, sir, I am ever in your debt sir, 'umblest apologies, sir."

"Away with you. Light the torches another time."

"As you wish, sir. The servant bowed again and shuffled quickly away.

Barin, clenching his right hand against the pain, shoved the note from the servant into his vest pocket. As he took a few steps down the stairs, his foot slipped on a small piece of parchment. Momentarily losing his balance, he shoved out his arms to steady himself, slamming his right hand into the wall again.

"Gods!" He bellowed.

Barin pulled the first note out of his tunic after picking up the second. The seal was indeed the royal seal of the King himself. *What does His Majesty want with Lord Hamstead?* He let his mind dwell on this question as he absentmindedly opened the second note. It was a map, a map of the castle, but it was more. He studied it carefully, it was a guide to a store room, and a small inscription telling the bearer to deliver the letter to a hidden storeroom.

He shoved both notes into his tunic pocket behind his tabard and carried on down the stairs. Crossing the doors to the Main Hall he found them open. The chaos of the room mirrored the fear in his own heart. *I might have had a place at that table.* He mused as he saw the servants begin to set up the King's table. *I must not dwell on that. I have been released by my lord, I will find a new Vassal.*

Retiring to his room, he carefully removed the two notes and studied them at the small desk. His room was comfortable, furnished with a simple bed and desk, a small chest and warm rugs. *I will have to move now.* He thought before he melted the wax off the seal and forged his way into the document.

He stared blankly at the paper. *This can't be. Where is that other...* He grabbed the second note and quickly unfolded it. A map to a secret storeroom was evident, and the small handwritten inscription was a password. He held it up to the light. 'Meet here to plan.' In that moment he found his mind. *If I am no longer in my lord's service, then it is not my duty to bring it to him.* He smiled to himself.

***

A dark figure moved quickly through the smoke of dying torches. Echoes of soft pattering feet bounced around stone walls of the narrow hallway. As Barin passed the torches, he inspected them. Running a few fingers through the flames, he shuffled quickly to the next one in line. Each torch received the same treatment, and his bent frame disappeared down a flight of steep stairs. The map was crude but accurate. Each turning and staircase was represented but nothing else. One wrong turn and he would have lost himself in this labyrinth below the castle.

Circling down into the depths of the earth, he quickened his pace. The echoes stopped; there was no sound to announce his presence. Consulting the map for a final time, he repeated the instructions he read several times in his room while waiting for darkness. "I hope this is the right door." His voice sounded muffled in this echoless tunnel. When he reached the large wooden door, he bent down and slid a small parchment through the crack. "I hope my answer was right." Before he had a chance to turn and leave, the door slid silently open and a hand grabbed the hood of his tunic and pulled him into the room.

"Sir Fairclough, I did not expect to see you here." A large man filled most of the small room with his girth. "With the royal welcoming tonight. Should you not be at the side of your young charge?"

"As it happens, I have been relieved of my duties by his lordship himself. It seems he would rather pursue his own petty interests than have a Knight of the Realm as his Captain."

"I have heard little about the young lord. Please come have a seat, tell me all." He spoke genially and loud, until he closed the door. "I see you have brought some correspondence for us." He pointed at the letter still lying on the floor.

"I shouldn't be here."

"But you are." The large man stepped into the small halo of light from the torch. Barin had no difficulty recognizing Mystic Grahm.

"Why do you have such an interest in this young man?" Sir Fairclough scanned the small room.

One wooden bench was against the far wall, and one chair sat next to the door. The walls were stone, except for the door. The room was cold, dark, musty, and the last place he would have assumed he was going to meet the High Mystic of the Temple.

"You know as well as I do, that message was meant for you." The mystic smiled. "Beggin' your pardon me'lord. Me 'umblest apologies me'lord."

A wave of understanding washed over the knight as he crossed his arms. *What does he know?* Barin tried to hide his thoughts.

The large cleric waddled over to the far bench and motioned for Barin to follow. "Please walk with me. We have important matters to discuss." He bent the arm of the bench and a crack appeared in the flat stone wall. Sliding back slowly, the wall revealed a passageway back under the castle itself.

"Where does this lead?"

"Do you not trust your spiritual leader?"

"At this moment, no, I do not."

"You will soon enough. Please." He motioned again and stepped into the passage.

Barin followed, hesitantly. There were no torches in this hall, no light. A few hundred yards of stumbling behind the surprisingly fast cleric and they emerged from the tunnel into a large round room. A stiff breeze pushed the two men over the threshold.

"What is this place?" Sir Barin Fairclough managed to ask through his shock.

The ceiling was at least a hundred feet above their heads and lost in darkness. Large torches were positioned in gold hangers every few feet along the walls. The flames flicked with the wind that was circling the room. The stone of the walls seemed to be carved in a dome leading up to the capstone, hidden by darkness. The sound of distant rushing water filled the background of the room, and the smooth stone floor clapped as Mystic Grahm quickly crossed the room and found a seat on a golden bench near the far side. Several other benches of expensive metals lined the outer rim of this circular room. The inner circle was a large hearth with a dying fire still burning. *The smoke from this has to be visible from the outside.* He slowly followed his companion and sat next to him. Every inch of the walls were covered in some form of ancient writing, symbols he recognized from his youth. The ancient writing of the Veldorians.

"How is it that I have served this King my whole life, spending more time here in the capital than at home and I have never heard of a place like this?" He marveled.

"There is much about this city that even I do not know. The wonders built by the Veldorians surprise even the most learned of us. To answer your questions and move the conversation along, I will say this. As far as I can understand this room, it opened to us on the moonless night. While wandering the passages below the castle I found the cellar were you slid the note under the door. I, no doubt like you, surmised that room to be a storage room of wines or spirits, such small alcoves are not uncommon in ancient buildings, but on the night itself the door was open. This is the secret high chamber of the Veldorians. Upon first entering the room we found the remains of King Haydn."

"The Lost King." Whispered Fairclough

"Yes, the Lost King, and the last. This means there is something moving against us. The last time this room was used it was by King Haydn, the last true Veldorian King, and thousands of years before the War of the Feathers. The magic left behind by the Kings of old felt it, I feel it, and this room has presented itself to us."

"But where is it?"

"According to our best calculations, it is under the Golden Bay."

Barin grabbed the bridge of his nose with his right hand, in a show of impatience. "Tell me, Mystic Grahm, why have you brought me here?"

"To show you. The simple fact that this room exists, added to the fact that it opened itself to us, proves there is evil rising in the world. We need every good man to join arms against this coming doom."

"What does this have to do with me?"

"Sir Barin Fairclough, why were you delivering a sealed letter to a storeroom in the basement of the castle at night with a hooded cloak, while under the impression that your correspondent expected Lord Hamstead?" The bulging cheeks of Grahm's ample faced turned upwards in a smile. "Because you are a good man. The gods need good men."

How much does he know? Why did I agree to this? Can I trust him? He shifted slightly on the bench and scanned the room a few times. Looking down at the folded parchment in his hand, he made his choice.

Passing the note to the swollen hands of the head Mystic, Sir Fairclough stood and took two steps toward the center of the room.

The Mystic followed him and handed back the paper. "Open it. There is much you need to know."

"I have already read the contents of this letter."

"As I assumed." Mystic Grahm laughed. "Let us not play games, Sir Fairclough." The Mystic retook his seat on the bench. "What is to be done? If this is true, and all the acolytes agree it is, what is to be done?"

"If this is true, the King will need to be told, and he will not be pleased." Barin sat beside him. "We need to confirm this before we assume its truth. I want to see it with my own eyes."

"A wise suggestion. I know where to start." Mystic Grahm put the note away and shifted in his seat. "But what of the Valley? All communication from my brother has ceased. Lord Bryne was kept unaware of the situation for his protection, but now he blames the Colbralians for the disappearance of his daughter."

"But it was you, or rather your brother operating under your orders, that took his child."

"Yes. You do not know everything she represents."

"The Bryne's will want retribution from the king."

"We mustn't let that happen. Any dissension now will sacrifice our strength, and we will need all of it for the coming battle."

"The coming battle against The Valley?"

"I do not know, I only know what was shown to me. There is a dragon, death, and a hero. There is one man standing between the forces of darkness and death, and that man can be you." Mystic Grahm stood up. "The God of the Veldorians has shown me this vision. I have seen the world burn in fire, the dead and the living alike running from the flames. Spirits controlled by an evil force pit us against our ancestors. War ravages this world and we are all laid waste."

"The God of the Veldorians?"

"I have seen much since the room opened."

Barin stood and paced around the giant hearth before responding. All this information confused him. *How am I to make sense of it all?* After returning from the great circle, he took a deep breath. "I have heard the rumors. I know the tales of the moonless night. When I was but a child growing up in the Riverlands, our people would tell stories of a powerful lizard, larger than any that have lived, with the ability to breathe fire. It was said that on the first moonless night, the first of its kind was born, over two thousand years ago. Now another moonless night happens in our life time." Sir Fairclough tried to read the face of his partner.

"Sir Barin Fairclough, you remember your lore well, but remember what happened after the first moonless night? I ask you again. Will you stand for good, will you stand for the God of the Veldorians, and will you stand against evil?"

"I was told, by your young acolyte that I could find a friend in the temple. I did not suppose it was going to be like this, Grand Mystic."

"Trust me. You have found an ally here."

Sir Fairclough returned to his seat on the golden bench. The large fire had all but gone out, and he followed the last string of smoke as it floated towards the center-top of the massive room. As his eyes watched the accent, he noticed how this chamber was built. A dim blue light was glowing at the very apex of the room. As the smoke floated towards it, it began to fly around gaining in speed until it reached the center. A small hole no bigger than his head. He watched as it passed through the threshold and turned into a bubble on the other side.

"My dear Mystic Grahm." He said rising. "We are indeed under the Golden Bay."

King Robsfeld

The King sprawled out on his oversized bed. It was made for him after the last bed crumbled during the night. Two trays shared space with him on the goose-down and straw mattress. One had various fruits shipped in from the far reaches of the Broken Lands, and the Midlands. The other had a flagon of spiced honey mead from the Gold Coast and a flagon of red wine. He did not bother with cups.

A few small baldheaded boys were scurrying about the room cleaning spots of food off the floor, or refilling the two flagons. Many people knew about the King's odd choice in servants, but not many had seen the extent to which he collected them. Through the commotion of the boys coming and going to and from his room—there were at least three in the room at all times—King Robsfeld did not move. He sipped from his wine, he nibbled on the bits of food left over from his second lunch, but most of all he watched. He watched boys fill the ever emptying flagons, and he watched them scamper around his room doing random tasks.

Downing the spiced honey mead, he rose from his bed and grabbed the nearest servant boy. "Bring me Lord Tobin." He rubbed the bald head of the terrified looking child before letting him run off into the castle.

Exiting the bed completely and dressing himself in his royal robe and belt took a quarter hour and three boys. By the time Tobin was announced at the entrance to the King's chambers he was only just entering the sitting room.

"Show him in," he said. "And bring me wine and grapes."

Tobin entered. The King loved the way this young Lord of the Blackwatch moved. The youthful bounce of his step, the way his hair moved while he spoke, even the timbre of his voice gave the King a warm sensation that grew in his lower stomach.

"Lord Tobin, so kind of you to join me. Won't you please sit." He motioned for a chair to be brought up close to him.

The room was lavishly adorned with red cushioned chairs and deep mahogany wood tables. It was one of the only rooms in the castle to have thick rugs covering the entire floor and muffling all sounds, giving the room a dark feel, even though all the curtains were open and a warm sea breeze was drifting through the windows.

The sweet scent of wine and roasted meat danced around royal chambers on the smoke of several sticks of incense that burned quietly in the corners of the room. King Robsfeld rarely bathed and he liked his room to mask the odor that haunted his movements, but was pleased that Tobin visibly blenched when entering. *Welcome to my room* he thought with a smile.

A bald boy set a chair slightly too close to the King and Tobin sat without a pause.

"Your Grace, I thank you for inviting me to meet you in your own chambers, and I would be even more pleased to dine with you this afternoon."

"As you wish, Lord Tobin." The King shifted awkwardly in his chair. "Boy, bring pheasants in cranberry sauce, roasted nuts with goat cheese, two more flagons of mead, and soda bread." The bald boy bowed and scurried out of the room. "Leave us." He told the rest of his servants.

Once they were alone he leaned forward in his chair and eyed the young lord. *He looks calm, does he not know why he is here? Or does he?* He smiled. Tobin returned the look and reached for a glass of wine from the near empty flagon.

"Your Grace, I am new to the capital, and I have no friends here. I am eternally grateful that you have shown an interest in my career here."

"Tobin," He paused to see how the change of tone would affect him; it did not. "Tobin, I knew your grandfather quite well. It came as a great sadness to me when I learned of his death."

"I thank you for your sentiment, Your Grace, but

he had been serving in the capital for several years by the time I was born. I never met him."

"That is a shame." The King paused as two bald boys entered with trays and flagons. "Ah our meal has arrived." The King filled his tankard and ripped off a large chunk of pheasant. The bald boys left as quietly as they came, and he continued. "I wish now that you could have met him. He was a wise man."

"Your Grace, you honor my family. I wish I could have known him," Tobin paused and made eye contact with the King. "I have never had a good father figure in my life; there is so much I could learn from you, and my late grandfather."

King Robsfeld roared in laughter, "Your grandfather talked about the 'tick of a son' he had back in the Blackwatch, and 'that house of ticks,' the Murrays. I am sure there is little you could have learned from that cranky old man. Tell me young Lord Tobin, how is life back in the Marsh? Is it as backward and terrible as I hear?"

"No, Your Grace. I lived a quiet life; as the youngest son of my father, I had no responsibilities. My eldest brother is being groomed to replace my father, Marcus is a member of the Merchant Guild and hardly spent time in the Blackwatch, being off in the Broken Lands, and my—" he cut short and took a sip of honey mead. "My life was happy. On more than one occasion I have heard my father complain about the Murrays and how they kept to themselves and care not for the rest of us."

"As I thought." He shifted again in his chair bringing his massive frame even closer to Tobin. "And your life now? Is it not happy?"

"Oh yes, Your Grace. I am very happy here in Aurorum." Tobin smiled what the King thought was a forced smile.

"You know, you could forget all that, and change your life?"

"Your Grace?"

"You are here now, at court, several hundred miles from your father. You have to make your own decisions, and your own friends." He scooted closer to the young lord.

"My own friends, Your Grace?" Tobin looked at him with large eyes.

"Friends in high places that may require you to do certain things that you may not be accustomed to." He gently rested his arm on Tobin's leg.

"Your Grace, I have only been here for a short time, and I am not accustomed to a great deal of things," he said, with a look of innocence in his eyes that egged the King to further action. *He wants it.*

King Robsfeld felt Tobin's legs move slightly, widening for his massive hand. *I knew it. I have him.* "Young Lord Tobin, how old are you now?"

"Only fifteen, Your Grace, though soon enough I will see my sixteenth birthday."

"So young to have a wife, and she is too young to know how to properly please a man." His hand slipped up Tobin's leg until it covered his crotch.

"Yes, Your Grace. I would choose you as my friend if I were able."

The King smiled down at Tobin, and squeezed his hand that cupped Tobin's groin. "I would like that," he whispered as he grabbed Tobin's hand and led him to the bed.

***

Tobin had long since left his chamber, and the bald boys had returned to clean him. He enjoyed it, but the solitude was now crushing on King Robsfeld's soul again. He lay in his bed, avoiding the mess made by his lust, staring at the ceiling.

A voice spoke near his feet and his heart skipped a beat and tore at his left shoulder with a pain that he never felt before.

"Your Grace, is it done?"

"Felter, you scoundrel. Would you kill me? Announce your self when you enter my presence."

"Just as you say, Your Grace. I am the very portrait of apologies." He bowed deeply. "Is it done?"

"Yes, it is done."

"Good, and he doesn't suspect a thing?"

"No, It was my impression he was trying to manipulate me." The King looked at his hands. "I...had him."

"I knew you would, Your Grace, you deserve what you want. You are after all the King."

"Enough of your cheep words. He is ready to assume the position as my heir. The kingdom will go on."

"Good. I will take my leave of you, Your Grace."

"Why him?" The King asked, sitting up in bed.

"Why any of us, Your Grace, because it is the will of the gods." Sir Felter Morris drifted out of the King's chambers silently.

King Robsfeld fell back hard against the mattress of his bed and drowned the remainder of his evening in a fresh flagon of wine. He did not sleep that night.

Aislinn

A sword slashed down onto her neck.

"Ouch!" She screamed.

"You shouldn't have run away." Rebecca yelled as she kept battering away at the now crouching Aislinn.

Throwing her shield up to protect her from the wooden practice sword, she managed to get some distance between her and the blonde twins by kicking dirt in their faces and pushing back. "You would have done the same." Aislinn shouted, gaining her feet again.

"I would not have come back." Rebecca kept throwing slash after slash at her.

She is wild, I see an opening every time she

backhands. Damn! Another weapon struck her in the back of the head. "Margery!"

Aislinn rolled out of another swing and turned to face the twins. Rebecca brandished a short sword and a small shield just like Aislinn, but Margery had a trident.

"There is no escape for you." Margery hissed.

"We know what you did in that tent. Don't think he didn't have us the same way, you are not special."

"Shut your mouths." Aislinn knew she could take them one at a time, but together might be too much. Even though they only had practice weapons, Aislinn was not sure if they wanted to kill her or not.

She took a few steps backward and they advanced. Following this routine, she backed around the entire practice grounds. *Why won't they attack? They must be scared of me!* The thought dawned on her like a ray of sunlight.

"We know why you cry at night." Rebecca started.

"It's 'cuse you miss the Prince's prick, not your mom."

Aislinn let out a scream and flew at them, waving her sword widely in front of her. Rebecca fell backwards and Margery dropped her weapon. Aislinn managed to land several blows on both of them before the guards pulled them apart.

"Save it for the ring, you three." His boredom more than apparent. "Prince Naveed is putting you on display tomorrow."

***

After her mother had died so had Aislinn,

inwardly. She was aware of less than half of what was going on around her. She had no memories of inside the prince's tent, or the following week. Only a few days ago did she snap out of her depression long enough to realize that she was in a sort of gladiatorial battle with another slave around her age. It was then she realized why they had taken so many people. *We are to be entertainment for the realm.* The thought was nauseating and she was sick on the dirt floor right before the bell rang to begin the battle.

He ran to grab a spear and a buckler and started to advance on her. Realizing she had no weapon, she scanned her surroundings. It was a dirt oval ring with one podium in the middle. The stone walls surrounding were ten feet high and there were wooden seats above that. She saw Prince Naveed and Cor Donovan staring down at her and pointing.

A spear thrust just missed her stomach and she started running to the podium. She was faster than he was and reached her goal with enough time to find a short bow but no arrows. She ducked below the podium just as he jabbed at her face. *Why does this guy look so familiar?* She asked herself as she inched around, keeping the cover between her and the spearman. Still no arrows, although he never gave her long enough to look. *He was the baker's boy!* She remembered in a flash the young boy, one year younger than her, and how they would play together in the streets before his mom would bring them both in to help bake bread in the mornings of Little Town. *What is his name? Remember!*

"Jonathan!" She shouted.

"Shut up, Aislinn. We will both get killed, and I

am not going to die."

"Jonathan, stop!" She dodged another spear thrust and rolled around to the other side. There on the ground was one arrow. She snatched it up and ran to the other side of the arena. *I need separation. I have always been faster than him.*

"Jonathan, stop please! We are friends." She hated this world. She hated Prince Naveed, she hated Cor Donovan, she hated the gnomes for letting her get caught again, and she even hated Princess for saying her mother would die.

As he ran towards her, his clumsy form reminded her of their childhood together when he would chase her with a cart with the sole purpose being to capture her as his prize.

"No!" She screamed.

Tears streamed down her cheeks. Her heart beat furiously against her back teeth. She watched him run. Time slowed. He was almost to her. Without thinking she drew, fired, and ran to him, almost beating the arrow.

"Jonathan." She threw her weapon aside. "I am so sorry."

"Don't be. I would have killed you." He coughed twice sending blood all over Aislinn, she did not notice. "I am sorry about your mother. I will tell her you are well." His body relaxed and she was holding the head of her dead childhood friend.

Ripping the arrow out of his heart she notched it again and pointed it at Prince Naveed. Immediately, three people with large tower shields stepped around him completely blocking any shot she had.

"Well done, little rat." His voice flowed musically

down into the arena. "But in a few days we will see how well you do without your bow."

Guards with similar shields streamed out of unseen doors in the stone walls. Their bodies completely covered in plate mail but for a small slit for the eyes. The metallic clinking as they ran almost soothed the anger from Aislinn.

"Throw down your weapon and come with us." One of them shouted.

She did as she was told and was led off into the caves below the arena. There is where she spent her nights.

***

Lying in her bed, her ribs bruised from where Margery had slashed them with the trident, she stared at the cold stone ceiling and pondered tomorrow; sleep would not find her tonight. *What did the guard mean by 'You will be on display tomorrow?' Display?* She could not control her thoughts, and they darted in and out of reality at will. Taking a cue from them, her heart beat furiously. Her hands started shaking, and her breath came in short shallow gasps. *No. Don't let this happen.* She ordered herself. *I don't care if you sleep or not, just don't panic.*

A crash on the far side of the room sent her bolt upright. She silently rolled out from underneath the musty thin blanket and onto the cold stone floor. Creeping slowly to the wall of bars that kept her confined, she tried to poke her head out to see what happened. Finding a way she could manage to see down the hall proved difficult at first, but after a few moments of adjustment she had it.

The crash seemed to have come from one of two large crates. The lid was lying on the ground and there were five or six fully armed guards with long two pronged forks and nets.

"Watch it, move slowly, they see different than we do." One guard was saying.

"Get that lid back on!" Another one shouted.

Four others grabbed up the lid and slowly secured it back on top of the crate.

"There. Don't want to be those three girls tomorrow."

"Why is Naveed wasting them like that? If he doesn't like 'em, send 'em to us. I could do with any of those three." The first guard asked.

"Prince Naveed is not wasting them." Aislinn shuddered. The melodic sound of his voice left no confusion as to who was talking. "I think that they will beat these exotic animals."

There was a clamor of excitement as he was obviously unnoticed by his men. Aislinn could hear half of them cursing each other while the other half seemed to just shuffle their feet and keep their eyes on the floor.

"No one has, not even our most experienced gladiators." It was the same guard as before.

"If you feel so scared for them, you can join them." Prince Naveed laughed. "Take him."

The guards leapt into action. Aislinn could not quite see what was happening, but, by sound alone, she could tell the guard was losing and she would soon have another cell mate. Her inclination was correct. Not five minutes after the fight started the sounds of dragging started coming her way and she flew silently back into her bunk and shut her eyes.

The cell door slid open and a large body was thrown inside, accompanied by laughter and jeers from the other guards.

"You should never speak ill about our Prince!" One guard shouted.

"Now you get to feel what those girls will feel." Laughed another.

The forsaken guard crawled to the far end of the cell and rested his back on the dirty cold stone. His uniform had been stripped off, the armor was gone, the cloak was gone, the helm was gone. The only thing he had left was a tunic and a short kilt. He wrapped his thick hairy arms around his legs for warmth and started shuddering.

After what seemed like hours of ridicule from his ex-companions, they left him. Aislinn rolled over.

"I am sorry for you." She ventured.

"Not half as sorry as you should be. I know what it is you fight tomorrow, little rat."

"What it is *we* fight, if I understand the situation."

"Indeed." His rough masculine voice echoed in the large cell. "Little rat has a point."

"*Little rat* is the only thing standing between you and death." She chose the forceful approach.

The muffled laughter told her it was a poor choice. "You are beyond hopeless. Look at you. You are scrawny, you have no training, your beauty is hidden behind rags and dirt. There is nothing of note that sets you apart from anyone else, yet you, little rat, tell me that you stand between me and death? Why?"

He burst into another fit of laughing.

She brushed her hair behind her ears and tried to wipe the days of captivity from her face. Opening her eyes wide and looking up at him she whispered. "What is your name?"

"Jarret." He followed her example of voice lowering.

It's working. I knew it. "Aislinn." She smiled. "We seem to be stuck here, together, in this awful situation. Is there no bargain that could be struck between us?"

"I wish we could have met under different circumstances, little rat," He barely looked at her. "But tomorrow will bring out death regardless of any deals struck between us."

"I heard what you said about wanting to take any one of us." Aislinn knew she was walking a thin line. *He could snap at any moment, and I am not sure I could fight him off if it came to it.* "I will ignore this slight on my honor as long as you help us stay alive tomorrow."

"And if I let you die and save myself?"

"From the fear in your voice, I know you don't think you can do it alone." Her voice did not betray her own fear. "But if two can work together? Perhaps we have a chance at surviving?"

"What about the twins?" He motioned to the sleeping bodies. "Perhaps they will give me something more tangible tonight?"

"They might, but come the morning they would surely sacrifice you to save themselves." Aislinn rolled off her bed and crawled to his huddled form. Resting her warm hand gently on his knee she looked past his short thin beard and into his misty-blue eyes. *He is handsome.* "Tell me what it is we fight. If we pledge our loyalty to each other we *can* defeat it."

"Dire tigers. Two of them." His once blue eyes were clouded with fear.

***

The rattle of the cell door opening startled Aislinn awake. *When did I fall asleep?* After Jarret told her what they were going to face, she had spent the night curled up on her bunk trying to put it our of her mind. She, like every little child in the Gold Coast, had heard stories of the large evil beasts that would roam the hills north of the capital. They killed oxen with one swipe of their massive paws, and would think nothing of attacking a knight in full armor if they were hungry. *I can only assume they are hungry.* She thought to herself as she followed the twins out of the cell.

Jarret caught her arm before she left. "Remember what we spoke about. I pledge to you if you to me?"

"I swear it." Aislinn felt comfort in the terror of his eyes. *At least I am not the only one who is scared.* "Together we will survive this."

Jarret's eyes filled with tears. "From your lips, little rat," he paused. "Aislinn, I believe it."

I just hope I believe it. She tried to comfort herself.

For once the twins were not talking or thinking of new ways to torture her. The gravity of their situation had probably been impressed upon them when they were handed real swords, and heavy shields. Aislinn and Jarret both grabbed spears before leaving the armory. The four were led in silence to the main entrance of the arena by five fully armored guards, none of whom Jarret had seen before. The darkness of the clay-walled tunnel did little to hide their fear.

The large wooden doors ground open. A sun-baked sandy floor stretched out before them. Four ten-foot columns had been added in to the normally barren fighting area. They marked out a large square near the center of the oval ring. Inside this new square were two very large beasts. Aislinn had never seen any animal larger than herself—outside of horses—before, and these were bigger. The shock of such a large creature gave her pause. Their eyes were black as polished obsidian and their fur a striped mix of black and orange. The two lower canine teeth were three times longer than her hand, and nearly twice as thick. Their claws were also much larger. Guttural deep growls reverberated through the arena floor.

The guards prodded them cruelly in the back and shoved them forward, into the blinding sun. The stands erupted with cheers and shouts. Scanning quickly, not wanting to take her eyes off the dire tigers for too long, she could not find one set unfilled. *Where did they all come from? And they came to watch us die.*

"They came to watch us die." Jarret whispered in her ear.

"We will not give them what they want." Her face became hard and set. *Gods help me, give me the rage I felt before. I will need it.* She tried to wake the inner beast she felt before. Gripping tighter onto her spear she shouted at the roaring crowd, "We will not die!"

Just then Prince Naveed and his guards arrived at their usual spot, and he raised his hands, quieting the crowd. "Brothers, friends, delegates, and anyone else that managed to stumble onto our shores. We welcome you." He was interrupted by cheers. After a few moments, he began again. "As you know we have the reputation for finding the best and bravest gladiators. Today is no exception. Hailing from Aurorum, your grand capital, Little Rat and her band of minions." A cheer cascaded down on the four warriors. *They are not cheering for us, they're cheering against us*. Aislinn realized.

"Twins, Jarret come." She commanded, doing her best to ignore the rest of Prince Naveed's speech. "If we stand together we can win."

"Who made you our queen?" Rebecca snarled.

"We have the shields, we will be in charge." Margery gave Aislinn a look of disgust.

"Don't you understand? We are going to die!" She was almost in tears now pleading with them.

"You are nearer to death than us, Prince Naveed visited us last night. We will live, he gave us these shields to protect us."

"Leave off!" Jarret shouted. "Incoming!" He pointed with his spear to the animals as they advanced quickly to their position.

Rebecca and Margery ran to the left of the closest column and sandwiched themselves between the hard stone and the forged iron of their large shields. Jarret thrust his spear into the fur of an advancing beast, barely drawing blood and sending it into a frenzy. Aislinn froze.

Move! Move! She shouted to herself. *I can't move!* She watched, spear lowered, as Jarret and the monster became one mass of tangled flesh. She could see his spear still moving, hitting and pushing the beast away from him. For now he was holding the dire tiger at bay. She looked left and watched the other tiger creep slowly to where the twins were huddled. The creature's fierce black eyes were fixed on the shields.

"Run, it was a lie!" She shouted to the twins.

It was too late. The powerful front paw had already ripped through the hollow wood of the fake shield, leaving Margery bleeding from a wound that stretched from waist to neck and opened her body. She was dead within seconds. Rebecca scrambled back around the pillar and grabbed her knees to her chest.

The sight and smell of blood broke Aislinn free from fear. She felt the power coming back, and smiled. Rushing to Rebecca she threw her spear aside and pulled the mumbling girl to her feet.

"Run to the far wall and stay there." She ordered, ripping the short sword from her hand.

"She was my sister. He lied." She stared back at Aislinn with the blankness of clean paper.

She is already dead. Aislinn thought as she whirled around to face the creature. Crouching into combat position she shifted rhythmically as she stared down the tiger. Two animals ready to kill each other. A scream erupted from behind her, and Rebecca rushed towards it, Aislinn's spear in hand. One lightning fast snarl and the headless body of the twin fell to the earth. The tiger chewed slowly as it advanced on Aislinn.

Trying to work in circles around to the body of Rebecca she moved to her left. The tiger bounced after her, never getting too close. *It is playing with me.* She realized. Its massive paw swiped at her and she raised her sword. The impact nearly broke her shoulder. She felt the blade pierce the padding of its foot and a terrible inhuman scream filled the arena. Her left arm protested every movement. She seized her moment. Leaping forward and kicking the sword deeper into the wound, she grabbed the spear and thrust it into the tiger's side. It spun around and bit at her with its oversized teeth. Without thinking she grabbed both jaws and held them apart. *Don't let him eat me, like he did Rebecca,* was all she could think. Her palms were bleeding from where the teeth cut into her soft flesh, and her shoulder felt like it was on the verge of falling off. She felt the power inside her double, she felt the beast come to the surface and give its strength to her arms.

"Die!" She shouted, followed by an incoherent yell. She ripped the two jaws apart.

"Aislinn!" Jarret shouted.

She turned and saw him laying on the ground with a gouge in his side and teeth marks on his face. He was pointing.

She saw it. The second tiger was flying through the air at her, trying to pounce. She only had a second before it was on her. In half that time she snatched up the spear and held it point first above her. The last dire tiger impaled itself on the spear point, running its head clean through her weapon.

The shaft broke, and the carcass fell to the earth next to her, its claw tearing her cheek open on the way down.

She looked up at Prince Naveed. Covered in blood, some of it her own, her left arm hanging uselessly at her side, she threw the broken shaft of the spear at him. It bounced harmlessly of the first row of seats.

"I win!" She shouted and limped to the door that was now open.

Tobin

"We need to make this appearance, my love." Tobin urged his sister. "The empire is our stage, and we are the main players tonight. The King's Feast will be special this year. I can feel it."

"The crowd, Tobin, the crowd." Her voice betrayed her fear. "The King." The last words were almost a whisper of horror.

"Do not worry about the King, what I suffered through should solidify our place here in the Capital. You will have everything you ever wanted because of him, and his unquenchable lust."

The siblings were in their chambers, Tobin standing by a chest of drawers near the door opposite the bed, while Fallia finished preparing behind a dressing screen on the opposite side of the room.

"So be it. I just wish you did not have to endure that man's advances." Tears were never far from her eyes of late and now they were on her cheeks.

"I know, but I will be there for you, the whole evening. I will have our personal guard never leave your side." Tobin strode to the door and opened it. Grabbing the first knight he could see, he brought him into the room. "Sir Moor, you will escort my lady and myself tonight. No one will get close to her, is that understood."

"Yes, My lord." He bowed to Fallia, before continuing "I heard all about what happened with Sir Fairclough. I will serve you well." He whispered to Tobin. His shield bore a squirrel on a field of brown. Tobin thought he had seen that device before, but ignored it and focused on his sister.

"My lady? Are we ready?"

Fallia rose from her desk, folded a piece of parchment, and tucked it into the bosom of her dress. "I am ready."

Coming out from behind the screen, she smiled at her brother. She was wearing a long white gown made from a cotton silk blend, embroidered with gold trim around the hem. She had a belt made from gold squares locked together with two thin chains. The shoulders were slightly puffed out and a silk cloth wrapped around her upper arms leaving the rest of the sleeves to hang nearly to the floor. The neckline dipped low enough to show the beginning of the crevasse created by her young breasts, causing Tobin to stop and stare. He had never seen his sister dressed like this. Even the gowns she wore to feasts in the Blackwatch never came close to being this fancy.

"You, you look amazing!" He managed to stammer out.

"You flatter me." She blushed. "Come, let us away to the King's Feast."

He grabbed her and kissed her deeply. Brushing her loose curly hair behind her neck, he rubbed her shoulders. "I love you."

"Tobin, please." She pulled away. "I love you too, but we have to go."

"But you just look so amazing tonight." He slipped his hand under the neck line of her dress. "You are beautiful."

"My lord. Someone approaches." Called the Squirrel Knight.

The two broke their embrace and Fallia straightened her dress. The dull slap of boots coming up the stairs told them their new bodyguard was correct. A few moments later Lord Morris rounded the corner and walked quickly up to the couple. He, too, was adorned for the King's Feast. He had a silk shirt with an embroidered overcoat showing the black snake on a field of gold, that was his house sigil. Large black leather boots and black trousers were complemented by the sash of his office as Royal Council Member. *I need to put my sash on.* Tobin thought to himself as he studied this newcomer.

"Lord Hamstead. May I have a word?"

Fallia grabbed Tobin's hand and squeezed vigorously.

"I fear not, my lord...ahem, Lord Morris." Tobin

closed the door to his chambers behind him and started to lead Fallia towards the stairs.

"Lord Hamstead, it is about your grandfather." Lord Morris accosted him again.

The hallway was narrow and Tobin had to push passed Sir Moor to stand face to face with Lord Morris.

"You will not speak of him." Tobin's face burned red with rage. "I am here on my own merits."

A sly smile stole across Lord Morris's face. "As it is, Lord Hamstead. I just wanted to inform you to the killer of your grandfather."

"Leave us." Tobin yelled. Looking back at Fallia and Sir Moor.

"My lord." Sir Moor bowed.

"Tobin?" Fallia quavered.

"Take her, I will catch up with you."

"My lord." Sir Moor bowed again and grabbed Fallia by the hand. "It is just such a shame that you two have to deal with court. A young married couple thrown into this lion's den. It is sad." He said with a slight lisp that Tobin had not noticed before as he walked down the stairs. *He was at the Dam!* Tobin remembered.

"Lord Hamstead," Lord Morris began, "I regret to inform you, that as you know, The King's Feast this year will also be a remembrance for your late Grandfather. He did not die of old age as is supposed by the people. He was hearty and strong. Nowhere near death. There was a strength in him that I now see in you. But enough reminiscing. He was murdered by a fellow member of the council. Lord Lynch."

"Why do you tell me this?" Tobin asked, unsure of himself for the first time since his arrival.

"I tell you this so as his heir you can exact revenge on this man."

"Was he not banished?" Tobin bit is lower lip. "How?"

"There are ways to reach out passed our city walls."

"I don't care. Let him rot in exile." Tobin tried to stand his ground with the much older council member.

Lord Morris grabbed his arm. "Do you not wish to make the man that killed your kin suffer?"

"Silence." Tobin tripped on the bottom stair. "When I first arrived, the King said I was responsible for capturing him. I now see it was you."

"With help." The older man smiled, revealing his pointed teeth. "Consider it a welcome present."

Tobin jumped back. "I want nothing more to do with you. No more presents, no more welcomes, and I will not have you or Lord Corbett around my chambers again." Tobin left him quickly, his heart beating furiously in his chest.

He rushed to the Great Hall and found Sir Moor standing with Fallia near the entrance.

"Why are you so pale?" Her fear showing through the finery of her dress.

"It is nothing, my love, it is nothing. Please enjoy yourself at the Feast." Tobin brushed her face. "I love you." He finished.

Fallia brushed her hair out of her face and smiled. Her red lips were the perfect accent to her blonde curls. *I will not let politics get in my way. My plan will work. Tonight.* He thought.

They stood at the threshold to the Great Hall, waiting their announcement. The room was transformed since the last time he saw it. Replacing the barren walls of the room were woven tapestries of epic battles. The normally empty floor, where peasants and lesser knights gathered for audience with the king, was filled with long tables, benches, and standing candle sticks. On the tables were a vast array of dishes, some steaming, some not, some covered, and some being heated from below by small candles. The vaulted ceiling was filling up with steam and smoke, and there was a slight fog in the room. Aromas of cooked meats and fried vegetables wafted around on the smoke of the large fire burning in the oversized hearth.

"Follow me. Ignore the stares of the others." Tobin whispered to his sister.

"I know, I know."

"Lord Tobin Hamstead, of Blackwatch in the Marsh, ambassador and member of the Royal Council, with wife Lady Fallia Black Hamstead." A voice echoed through the hall as they crossed the threshold, followed closely by Sir Moor.

The two took their seats at the foot of the head table, and Sir Moor stood behind them. Several lesser lords lined the tables across from them and, faint murmurings and whispers floated throughout the room as they walked, but Tobin and Fallia ignored them. 'It is normal for the peasantry to gossip about their lords.' Tobin would constantly remind Fallia, 'even if those peasants happen to be knights and lesser nobles.'

They were seated for only a few moments when a servant filled their goblets with a sweet red wine. The fragrance was irresistible and both Fallia and Tobin reached for and drank from their goblets at the same time. Wiping their mouths with the back of their hands identically, Tobin noticed Lord Morris and Lord Corbett watching them, whispering together.

"We are being watched." He whispered to Fallia.

Before she could respond the voice called out again. "His Royal Majesty the King. King Robsfeld Colbralian. Ruler of the Old Kingdom, Lord Protector of the Gold Coast, Ruler of the Wild Islands, and rightful King of the Broken Lands."

Trumpets blared into the hall as the large round body of the King stomped heavily towards the head table, surrounded by little bald boys like planets orbiting their sun. His thin beard already littered with specks of food. The crown sat sideways on his head and the King's round arms made no attempt to straighten it. Whether this was because he didn't want to or just because his arms could not reach up that far, Tobin did not know.

The hall was silent as the King took his seat and raised his hands. *So he is just lazy then.* Tobin thought.

"Let the feast begin!" He roared into the hall.

Servants streamed into the room from the outlining passages bearing trays and jugs filled with the finest foods. In a moment the entire hall was filled with aromas of cooked meats, and fried vegetables. Tobin's mouth began to water. Watching the food stream past him on its way to be presented before the King, he almost forgot he was at the

Capital, surrounded by people who were his enemies.

"Who is that man, staring at us?" Fallia grabbed the fabric of Tobin's sleeve.

Tobin followed her gaze. "That is Lord Felter Morris." He whispered. "He is the one watching us, so mind yourself."

Before she could respond, a large platter of roast duck crashed down in front of her. A servant quickly began carving the bird and dividing the meat between the two siblings. Fallia and Tobin began enjoying the feast, and thought no more about the two lords who watched their every move.

Hours passed, and course after course filtered in from the kitchen. The two young siblings from the Marsh lost themselves in the rich foods and sweet wines. Oblivious now to most of their surroundings, they gave in to the mounting pressure of their lust, and on more than one occasion were separated by Sir Moor.

One of the lesser lords, with a troubling sigil of a man hanging from a gallows, sat across the dais from where Tobin and his sister were eating.

"There have been disturbing reports coming back from the Riverlands." He commented to his companion.

"I have heard them as well."

Tobin inserted himself into their conversation. "What reports?"

Both nobles gave him a disdainful look but neither wished to challenge his office as a council member. "My lord. There have been reports of the dead rising, and walking amongst the river mouths."

"The dead walking. Simple folk give simple

stories." Tobin laughed and checked to see if Fallia had heard the rumor. She was engrossed in a fruit desert, covered with mixed nuts and a sugar sauce. "Do not pollute this night with your tales of fantasy."

"My lord, it is not just the simple folk that spread these rumors. Lord Noristrall himself swears that his grandson has seen these walking dead."

"Speak no more of this nonsense. I will not have my lady listening to your gossip and rumors." Tobin admonished the two lesser nobles.

"Yes, my lord."

"As you wish, my lord." The two nobles bowed their heads and leaned closer to each other after lowering their voices to whispers.

"What were they saying, my lord?" Fallia whispered into his ear.

Her hot breath and close tongue acted on Tobin quickly, and powerfully. He grabbed her around the waist and pulled her mouth close to his. "Nothing, do not worry about the lesser nobles, you are mine and you will always be safe." He said as he drew her tongue into his mouth.

After the last pie was served and the wine was cut off, Tobin stood shakily to his feet, but before he could leave the King also stood. His large voice bellowed and echoed throughout the Great Hall. "My fellow nobles and lords, esteemed guests for the King's Feast, you have all been brought here for this the King's Feast." The King swayed under the influence of wine. "I hope you have enjoyed the output of my chefs as greatly as I have. But I have not." He paused with a confused look on his face. "I, however, as your king, here at the King's Feast, and as the heir to the line of Veldorians, Ruler of the Old Kingdom, and Protector of the Realm, do hereby declare myself Emperor of the Kingdoms. I abolish the royal council and name Lord Tobin Hamstead as my sole heir." He pointed at Tobin. "All Lord Protectors are to swear fealty to me as their emperor in two months time. Furthermore, I am retiring to bed." He staggered off the dais, and out of the now deathly silent hall, with the help of his young bald boys.

Tobin looked around. Every face was on him, most smiling, some too drunk to understand, but the faces that he feared the most were not there. Lord Corbett and Lord Morris, sometime during the king's speech, had left the Great Hall.

"I, as your Prince," Tobin yelled slurring his words. "Order the arrest of both Lord Corbett and Lord Morris. The charge is plotting to kill the Emperor."

"Tobin what are you doing?" Fallia pulled him to his seat.

"Do not question me in front of those I mean to rule." The venom in his voice sent her reeling. "Those men are plotting against us, and I will see them behind bars." He noticed her shrinking from him and changed his tone. "My love, worry not about these matters. I will join you shortly." He kissed her hand, and stood up. "Sir Moor, take her back to our room, stop for no one, speak to no one."

"Yes, my lord."

"I am not your lord anymore, remember, I am now your Prince."

"Yes, my Prince." Sir Moor bowed and left the

Great Hall with Fallia in tow.

Tobin addressed the room again. "Did you not hear me. Guards, find the Lords Corbett and Morris. Go!" The city guard leapt into compliance and the guests of the King's Feast murmured amongst themselves.

"Who are you to take this honor." One man called out from near the back. "You have just arrived here."

Tobin jumped off the dais and nearly ran to face this lesser knight. A young man, only older than Tobin by five years or so tried to hide his fear as the much shorter Prince descended upon him. The knight wore a black and red tunic, and a device that Tobin could not quite make out. Even if he did, he would not have recognized it.

"Who are you to speak to me this way?" He bellowed into the taller man's face.

"My Prince, I only mean-"

"Silence!" Tobin drew his dagger from his belt and slid it quickly and carefully into the knights belly, turning slightly as he did so. "You will never speak again." Turning to the rest of the room he called out. "Leave."

After the room was clear, Tobin followed his own advice, heading directly for the king's personal chambers. The guards near the door must have already received the news and let him pass without question. Upon entering the bedroom he could smell the burning of incense and the stale aroma of dried wine. A large fire burned peacefully in the hearth, across from a large four-post bed that had dark curtains hiding the mattress from view. Tobin padded softly around side table to stand at the foot of the bed.

"Your Grace, Lords Corbett and Morris are still at large. I fear for your safety." He began, struggling against the wine to remain standing. *Just focus a few more minutes and you will be free to sleep.* "I have already slain one dissenter, I fear there may be more. We need to double the city guard and patrol the streets, Your Grace." The only sound Tobin heard was the faint crackling of drying wood in the flames. "Your Grace?" *There is no snoring, shouldn't he be snoring?* Tobin pulled back the heavy curtains.

On the bed lay the large form of Emperor Robsfeld Colbralian. A sword was buried deep into his gut with only the hilt remaining outside the carcass. Blood covered the sheets and the late Emperor had already voided himself after death.

Tobin calmly left the room and addressed the guards outside.

"Who else has been in this room besides me after the feast?" He asked calmly.

"Just you, my lord, and Lord Morris." The guard responded.

"You allowed him entry?"

"The Emperor said if Lord Morris or Lord Corbett were to come calling that he would give them an earful. He wanted to see him."

"And you didn't think to disarm him before you let him pass?"

"He was not armed." The guard shifted. "What are you saying, my lord?"

"You will address me as Your Grace now." He said as he turned and walked away from the carnage. The sounds of scrambling guards and the castle alarm followed him up the tower stairs to the waiting arms of his sister, and now Queen of the Five Kingdoms and Empress of the New Empire.

Aislinn

Several days of fever and agony had left Aislinn weak and broken. Time had no meaning in her recovery room. She drifted in and out of consciousness freely. Only vaguely aware of the guards that came to take her away, but they were not guards at all, they were women, with veiled faces and soothing songs. She drank sweet honey, and ate oatmeal and cakes. Bandages, salves, wines, hot presses and rolls of strange smelling parchment filled her thoughts and dreams as she was cared for by these strange healers. The cuts on her body and face stung and burned from the treatment, and her left arm was all but useless still. She was force-fed a sweet honey wine and the blackness of unconsciousness took her again.

Opening her eyes slowly, she became aware of the change in her surroundings. The cold stone walls were replaced by soft rugs that hung about her room. A fire burned brightly in the hearth, giving off a warm glow that comforted and soothed Aislinn. The room was small, but still had a dresser, a small table with a chair, two throw rugs—one in front of the fire and the other under the bed—and the bed itself. Aislinn forced herself to sit up.

The hanging rugs on the wall were pictures of past battles. Some she recognized and some she didn't, but all of them depicted great champions. The rich wooden smell of this room washed over her as she tried to stand. Her head spun with pain and something else, something on the edge of her mind that was dulling her wits. *I shouldn't be here. What happened?* She staggered to the table and pulled one of the small chairs onto the large rug in front of the inviting flames. Looking down she realized that both the rugs were made from the hides of dire tigers. *How long have I been asleep?* Feeling the scabs that had formed on her face she stopped horrified. I must be hideous. My arm can move though. She tested it by swinging it around in a large circle, and was surprised by the large amount of pain accompanied this action, almost knocking her unconscious again.

A large slam on the door nearly sent her into the fire.

"Who's there?" She inquired feebly.

"I was told you would be awake." Prince Naveed stepped through the threshold. "I was most anxious to see how you were progressing. My star fighter will have to battle again soon."

"And if I refuse to fight for you again?" Aislinn sat carefully in the chair, trying not to reveal how weak she was. "I have already defeated your worst-"

"My worst!" The Prince cut her off. "My worst? You have not dreamed of what is to come. I have seen it." He pulled the patch off his eye, exposing a rotten mass of maggots and moist flesh.

Aislinn gagged and felt the sick in the back of her throat. *Don't show weakness.*

"I have seen how death comes and rules us all." He continued. "I have watched you die. I have watched the armies of death march across this land and burn all that is in their path." He paused, replacing the eyepatch. "You speak about my worst. My worst is nothing compared to the beast you will have to kill for me."

"I have to kill it for you." She saw her opening. "So you need me. What will I get in return for this killing?"

"I have been gathering here an army, an army to protect us from this coming doom and you, if you so choose will be the general that leads the army of life against its most dire foe. Or, if you so choose, you can be free of me." He pulled the other chair next to her and sat down.

Turning to the door he snapped his fingers and a young boy ran in with a tray of two goblets and a decanter of wine.

"Drink with me."

"No, thank you."

"It is a good vintage. I have much to discuss with you. Please drink."

Aislinn noticed the change in his tone. *What is happening? He is not himself.* "You most surely do not. Tell me what it is I must kill for you so I can quit this island." She tried a half smile. "And be quick about it."

"A dragon." A shiver took him. "We have existed here for hundreds of years, hidden on this island."

Why didn't the gnomes tell me that? She cursed to herself.

"I have pitted many a soldier against the dire tigers, but in those hundreds of years, my predecessors and I have only found three people to ever survive, and only two to have ever killed them."

Aislinn looked up at him. "You?"

"Yes, you and I are the only two people to have bested a tiger in the arena. It cost me my eye, but for that I am grateful. It cost you two friends, and your injuries."

"Two friends, does Jarret live?"

"Aye, the boy lives." He shifted closer to her and leaned in. She could feel his warm breath on her face. "I will throw him against the dragon if you refuse to fight."

"I will fight." She blurted out. The thought of losing Jarret, her only friend, was too much. "I will fight, but tell me why you need this creature destroyed?"

"The heart of a dragon makes a man immortal. Not only that, with the power of this beast I will be able to use its blood and flesh to fortify ourselves against the coming death."

He is telling me everything. No more secrets between us. Why?

"If what you say is true, why should I give you this heart, when I can give it to Jarret or myself?"

"You are cunning, and strong, and brave, little rat, but you are not omniscient." He smiled. Aislinn thought of what was behind the eye patch. "I will offer you money, and riches, and power, and most of all safety. For you and the boy."

"Why have you not killed this creature yourself?"

"Ha!" He erupted. "Do you know nothing of dragons?"

Aislinn shifted uncomfortably, the truth was she had heard the word before, but had only a vague idea what this creature was, but she was nervous to allow him to know that.

He continued. "No, you must not. A meaningless girl from Little Town, no. It matters not, you have given your word to fight it." He crouched off his chair and added a few logs to the fire. Staying crouched he stared into the flames for what seemed like an eternity.

"Get used to the heat, Little Rat." He chuckled to himself as he stood to leave.

The rage that filled her in the arena rushed back into her limbs, the pain from her wounds disappeared. Grabbing the nearest thing to her she swung it at him with deadly accuracy. His body flew limply to the far wall and snagged a rug, pulling it to the floor to cover him.

"Stay there!" She shouted, running out of the room.

The hallway was narrow and lined with dull rock. Torches every few feet showed her the way to the exit as she ran passed several doors. *This must be a barracks or something like it.* The heavy wooden door was open when she reached the end of the hall.

Cool night air did little to shake her fury as she did not slow down but ran straight to the arena. The stars were blinking through the sparse cloud cover. The sand under her feet grabbed and pulled at her ankles while it imbedded itself between her bare toes. The gate to the underbelly of the arena stood only a few yards before her; two fully armored guards stood beside it.

Without slowing down she leapt to the closest guard and ripped his helmet off, throwing it into the face of the other. Driving her thumbs into the eyes of the first guard and continuing down the passage inside the gate, for her, took only a moment. A large bell began to ring out in the night to accompany the shouts and screams that became the backdrop to her sprint across the camp.

Turn after turn she weaved her way lower into the building, until she saw it.

A massive red mountain lay curled up behind its tree-trunk like tail. Its thick chest rose and fell softly with its sleeping breath. Large spines lined its back, connected by a thin layer of rubbery flesh. Its red scales gleamed and glistened in the fire light casting strange reflections around its room. The dragon adjusted one of its wings and Aislinn gasped. It was a massive thing, dwarfing any other part of the dragon, made of thick bat like skin with one long bone that lined the front.

The creature opened one eye and looked as Aislinn. Staring into her mind, she saw a flash of red and felt a searing pain in her left eye. Reaching for it she screamed when she felt it wasn't there. The dragon stood before her now, with her eye resting gently between its jaws. He rolled his head back and swallowed it whole, leaned forward and breathed into the empty socket.

Instantly the pain fell away and it burned. Burned with a fire so hot that the pain turned to pleasure. Fire warmed her, filled her, burned her insides. She was consumed by the flames that flowed into her head.

"Enough!" A deep resonating voice bellowed inside her head. It was the voice of ages, the voice of time itself. *"You need no more. I have been waiting. Come let us away."*

Without thinking she leapt on his back and grabbed the two long spikes by his neck. The dragon stood. Thrusting his neck upward he shattered through the ceiling; spreading his wings, he burst through the walls. The building started to collapse around them. The pain in her body returned. Aislinn clung to the neck of the dragon.

With two powerful beats of its wings the mighty lizard took to the sky. Jumping in altitude faster than Aislinn thought possible, her ears popped and cracked as she felt like she left her stomach far below them. The strain of holding tight to its neck was wearing on her already worn body. *I am going to fall.*

"No one I allow to ride me falls." The voice was back. *"I have waited for you Aislinn Godschild. I am Erlind. Focus on my voice and my skin. We will be well away from here shortly."*

"How is it I can hear you?" She screamed into the

torrent of wind that surrounded the two as they flew ever higher.

"I have breathed into you the fire of my life. We are linked. I to you and you to me. It was foretold that one who was born of the gods should ride before an army to vanquish death."

"I am nothing, a little rat from Little Town..." She closed her eyes, expecting to see her cold stone cell when she opened them. "This is what death feels like then..."

"Aislinn Godschild, you will never know what death feels like."

The voice continued speaking but she could not focus as they turned sharply and her vision narrowed to a small tunnel and her ears pounded against her skull. When she recovered he was still speaking.

"...and that is what brings you to me. Farther east we must go now. There we will find answers for you. The other two have already gathered. We are late."

"Late?"

Before Erlind could respond a shape flew at them from the blackness. It was another dragon. The two beasts circled and snapped at each other in the air. Aislinn felt sick. The viciousness with which both of the creatures attacked terrified her. She felt she was witnessing the terrible world before the first men came to inhabit it. The primordial power and destruction that formed the earth was present in these two creatures.

They are playing! She realized in a moment of clarity. *Gods! They are playing.*

Without warning the ground rose up to meet them and they landed with a jolt that sent Aislinn careening off Erlind's back and into a large patch of long grass. Pain racked her body and she tensed up trying to contend with it. Slowly the pain subsided enough for her to regain control of her mind.

From her vantage point she saw the ocean slowly lapping against the gentle sandy beach. A large moon shone down, casting a pale reflection in the calm water and giving the world a light glow. A halo of alabaster light circled the god of the night sky keeping the countless stars at bay. They twinkled and sparkled through the cool air, shining down on Aislinn and the two dragons.

A gentle breeze toyed with the dune grass that grew in the soft sand, bringing with it the faint chirp of a faraway cricket and the smell of campfires and cooked meats. Aislinn watched as Erlind pawed and pushed the new dragon, pinning it and snapping tenderly at its neck. It's a girl. A warmth filled her as she watched the two creatures of old dance and celebrate together. Erlind reared back his head and sent a jet of fire streaming into the night sky. There was a magic in that moment that filled her soul. Turning slightly she saw Princess dropping down off her unicorn and walk up to where she lay.

"You have arrived." She smiled as she helped Aislinn to her feet.

The two women stood on the sandy beach and watched the dance of dragons. A sight that had not been seen in the world for thousands of years.

Epilogue

The crunch of snow being packed by a large boot was the only noise filling the still winter air of the city center of Riverspring. John Bryne paced the empty early morning streets of his castle with a heavy heart. Almost a year had passed since the moonless night, and since that time his rangers had disbanded, his daughter had left, half the towns folk fled the Valley, and he felt that a doom descended on him. The once busy town was little more than a shell for him and his wife and only a handful of others. After the disappearance of Lonessa and Mr. Grahm, shortly after two other citizens died in the night, rumors spread quickly and his people all seemed to agree that his family had been cursed.

A light snow started to fall, adding a thin layer over the two feet already on the ground. Early winter always brought heavy snows and this year was no exception. The mountain breeze whipped down off the peaks surrounding the city and tore at his heavy woolen cloak. Wrapping it tightly against this battering, he continued his pacing. After a few moments of blowing into his hands and grabbing his ears he saw her, tall, thin, graceful as the day they were married. Beautiful. Only she had changed since that night, since Lonessa ran away, since the rumors that they were cursed scared away most of her people. Her face did not shine any more, her smile did not warm him, and her eyes were empty. Reaching out for her hand he led her across the abandoned city to the temple, where there was a fire burning, ever burning in memory of his daughter.

"We come here everyday, and everyday nothing happens." Aviana's voice mirrored her inner emptiness.

"We must trust the mountain gods, if we have displeased them we will make amends, if they are testing us we must prevail." John's voice hung in the snowy air.

He pulled open the heavy wooden door and ushered his wife into the shine of the gods; his large hand pressed gently into the small of her back. The center of the round room was a giant fire pit, only half filled with burning wood. The flame that was lit on the day Lonessa left the Valley had not died. An acolyte stood before it in a long white robe with fur on the ends. He was throwing more logs into the flame, and the hiss of melting snow and drying wood was echoing inside the small building. Along the outer walls were statues to the gods, some depicted as animals, others as humans, but all of them divine creatures of the mountains.

Still with his hand on her back, John led the two to the center and they both knelt before the flame.

"Leave us." He said to the acolyte, who did not move. "I said leave us. We would be alone."

"Almost a year and you no longer recognize your own daughter." Lonessa pulled back the hood to reveal her face. Her voice was soft and sad.

"Thank the gods you are alive!" Shouted Lord Bryne jumping to his feet.

"My daughter!" Aviana burst into tears and grabbed Lonessa's hand. "I love you. I missed you. Where did you go? Are you safe?" Tears choked her words, and she kissed her face and forehead between speaking.

"The gods have not forgotten us!"

"Father, you are wrong." Lonessa's voice startled both of her parents.

"Wrong?" John took a step back. "Lonessa, my dear child, you have been through an ordeal, only the gods know how hard it was for you."

"Father," Lonessa stopped. The gods left you when you let Garon die."

Her skin was pale, almost translucent, her eyes were pits of black velvet with dark circles around them.

John rushed to her side and grabbed her hands. Lonessa's body began to twitch and writhe in his arms, Aviana screamed. A shadowy form manifested itself on Lonessa's back and took the shape of large feathered wings. They flapped twice causing the flames to dance and flicker and grow as they consumed the wood she had been adding. As the light increased John and Aviana could see the statues faces, all of them were scratched and broken, as if vandalized by large claws. Only the face of the mountain wren was untouched, but its neck was broken and the whole head lay on the ground opposite Lonessa, its stone eyes pleading with anyone to help it.

"What is happening?" Aviana screamed.

"This is not our daughter, but a demon from the Underworld." John roared, as he pulled his sword from its scabbard.

"You are wrong again, father. I am your daughter." Her voice was the layered rasping of two people. "I am Lonessa Bryne, and I am so much more than that. You have prayed I would return to you. You have asked to give anything so that I may be with you again. Your prayers have been answered. You can give up your life, so that I may live."

Her shadow wings swept down and hit both of them in the face knocking them back onto the cold stone of the temple floor.

Before their eyes, Lonessa seemed to grow to twice her normal size and she moved with an inhuman speed. Before John and Aviana could even react to being thrust on the ground Lonessa was on top of them, digging her nails into the soft flesh of her mother's neck.

"You should not have birthed me mother. I am a failure." Tears poured out of her large black eyes, and cascaded down her cheeks landing near her mothers mouth. "Why? Why did you..." Lonessa kept up the assault until a large pool of blood covered the floor beneath her mother.

"What have you done? What have you become?" John shouted. "Who are you?"

"I am your daughter. I am death."

"In the name of the gods, leave this holy place demon." He tried to stand and run.

"You mean nothing to me now." She leapt from her mother's corpse to land on her father.

Her nails grabbed the sides of his face leaving puncture wounds on his cheeks and her teeth sank easily into the flesh of his exposed neck. She drank deep from his blood and threw his carcass aside.

"Gravous. Enter." She called out once she had returned to normal form. "Clean this mess out of my temple. Gavrill, Renyard, make this place mine." The three entered the room. Gravous, weak and tired, began dragging her parents out of the temple. Cringing and gagging at the sight of the mutilated bodies.

"I do not trust that man." Renyard whispered to Lonessa. "We should not have left him alive."

She stepped over the pools of blood that were once her parents. "Sir Renyard, I have you to serve me, to love me, but I need one living body from which to draw my power. I need him." She caressed his face with her cold hand. "Once my power is complete I will have no use for him, and then you can do what you will."

"As you wish, my Queen." Renyard bowed.

"But as I say, I only need *one* living body. Kill everyone."

Appendix

The Creation of the Five Kingdoms and their houses

When the Veldorian Empire fell, three thousand years ago, some of the prominent families built for themselves kingdoms out of the rubble. The great houses struggled against each other, and against the native peoples, for control over their own lands. Without the power of the Veldorians behind each separate house, it was a grueling time for everyone. After hundreds of years of war the five family heads met to form an alliance, or at least a truce. This is when the Royal Council was created, a reflection of the Veldorian Senate.

The five Great Houses are listed here with their sigils and a short genealogy showing the relation to other houses.

COLBRALIAN

The Colbralian Family is the newest of the great families. Their linage cannot be traced back to the Veldorians. However, after the War of the Feathers this family settled on the Gold Coast, founding Aurorum on the ruins of the ancient capital city of the Veldorians: Veldoria. They found massive deposits of gold, allowing them to buy their way into power.

Later, when the houses were in the midst of the War of the Feathers, the Colbralian family bought peace for the realm and bought themselves a crown.

Sigil: Three interlocking gold coins.

Robyn Colbralian m. Justine Noristrall
          b. (King) Robsfeld Colbralian.

RAWFIELD

There has always been a Rawfield in the Midlands, and there always will. This is the motto of the oldest family in the Kingdoms. They claim rights to the largest portion of land extending from the southern border of the Gold Coast down to the Frozen Plains on the steps of the Grey Mountains, and from the mighty River Dirgo to the sea. This powerful family claims to descend from Vorlian the Great, who lived over three thousand years ago.

Content to stay in Fieldhaven, their capital city, the Rawfields are not aggressive but they will not be owned.

Sigil: Oxen

Justin Rawfield m. Mariah Wallin (d.)
      b. Richard Rawfield
Justin Rawfield m. Emily Murray
      b. Aviana Rawfield (Bryne)
      b. Rormir Rawfield

MURRAY

The Murray's have always claimed the throne for themselves. Being an older house than the Colbralians, and having some evidence that the Colbralian name came from an offshoot of house Murray, they feel cheated out of their rightful crown. They stay in the Marshes, secluded from most of the rest of the kingdoms, and they are the only major house to openly trade with the savages from the Broken Lands.

The Murray's and the Rawfields have always been closely allied, and in an unfortunate turn of events, both of the Murray twins, Jondavid and Fergison, contracted a childhood disease. Rormir Rawfield will take the name Murray from his mother, as he stands to inherit the throne at Mergorod, the Capital of the Marsh.

Sigil: Fish with a gold coin in its mouth.

Madison Murray m. Fiona Wyllallia
      b. Emily Murray (Rawfield)
             b. Rormir Rawfield
      b. Jondavid Murray
      b. Fergison Murray

NORISTRALL

The Noristrall Family has lived in all of the kingdoms, as guests, for most of the modern era. Pirates, raiders, savage folk, and even some of the Posli people from the Broken Lands took up residence on the large island of Blackpool. They stormed Headwater, the capital of the Riverlands, several times and drove the Noristrall family out and into exile. Not until the kingdoms were united after the War of the Feathers did the Noristrall's have the strength to retake their homeland. Even then Riven had to enlist the help of the Colbralians by marring his sisters to Robyn Colbralian, and James Bryne.

With the Riverlands back firmly under the control of the Kingdom, the Noristrall's can now focus on the clearing the Island of their enemies

Sigil: Fox

Riven Noristrall m. Sorista Morris
　　　　　b. Arian Noristrall m. Dorli Corbett
　　　　　　　　b. Regen Noristrall
　　　　　　　　b. Regina Noristrall

BRYNE

The Brynes have long lived in the mountains, holding true to the values and customs of the Veldorians before them. Tucked safely away in a small valley high in the mountains the Brynes are well fortified but also isolated from the rest of the kingdoms.

The refusal of the first Bryne to send a representative to the Capital to sit on the council of the King is a tradition carried on to this day. The Brynes feel they don't need anyone else to survive.

Sigil: Raven

John Bryne (d) m. Rose Colbralian (d)
    b. James Bryne (d) m Sarah Noristrall (d)
        b. John Bryne m. Aviana Rawfield
           b. Lonessa Bryne

ABOUT THE AUTHOR

Benjamin Andrus is a student at Grand Valley State University. He currently lives in Hudsonville, Michigan where he enjoys writing and brewing beer and mead with his brother. He returned to school after spending eight and a half years in the United States Army. Now, after two deployments overseas, he is pursuing a BA in Creative Writing. This is his first full length novel.